Back to Life Again:

Love After Heartbreak

Back to Life Again:

Love After Heartbreak

Shantaé

URBAN Renaissance

www.urbanbooks.net

Urban Books, LLC
300 Farmingdale Road, NY-Route 109
Farmingdale, NY 11735

Back to Life Again: Love After Heartbreak
Copyright © 2019 Shantaé

ISBN 13: 978-1-60162-921-0
ISBN 10: 1-60162-921-4

First Trade Paperback Printing August 2019
Printed in the United States of America

10 9 8 7 6 5 4 3 2 1

Distributed by Kensington Publishing Corp.
Submit Orders to:
Customer Service
400 Hahn Road
Westminster, MD 21157-4627
Phone: 1-800-733-3000
Fax: 1-800-659-2436

Chapter 1

There's Been a Mix-up
(Recap)

Dakota

"Baby, did Breelyn pick the car up yet?" I asked with my cell phone faceup on my desk on speaker. I was at the office for a few hours sorting through and signing some paperwork, so Giannis agreed to stay at the house until my cousin showed up. Her car was down, so she would have my whip for the next few days. Giannis was basically living with me now and hardly ever went home to his condo. I couldn't wait for it to be permanent because I loved going to sleep and waking up wrapped tightly in his arms.

"Not yet, but after she leaves, I'm going to step out to get dinner, so don't worry about stopping on your way home," he replied.

"Thank you, bae," I responded. "You know I wasn't trying to stop anywhere."

He laughed. "I already know. I got you though. And make sure you check your email while you're there. I sent another listing that you need to take a look at."

"Okay. Just let me finish up and I'll check it out," I replied, shuffling around the papers that were on my desk.

"Cool. See you soon, baby."

"I love you."

"I love you too, Kota B," he said before hanging up.

Goodness, I just loved me some him. It just seemed like everything about him was made just for me and vice versa. No longer did I give a fuck about all the bullshit I had to endure to get to this point. Exes getting married mere months after dumping me, being cheated on and disrespected in the worst ways possible by someone who claimed to love me. Again, none of that mattered to me as long as it led me right here with this man in my life.

Quickly signing the documents remaining on my desk, I logged into my Gmail account to check out the listing baby had sent to me. We were currently looking for a home in the Frisco area but hadn't found anything that we both liked. My current home was nice, but Giannis and I wanted to live in a home that we picked out together. I knew it wouldn't be long before marriage and children came into the picture, so we wanted to be prepared and settled before that happened. As much as we got it in, I was surprised I wasn't already knocked up despite being on birth control.

"Damn, this is nice," I said to myself as I flipped through the pictures of the five-bedroom, four-bathroom, two-story home. The property had a pool, which was a must for me. It was huge, yet there was still enough yard for entertaining family and friends, which was something both of us required. Family was number one in both our lives, so it was important for us to have enough space for everyone to mingle and be comfortable while visiting us. The game room, theater, and brand-new stainless-steel appliances in the kitchen basically sealed the deal for me. I could use the office downstairs for myself, and we could turn one of the bedrooms upstairs into an office for Giannis. He had a lot of shit popping off with his businesses, so he needed a separate space to organize and manage things. We would need to see it first before making a decision, but in my heart, I felt it was the perfect first home for us, so I quickly shot him a text.

Kota Love: I want it! I want it! It's perfect!

My Honey: Lol. I figured you would like it. We can take a look at it on Monday. Love you.

Kota Love: Love you too.

As I was shutting down my computer, I heard some movement up front. I was here alone this afternoon and had stupidly forgotten to lock the door. Glancing down at my schedule, I saw that I wasn't expecting any appointments, so I had no clue who was walking through the door of my business right now. I wasn't tripping though because y'all know I had my .22 sitting on my lap where only I could see it. Not to mention there was the pepper spray and Taser that sat in my top drawer, which was slightly open for easy access. There ain't a soul alive who can say they caught Kota B slipping and there never would be. Cool, calm, and collected, I leaned back farther into my plush chair and waited, ready for whatever. That was, until Montell poked his big-ass head in the doorway. All I could do was lean back and roll my eyes to the ceiling. Hadn't heard a peep from him since the night of my book release and I was happy about that. Figured he'd finally gotten the picture and decided to let go of any thoughts of us being together again. Obviously I was wrong.

"I see you're already rolling your eyes, so I'll make this quick," he said with his hands out. Guessed he saw me move mine to my lap, and trust he knew exactly what that meant.

"Please do, because I have no idea what we could possibly have to say to one another at this point," I stated calmly.

"I'm not here to cause any problems, so chill," he said, looking down again at my lap before taking a few steps toward the desk.

"Talk, Montell. If I ain't home soon, my nigga gon' be up here, and neither you nor I want those problems," I said, being petty.

"Whatever, man. I just came here to talk to you about David," he retorted, clearly bothered by the mention of my man.

"I don't give two fucks about yo' ho-ass cousin. If that's what you're here for, you can leave now. Anything to do with that coke-head nigga I don't want to hear or have anything to do with."

"Even if it got something to do with you and your cousin?" he snapped.

"Bree don't fuck with David no more, and I ain't never cared for the nigga, so no, I still don't give a fuck," I clapped back.

"I'on mean like that, Kota, damn! I'm saying the nigga been tripping lately talking about doing you and your cousin harm. I went by his spot after that book release shit, and the nigga was still heated about Breelyn being there with that nigga and mad because they whooped his ass. For some reason, he thinks the only reason that Breelyn won't take him back is because of you. Says you have too much influence over her and that if he gets you out of the way she'll come home." He sighed as if telling me this was hard on him.

"I think I'll be okay, Montell, but I do appreciate you coming to tell me this. I know how close you are with Dave," I sympathized.

"Look, Kota, I know you can take care of yourself, but this nigga ain't been in his right mind for a minute. I know you keep your protection on you at all times, but it's deeper than that at this point. Shawna left his ass, and before she skipped town with Davy, she stopped by Mom's and told me all the shit that's been going on over there. Nigga got off the coke, but now he's popping pills and is a full-fledged alcoholic. Said she just couldn't take the beatings anymore or being around him period. She also told me he was asking around, trying to find someone to kill you, but his broke ass couldn't afford the fee. Now he talking about setting houses on fire and cutting brake lines on your cars."

After hearing that last part, I totally tuned him out as I felt all color drain from my face. My heart was literally racing. I picked up my cell, dialing my man's phone. The phone rang until his voicemail picked up. He must have left the house already to get food and forgot his phone in the car. I didn't bother leaving a message. Next, I dialed Breelyn and got no answer. This bad feeling suddenly came over me, and I just knew something was wrong. I was up out of my seat, grabbing my belongings, preparing to go see about my cousin. She was probably fine and the dread I was feeling was due to hearing of the plans David had for us. At least that's what I was hoping.

"What else did he tell her?" I asked, suddenly remembering Montell was sitting there.

"She says he was just out of it, rambling on and on about what he was gon' do to you. I tried to call you but you still got me blocked, and I didn't want to cause problems by stopping by your place. This is actually my second time coming here trying to catch you," he replied, standing when he noticed my panicked state. I was so out of it that I didn't hear another person enter the building.

"Dakota!" I heard Giannis call out, stopping me dead in my tracks.

"Shit!" I mumbled. The last thing I wanted was for him to be under the impression that Montell and I had some other shit going on. From the look in his eyes when he dotted the door of my office, that's exactly what he was thinking.

"The fuck is he doing here, Dakota?" he asked, grilling me hard as fuck.

"Had you answered your phone when I called, you would have known the answer to that, Giannis," I retorted, immediately jumping on the defensive. That was obviously the wrong move based on the heated look he shot me. I'd done nothing wrong, but I couldn't help but feel he was accusing me of something. My ass had been tripping and hella emotional lately, and he'd called me out several times in the last few weeks.

"Look, man, I ain't here on no bullshit with your lady. I just stopped by to warn her about some shit my cousin was saying he was going to do to her and Breelyn. Nigga been making threats about killing them both, and I took it serious enough to at least warn her," Montell spoke up. "I love my cousin, and I feel like shit even being here talking to y'all about him, but I would feel like shit if something happened to her and I had kept this shit to myself. Nigga been wilding since y'all beat his ass that night. I keep telling his ass to let it go but he won't. Talking real reckless about y'all, but mostly Dakota. Can't figure out why he hates her so much," Montell said, rubbing his hand down his head in deep thought.

I never told Tell about David trying to get with me before he approached Breelyn, or the comments he would make to me when he and Breelyn weren't close by. Giannis knew all about it because he confronted me the morning after my book release. My honey said that he just knew something was up based on the number of times David mentioned my name that night when Breelyn should have been his main focus. I could see his expression go from angry at me being in here alone with Montell to furious that David was making threats on my life. Right now, arguing was the last thing we needed to be doing. He came right over and wrapped me up in his arms because he knew that was what I needed at the moment.

Now, making sure that my cousin was straight was my main priority. "Babe, how long ago did Breelyn pick up the car?"

"Maybe twenty minutes ago. Why?" he asked.

"Just something Montell said to me about David threatening to cut the brake lines on my car and burning down houses and shit. I been calling her but she hasn't answered, and I just have a bad feeling," I said, getting worked up.

"That nigga said what?" Giannis's deep voice boomed. He pushed me back to look at my face, and all I could see in his beautiful eyes was pure rage. "You know his ass is dead, right?" he said, turning to Montell, who just looked off, not offering up a response.

I quickly began packing up my shit and dialing Breelyn back-to-back with no answer. "Baby, you have Rio's number, right?" I asked as I set the alarm and locked up the door to my business. "I remember Breelyn mentioning something about going to spend the weekend with him," I recalled.

"Yeah, let me hit him up real quick." He pulled his phone out, scrolling for the number before sliding his thumb to the right on the device.

"Kota, I'ma head out. I'm sure Bree is fine. Even so, I already know what's up once Rah hears about this shit," he sighed while looking to me with pleading eyes, trying to see if there was anything I could do to spare his cousin's life. Montell knew better than that. Shit was out of my hands, and even if it were up to me, his ass would still be out of there. I just shook my head, letting him know that I had no sympathy for that nigga. There was nothing that I could do to stop what would happen once Rah was put up on game. Just the fact that the nigga had plans and was actually seeking out someone to kill one or both of us sealed his fate. Montell knew as well as I did that his cousin was as good as dead. It had to be hard for him to be in the position he was in, though, and I sympathized somewhat. To be torn between doing the right thing or standing by your family and allowing some fuck shit to go down? Talk about a dilemma. I was just glad he made the decision to come here today so that we could at least be aware that we had someone lurking in the shadows who had a problem with us. Shit was wack as fuck if you asked me, but the way men dealt with rejection would forever be a mystery to me. Montell himself displayed some of the same bitch-nigga tendencies as David did when it came to moving on, but thankfully he'd come to his senses. Had he not, he would have been on the chopping block right along with his people.

Breelyn

"Okay, baby. All I have to do is stop by the store to pick up the food, then I'll be on my way out there," I told DeMario through the phone feature in Kota's Audi as I pulled out of her driveway. I had to put my car in the shop yesterday, so she loaned me hers until my baby was ready. Since I had the weekend off, I was spending it with my man at his place. I couldn't wait for our home in Allen to be ready so that I would no longer have to make this drive, but it was worth it just to be able to see and spend time with him. Soon we'd be living under the same roof, and I couldn't wait to have him with me every day.

Although Rio agreed to be the designated chef while I was there, I knew I'd end up cooking most of our meals. I didn't mind though. I loved cooking, and the fact that he enjoyed my food so much was an added bonus. I planned to stock up on all his favorites so that I could feed and fuck him for the next forty-eight hours. He'd been out of town, and I'd been working like crazy trying to occupy my time while he was gone, so this staycation was just what the doctor ordered.

"Take your time, and I'll see you when you get here. I've been missing you like crazy, so don't be surprised if I pounce on you as soon as you walk through the door."

He laughed, but I knew he was serious, too. We'd been joined at the hip since he came back into my life. This was the first out-of-town job he'd taken since we made things official, so this week without him was terrible. Daddy was back now, so it was about to be on and popping.

"If I don't jump on your ass first," I flirted.

"That's how you feeling, Breelyn?" The smile on his face was evident.

"Hell yeah. I missed you, daddy," I cooed.

"Breelyn, quit playing on this gotdamn phone and come home. Got me rocked up like a mu'fucka, talking like that," he groaned. "I'm seriously about to say fuck that food and just take you out to eat all weekend if it will get you here quicker."

"Okay, okay, let me stop. I'm coming up on Kroger right n . . . The fuck!" I panicked when the car wouldn't slow down as I approached the light. I wasn't going more than thirty-five miles per hour, but it was like the brakes were nonexistent right now. I'd noticed a little something when I first got in the car, but I just planned to tell Kota to have it checked out. "Rio, baby, something is going on with the car. Oh, my gosh!" I shrieked.

"Breelyn, baby, what's going on?" he shouted.

I was too worked up to even respond to his question. "Shit, shit, shit!" I screamed as the car continued into the intersection. I couldn't stop, and my blaring horn did nothing to alert other drivers that I was having an issue. *Fucking Texas drivers!* I'd barely turned my head to the right when, a split second later, the passenger side of the car was being rammed by an eighteen-wheeler traveling well beyond the forty-mile-per-hour speed limit. The smashing of metal, glass breaking, and my man's voice calling out to me in a panic were all I heard before everything went black.

Chapter 2

The Aftermath

Rio

In an effort to try to block out the chaos going on around me, I excused myself to the back of the room and sat with my head in my hands. In the aftermath of the accident, Breelyn's entire family was cutting the fuck up in the ER waiting area. But me? All I could hear was the blaring horn from that massive-ass truck and the cacophony of my girl's car being hit. Shaking my head from side to side and pounding at my temples with my fists did nothing to mute the sounds. It was a track playing over and over again in my head, fucking with my mental state. The breaking of glass and crushing of metal continued to replay in my mind. I didn't think I'd be able to forget that for as long as I lived.

Not even a full minute after I heard her scream, the call dropped, and my ass was already getting in my truck, headed to Dallas. I'd tracked Breelyn's phone to the intersection of Coit and Belt Line. As I was merging onto the ramp to hit the freeway, my phone rang, and I almost wrecked out trying to remove it from my front pocket. I prayed it was Breelyn calling, but my heart sank when I realized it was only Giannis.

"Yo, G, I can't really talk right now," I hurried to say as soon as I picked up. I was speeding my ass off, so I needed to be focused on the road, not on the phone.

"Ay, I realize you're busy but some crazy shit was just brought to my attention, and I need to know when you last spoke with Breelyn," he stressed, immediately sparking my interest.

"That's exactly who I'm on my way to see about, dawg. I was on the phone with her, and I heard what sounded like a wreck, and the call dropped. Been trying to call her back but she's not answering. I'm hoping I'm wrong but . . ." My voice trailed off when I heard someone cry out in the background. I guessed he had me on speaker, and the cry had to have come from Dakota. I wouldn't ever forget the sound of it, either. If you know what pain sounds like, then you'll know what I mean when I say that's what her cries were akin to. There was no other way to describe that shit. It was the sound of pain. The two were extremely close, so I thought Kota could feel in her heart that things were bad just like I did. I was sitting here remembering losing my mom years ago, and the thought of the agony I felt that day returned, having me ready to murder anything moving.

"Baby, calm down," I heard Giannis say in a soothing tone.

"G, what's up, my nigga? Why were you asking if I talked to Bree?" I asked impatiently.

His ass wasn't even listening, and I couldn't even be mad at him. Just like Breelyn was my priority, Dakota was his. Thing was, he had his lady with him and she was good, but I had no idea what was up with mine.

After he was able to calm Dakota down, Giannis returned to the phone and gave me the rundown. They weren't far from the area, so they headed to the scene, promising to hit me when they knew what hospital they were taking her to. I prayed the entire way here that if she was injured, it wasn't anything life-threatening. Those sounds, though. I couldn't get them out of my head for shit. I could tell the impact had been powerful, and that had me hurting for my baby.

When I made it to Medical City and Giannis told me that David's weak ass was likely the culprit behind this shit and that the car had been tampered with, I nearly lost it. I felt like this was all my fault because if I had handled his ass when I had him in my grasp, this shit wouldn't have been happening right now. I did this shit for a living, was a fucking trained professional, so I knew better than to let him make it that night at the club. I had multiple opportunities to get at him since the incident, but I let Breelyn talk me out of if each and every time. My love for her had me not thinking clearly. And to find out that Dakota was the actual target wasn't too shocking with the way that nigga kept saying her name that night. He hated her ass, and that much was evident. Giannis and I had already stepped away to talk, and as soon as we made sure that Breelyn was good, we were going to find him and murk his ho ass.

I lifted my head to see Rah storming through the emergency entrance with fear and rage written all over his face. Fear because he had no clue what the future held for his sister, and rage due to the murderous thoughts that ran through his mind for the person who was bold enough to harm her. The family was already prepared for him to come in this bitch on a fucking rampage about his one and only sibling. He was on his way back from Houston when Giannis called him and let him know what was up. Nigga must have sped the whole way back to Dallas, because it hadn't been that long since he talked to G and he still had about two hours to go on his ride, at least. Based on the foul language spewing from his mouth right now, it was clear that he wasn't feeling the update relayed to him by his family. The doctor had come out to speak with us about thirty minutes ago, and I was trying hard to recall and grasp all the shit he'd told us was going on with Breelyn. It was so much. *"Needs surgery . . . broken bones . . . blood transfusions . . . in a coma . . ." Blah blah fucking blah.* My lady could leave up out this bitch with one leg and two teeth, and I was still gon' marry her ass. I just needed her to make it so that I could take her home and continue to love her.

"Where the fuck is my sister? You!" Rah pointed at the female manning the registration desk. "What information can you give me on Breelyn Waiters? Nah, I'on give a fuck what they already told my people. I want them mu'fuckas to tell that shit to me! Lady, please tell me what's wrong with my sister! Greeedyyy!" Rah roared, causing me to blow out a harsh breath. Nigga was throwing a full-blown temper tantrum in this bitch, and I truly felt sorry for him. I couldn't stand his ass, but I couldn't help but sympathize with him after witnessing this scene.

Rah continued acting a fool, not letting the woman properly respond to his tirade. This man had her scared as hell, probably silently thanking God for the glass that separated them. He was damn near foaming at the mouth as he threatened to kill every doctor in the facility if the incompetent surgeons let his sister die. Those were his exact words. Several family members tried getting him under control to no avail. Giannis couldn't intervene because he was tending to an extremely distraught Dakota, who seemed to get worse when she saw the state Rah was in.

The closeness among Rah, Breelyn, and Kota might have been viewed by some as a tad unhealthy, but I understood it because I had a cousin back home I was just as close to. Breelyn's entire family loved hard, though, so it was natural for them to react the way they did when another was hurt or going through something. Hence Dakota's current state. She'd been inconsolable since arriving at the hospital. Seeing the wreckage and Breelyn in the condition she was in as they loaded her onto the ambulance was too much for her, according to G. He said she passed out and ended up in an ambulance herself, but after being checked out here in the ER, it was determined that she was straight physically. Emotionally, though, she was out of there.

I looked up again to see Mr. Bibbs wrap an arm around his nephew's neck from the back, saying something to Rah that only he could hear. Whatever it was calmed him some. I watched as another gentleman, who looked to be an older version of Rah, came to his side. There was no question that he was Breelyn's father. Looked like the man spit Rah out himself. A few words and an embrace from the man was all it took for Rah to lose his cool all over again. From conversations with Breelyn, I knew that the history between the siblings and their father wasn't great, which may have added to Rah's fucked-up state of mind. Any other time I would have made it a point to go over and introduce myself as Breelyn's boyfriend to the man, but I ain't have time nor was my mind in the right frame for introductions. Breelyn was my only focus right now, so me and her pops would have to rap some other time. I looked on as the father held his son as he continued to cry out for his sister. Nothing wrong with a man crying. Hell, we hurt too. He was terrified of losing his sister, and so was I. Felt like breaking down just thinking about it. What the fuck was I supposed to do without her? This shit was too much.

"Rio, sweetie, can I get you something? Some coffee or something to eat?"

I looked up to see Dakota's mom standing before me. "Nah, Ms. Syl, I'm straight, but thank you," I mumbled lowly.

"Oh, it's no problem, son. You're family now, so I had to check up on you," she said before taking a seat next to me. I didn't really feel like being bothered, but I'd never tell her that. "I'm sure you know this already, but my Breelyn is a whole lot stronger than everyone gives her credit for. Dakota always comes off as the tough one, but she's the more sensitive of the two. Even when Breelyn was younger, she was tough as nails. We just kind of babied her anyway because she was lacking her biological mother, and when you really think about it, she didn't have her father either. I mean, he was there, but he wasn't there if you know what I mean. She's older than Kota, but we just made her our baby anyway. If that were Kota back there going through what Breelyn's going through, I might be a little worried, but not Greedy. Nah, not her. Baby girl is going to come out of this better and stronger than she was before, and you need to believe that, okay?" she told me, wearing a confident smile.

She seemed so sure of what she was saying that it made me believe as well, so I just nodded in agreement. It was all I could do right now. I couldn't speak because one word from my mouth would have resulted in me crying like Rah's mark ass, straight up. I knew my baby's strength, and I believed she would make it through this. I just hated for her to have to hurt in any way, and to find out that someone she once loved was responsible pissed me off even more. Despite her moving on with her life and starting a new relationship with me, I knew that learning that David was the cause of her accident would devastate her.

"Thank you, Ms. Syl. I really needed to hear that," I admitted as I leaned over to give her a one-armed hug—a hug I probably needed more than she did. Breelyn was like her daughter. I knew she was going through it as well, and I appreciated her checking on me.

"Like I said, we're family. Keep a positive mind and let me know if I can get you anything," she offered before rejoining the rest of her family.

It really felt good to be a part of a family. I hadn't had that in so long I almost forgot what the shit felt like. The Sunday dinners, the laughs, and the genuine love between Breelyn and her people was everything and definitely an environment and group of people I wanted my children brought up around. They could get ratchet as hell and as a group was quick to gang up to beat somebody down, but it was all love with them. Love was something I needed. Wasn't even aware of that until I met Breelyn, and that was why I needed her to make it through this shit.

Chapter 3

You Needed Me

Rah

"Mind if I join you?"

I looked up to see my sperm donor standing tall as hell to the right of me. He caught me off guard when he approached me earlier, and now I sat here, looking unbothered, prepared to give his ass a hard time. Feeling eyes on me, I surveyed the room until I met my Uncle Kasey's glare. I guessed I would have to save the petty shit for another day. He was silently telling me to act like I had some sense, so I nodded nonchalantly, letting Kenneth know it was cool for him to sit down. Yeah, I said Kenneth and I meant that shit. Wasn't no Dad, Daddy, or Pops over this way. I was an exact replica of this man, and for years our relationship had been pretty much nonexistent. A phone call every now and then or seeing one another in passing was as far as it went.

I didn't see how he, as my father, let shit get like this between us. It was hard enough on Breelyn and me not having our mother, but having our father basically say fuck us was even worse. This shit with my sister already had my mind and heart fucked up. I'd never been so scared in all my life, and this pitiful-looking fool sitting next to me was about to have me in my feelings even more. This emotional shit was foreign to me and wasn't a good look, but I didn't care at this point. I just needed her to be all right. Breelyn had to make it because I didn't think I would if she didn't. I was sitting here kicking myself for the time we spent not talking. We'd just hashed things out, and boom, this shit happens.

"I fucked up, Elijah. I fucked up real bad," Kenneth said in a voice so strained that it caused me to raise my head to look at him. Our eyes locked but I didn't respond. "I fucked up with you and Breelyn, and now my baby girl is in there fighting for her life. I'm afraid that I might not get the chance to tell her how much I love her or how sorry I am for checking out after your mama died. How sorry I am for not being there for her when she needed me." He looked off in the other direction regretfully, not focused on anything in particular.

After a long pause and an extremely deep breath, he finally spoke again. "When ya mama passed, I was lost, Elijah. Felt like I was dead inside, and because of that, I didn't handle business like a man's supposed to. Shit ain't no excuse, but it's the truth. I should have sucked it up and done what was needed to be the best I could for my children, but I was in a fucked-up place. Layne was my world, son, and losing her caused everything to crash down around me. Made me forget that I had two people still here depending on me to be there, but I dropped the ball. You're grown now, but I'm hoping you're willing to work things out and give me a chance to show you that I've changed. Maybe God will bless our family and I'll get an opportunity to have this conversation with my only daughter as well. I want you to know that I love you. I've always loved you, and I'm sorry that I wasn't the man you needed me to be," he said, looking me right in the eyes.

For a moment we just stared at one another. In this family, I was known as one to hold grudges. You fuck me over just one time and you would never have to worry about me dealing with you again in life. But in this case, I just couldn't do it. I was making an exception for my old man. Yes, the way Kenneth handled losing my mother was some ho-ass shit, but he was trying to make amends for his shortcomings. He was humbling himself before me, and I had to respect that. I didn't know if Breelyn being in this accident was the cause of his change of heart or if he'd been meaning to talk to us. I really didn't care. I was just glad that he owned up to it. Standing up, I looked down at him for a few seconds before extending my hand. Once he grabbed on, I pulled him to his feet for an embrace.

A tortuous wail left his body as we held on to one another. This shit was awkward as fuck. Nigga was crying with his face torn the fuck up like that black dude from that intervention show. They had memed the fuck out of that video on the internet, and had this situation been different, I would have laughed so damn hard. To do that shit right now wasn't cool, so I just let him cry. On a serious note, I was willing to give him another chance and could only pray he got this opportunity with Greedy. If y'all thought I was bad? My sister really didn't fuck with this man on any level. With her, he was almost in the same category as Jada's ass, so you already know what it was.

"Elijah!" I heard that soft voice call out from across the room. Immediately, I released my father and took off to meet her halfway. I didn't think I ran, but I definitely jogged. I was on some sucker shit, but I didn't even care. That's just how happy I was to see her face. As soon as I was close enough, I pulled her into my arms. Having her here meant everything to me. I called her on my way here, but I couldn't believe she actually came. She said she was done with me months ago, but she came through for me, and that shit made me feel good.

"You came?" I stated the obvious as I studied her pretty face.

"You said you needed me, so here I am. How is Breelyn? What are the doctors saying? My God, how is Kota taking all of this?" She fired off questions one after the other.

"Shit's fucked up, love. My baby in there fucked up." I sniffed. Glad she wasn't here when I broke down and was crying like a bitch a little while ago. She knew what Breelyn and Dakota meant to me, so I was sure she knew I was hurting. I could feel all eyes on us as we embraced, but at the moment, I didn't give a damn. Like I told her on the phone, I needed her, and I was also realizing that I was in love with her, so folks' opinions of us dealing with each other was the furthest thing from my mind. That was, until I heard Kota's aggressive-ass tone behind me.

"Rah, what the fuck is going on here?" she asked, prompting both of us to turn and face her. I already knew this conversation wasn't about to go well at all, but it was long overdue.

Chapter 4

My Right Hand

Dakota

"Babe, I need you to eat something. I'm not for you falling out on me again," Giannis urged, shoving a sandwich and bottle of water from the vending machine my way.

"Ease up! How many times do I have to say I'm not hungry, Giannis?" I snapped. It wasn't my intention to come off so rude, but I was so distraught behind my cousin that I'd been lashing out left and right. On him, my parents, and anyone else who stepped to me. Shit, no one was exempt from my wrath. My dad had already cursed me out and banished me to this area of the waiting room with Giannis. I was ordered to stay here until I learned how to talk to folk. Straight up put me in timeout like I was a child. Kasey Bibbs was out of line for that, but I wouldn't dare challenge him.

"Dakota Layne, I'ma let you make it because I know you're hurting right now, but we're all fucked up about Breelyn. So what I need you to do is bump that shit down. I'm talking all the way down, baby girl. Just drink the water for me and I'll back off," he negotiated. I guessed he'd had enough of my attitude as well.

"Fine," I mumbled, snatching the bottle of water from his extended hand. I knew I was wrong for taking my frustrations out on everyone, but I couldn't help it. It was like I could feel her pain. My best friend was hurting, and it hurt me not being able to do anything about it. My body was literally aching right now, and that couldn't be good for me. Add in the constant crying and that only caused my head to pound harder. Every time I thought I had it together, I would once again be overcome with sadness and a fresh stream of tears would appear, covering the dry ones that stained my face. I was only causing more problems for myself, but the thought of Breelyn not making it consumed me. I felt like shit because all my thoughts were negative and I was in no way exercising faith like I knew I should be. To see her unconscious and bloody on that stretcher was too much for me to handle. She was barely recognizable when they lifted her on the back of that ambulance. The only thing that stood out was her platinum-blond hair, and even it was saturated with bright red blood. Really wished I hadn't seen that shit. Breelyn's situation wasn't the only issue contributing to this massive headache I had, but dwelling on that would only cause more anxiety.

"You know I don't mean it, right?" I asked Giannis, referring to my attitude.

"I know, Kota. Just let me take care of you."

"Okay. I'm sorry, honey," I said softly as I rested my head on his shoulder.

"We're good," he replied before placing a kiss atop my head.

Now back to that other issue of mine. Fuck that shit with Rah and ol' girl. I'd deal with that another day. I needed Breelyn by my side before I even attempted to approach him about those two anyway. Should have known something was going on with them but I ignored all the signs. Right now, though, I had bigger fish to fry. Some shit I didn't want to think about continued creeping into my mind. Upon arrival at the hospital, I was examined thoroughly. Out of the blue, the ER nurse asked me if there was any chance I could be pregnant, and of course, my answer was hell to the nah, nah, nah! There was no way that could be, right? Due to the fact that I'd lost consciousness for a moment, the doctor insisted on me taking a pregnancy test anyway just to be sure. I hadn't seen my cycle in a cool minute, but for me, that wasn't abnormal. I was solely basing my answer on how I felt, and I'd been feeling just fine. Nothing was out of the ordinary with my body, and I just knew that if I were pregnant, I would feel different or have symptoms.

Imagine my surprise when he came back in and told me that the test had come back positive. My ass almost passed the fuck out again. I mean, what the hell was the point in taking birth control pills if I was going to end up knocked up anyway? I admit that I hadn't been as diligent in taking them as I normally was, so this slipup was all on me. This shit happening wasn't in our plan at all. At least not at this point in our relationship. I just hoped Giannis wouldn't be too upset about it.

Luckily he was out of the room trying to get an update on Breelyn for me when all this was going down. Being pregnant was not something I could give my attention right now. Don't get me wrong, I was happy to be carrying Giannis's baby. He was the only man I ever wanted to have babies with, but I had to focus on one thing at a time, and at the moment my right hand had my undivided attention.

When I knew what Breelyn's fate was and we dealt with that as a family, then I'd tell my man about the baby. Hopefully we knew something soon, because I was already almost seven weeks in, so a visit to my doctor needed to happen as soon as possible. Despite me being perfectly healthy, Giannis's crazy ass would put me

on bed rest himself if he knew I was pregnant. Fuck a
doctor's order. And right now I needed to be here with
my family, not laid up in bed being hovered over and
put on restriction by my man. After I asked the staff not
to mention my condition when he was in the room, they
proceeded to give me two bags of fluids through my IV
to rehydrate my body. Dehydration along with being
pregnant was the real reason I passed out, but Giannis
didn't need to know all that. At least not right now.

Putting thoughts of my pregnancy to the side, my eyes
wandered over to my cousin. Just like Rio, Rah was in a
secluded area of the waiting room sitting tight until we
could get another update on Breelyn. He was straight
when ol' girl was here, but she left after we engaged in
a heated exchange. Since then he had slipped back into
himself. My big cousin was going through it, and it was
written all over him. His entire aura oozed despair. Head
hung back against the chair with his eyes closed, he
sported his infamous mean mug, the one that said
he wasn't to be fucked with. But me being me, I just
wouldn't leave well enough alone. I was sure he was upset
about me confronting him and ol' girl, but I didn't give a
damn. Now wasn't the time, but we would be addressing
that situation real soon.

"Baby, I'll be right back. I need to go check on Rah."

Giannis nodded his understanding, releasing me from
his hold. The closer I got to Rah, I noticed the tears coming from his eyes and flowing into his freshly faded hair.
Only other time I'd seen this man drop a tear was when
I broke my leg after a fall down some stairs, wearing
my brand-new skates when we were kids. Had to have
been around eight or nine years old. He cried because
I wouldn't have been hurt if I hadn't done the trick he
triple-dog dared me to do. One would have thought I was
dying the way he was carrying on when my folks brought
me to the emergency room. My leg was no longer hurting,

but I had his ass waiting on me hand and foot for almost two weeks before he peeped the game I was running. Now he was the one who needed some tender loving care.

No words were needed or exchanged when I took the seat to the right of him. He immediately draped his arm around me before resting his head against mine. My big cousin was one of the strongest men I knew, but I also knew that Breelyn and I were his weaknesses. Seeing him so torn up made me want to suck up my feelings to be strong for him.

After about ten minutes, Giannis joined us, sitting on the other side of me, interlocking his fingers with mine. I glanced across the room at Rio, and my heart instantly went out to him. It was obvious to anyone who witnessed them together that he was in love with my cousin. He was one of those men who turned inward when he was upset or hurting. Nigga was so much like Elijah Raheem that it was crazy. He remained quiet nearly the entire time we'd been here. Only spoke up when he requested that he be the first person to see Breelyn. Surprisingly, no one in the family protested or made a fuss about it, so it was established that he and Rah would go back once it was time. I didn't put up a fight because I really didn't want to see my boo like that again. I planned to wait until everyone had a chance to see her before I went back. We remained in the same spot for what seemed like hours, just waiting. It was more like forty-five minutes but time seemed to be moving at a snail's pace.

As soon as I knew Breelyn was straight, I planned to hit Montell up to see about getting a location on David. I wasn't going to share this information with Rah or Giannis because I was sure they wouldn't approve and I didn't have time for that. I was the one David wanted to hurt when he fucked with my car, so I wanted to be the one to deal with him. I knew he was pussy, but he had officially taken things too far. He was used to running females, so me always standing up for Breelyn and bucking up to him wasn't something he was used to. But that was his damn problem, not mine. God was the only one I bowed down to. Well, Him and Giannis's bossy ass.

I had some gruesome shit in store for Mr. Parrish. As I sat there thinking of ways to torture him, my hand instantaneously went to my stomach. It was like my baby was reminding me that he or she was there and I needed to think before I did something to jeopardize the life growing inside of me. Damn kid was already cramping my style. First Giannis and now this little person was forcing me to stand down. It was still hard for me to turn that switch off, that "I'm ready to pop off and fuck some shit up" switch. Remembering that I had a real man by my side to handle shit like this made it easier though. At least if Montell gave David up, I could pass that information on to the fellas. Knowing them as well as I did, I figured they were probably already plotting on ways to get at his ass anyway.

"The fuck you thinking about that got you smiling like that?" Giannis asked.

When I looked up at him, his eyes were trained on my hand, which still rested on my stomach. Shit, I didn't even realize I was smiling. I quickly removed my hand and moved it to push my hair behind my ear. I just knew his nosey ass was about to start asking questions. "I was thinking about getting a quesadilla from Qdoba. I'm getting hungry," I answered without hesitation, attempting to play it off.

"Hungry, huh?" he asked skeptically, finally lifting his eyes up to meet mine.

"Yes, Giannis. I haven't had anything to eat since this morning. Go ahead and pass me that sandwich," I requested to further convince him. He handed it over but was looking at me like he knew I was lying. This nigga here didn't miss shit. I swore that man watched me the entire time I ate that dry-ass turkey sandwich. It wasn't all that good but made me feel better almost immediately. Maybe I was hungry after all and had just been ignoring it. The ache in my head had even gotten better.

"Why are you looking at me like that?" I asked after gulping down some of the water.

"No reason, but tell me again what the doctor said about you passing out."

The way he was looking at me made me uncomfortable as fuck, and lying to one another was something we didn't do, so I was kind of stuck but proceeded to answer his question. "He just said I was dehydrated. That's why they gave me the fluids. Stop worrying, Giannis. I'm fine." I smiled and kissed his lips. Okay, I didn't lie. I just left out some key information. I was going to tell him. Just couldn't do it right now.

"A'ight, well, drink the rest of that water, and we'll stop by Qdoba when we leave here," he said, still giving me that look. I only nodded. My ass was scared to speak because if I opened my mouth to say anything right now, I knew I would break down and tell him about the baby.

The doctor calling for the family of Breelyn Waiters was what saved me. We were all up on our feet moving toward him and the nurse at his side.

"First, I want to say that the surgery was a success, but Ms. Waiters has a long road ahead and is not yet out of the woods. We repaired her fractured arm, left leg, and pelvis. Those injuries alone will require months of physical therapy should she make it through the next few days. The next forty-eight to seventy-two hours are critical, and we will be monitoring her closely."

All I heard after that was *whomp, whomp, whomp.* His lips were moving, but I'd tuned him out. Breelyn being that fucked up was doing a number on my emotions. Giannis squeezing my hand brought me back to the present as I once again tuned in to the doctor's speech.

"Once that is resolved, we will start to ween her off those medications and possibly remove her from the machine that's breathing for her right now. Like I said, she's not out of the woods, but I can tell she's tough because she's made it this far. Right now we have Ms. Waiters in recovery, and she'll be moved up to ICU within the hour. I'll have my nurse come out to let you all know when she goes up so that you can see her. They allow visitors up to two at a time in ICU, and we'll give you all an opportunity to quickly and quietly go in to see her before visiting hours are over," Dr. Stephens explained.

"Will one of us be allowed to stay with her?" Rio asked before I could.

The ride home was quiet. My mind was consumed with thoughts of what Breelyn would be facing once she made it out of that coma. Whatever it was, I would be there for her every step of the way just like I'd always been. After we stopped by Giannis's house, he was going to drive me across town so that I could shower and pick up some clothes from my place. I would go back to the hospital to relieve Rio so that he could make the drive to North Richland Hills, where he lived, to do the same.

"What the fuck is she doing here?" he grumbled.

Giannis's words jarred me from my thoughts, and I looked up to see exactly what, or should I say who, had my man irritated. I'd been so deep in my head that I hadn't realized we'd already pulled into his driveway. Looking through his driver's side window, I was able to see who had his attention. "Who the hell is that?" I asked. Whoever she was, she was a gorgeous girl, rocking a cropped haircut that was made just for her perfectly slender face. The bright smile she was wearing vanished when she noticed that Giannis wasn't in the car alone.

"Serenity," was his simple answer.

I didn't know why I expected him to elaborate, but he didn't. "Your ex-girlfriend Serenity?" He'd told me about her briefly.

"Yeah," he answered, looking from her then back to me.

"Well, Giannis, are you going to get out to talk to her and see what she wants?" I asked apprehensively. His reaction to seeing her low-key scared me and made me feel a little insecure. It was like she had him shook. Like he still felt a way about this bitch. I mean, this was the woman he thought he wanted to settle down with, but she wasn't ready at the time, so he decided to move on. I found it funny how not too long ago I was boasting on my man not coming with any drama or having hoes popping up out of the blue, and now this shit. Guessed I spoke too soon. As if I didn't already have enough going on, now this ho and her sudden appearance were about to be added to my plate.

"No, we're going to get out to see what she wants. It's been years, so I have no idea what she could possibly want, but when I find out, I want you by my side."

I was sure he said that last part to reassure me, but I still felt a way about her just popping up and him acting like he was stuck being in her presence. We were sitting in the car having a full-blown conversation while she posted up shooting daggers and shifting her weight from side to side. Guessed the bitch was mad that she had yet to be acknowledged.

"Whatever, Giannis. Just handle this shit quickly so that I can go back up there to see about Breelyn," I quipped with an eye roll.

"Nah, slow yo' ass down," he commanded, grabbing my arm to prevent me from exiting the vehicle. "Why do I feel like you're pissed with me and I haven't even done anything wrong, Dakota?"

"You sure about that? Got bitches showing up to your spot like it's some shit that happens often. Why would she think it's cool for her to just show up here out of the blue?" I questioned, getting myself hype with no real reason to be upset. I knew Giannis better than that, but I thought my hormones were out of control or something. I almost laughed out loud just then because I was acting like them two-minute pregnant hoes on social media Breelyn and I joked about. I'd just found out hours before that I was with child and was already blaming my irrational behavior on my baby. In my defense, I'd always been a hothead, so hopefully my man didn't read more into my actions than was necessary.

"I ain't even about to entertain the bullshit you're suggesting right now. I ain't no lying-ass, cheating-ass nigga, and you know that. If I say that I don't know why this bitch is here, then that's what the fuck it is. Now get your ass out the car so we can see what she got going on. Best believe we'll be having a conversation about this shit later," he said before shooting me a look that dared me to try him. I was Kota B, though, so I had to say something smart in return.

"Most definitely. And if this ho jump stupid, I'm popping her in her fucking mouth," I warned. He just laughed, which only further pissed me off.

"Yo' ass ain't 'bout to do shit. Stay talking shit like you can really fight. Ass probably got hands like a fish," he teased before smacking a quick kiss to my lips then pulling back just a little. I leaned forward to kiss him again before replying.

"Fuck you, Giannis. You already know what it is," I spoke against his lips. I was trying to keep that hardcore look on my face once we broke apart to exit the car, but I couldn't help but smile. As usual, his lips felt so good and could improve my mood in an instant. He immediately caused my smile to widen even more when he extended his hand for me. Ol' girl rolled her eyes and sucked her teeth as she watched our interaction. Giannis had me so caught up that I almost forgot the ho was standing there.

"Serenity, what's going on? What are you doing here?" Giannis finally addressed her. His tone didn't mask the fact that he was not happy to see her.

"Well, hello to you too, Zion," she said while smiling her cute little smile.

Her ass was already starting out on the wrong foot, calling my nigga by his middle name like that was supposed to mean some shit. Giannis knew my fuse was short, so I silently prayed that he got her ass under control before I fucked her up. Better yet, I had more serious shit going on, so sitting here going tit for tat with this bitch would be a waste of my time. I'd let him deal with his blast from the past who felt it was cool to drop by whenever she felt the need.

"Giannis—I mean, Zion—I'm going to let you handle this while I step inside," I said, attempting to walk away while fishing my keys out of my purse.

"Nah, fuck that. You ain't going no place. When we go inside our home, we'll go together," he said firmly while pulling me back to his side, placing a kiss to my temple. I noticed her eyes bulge when he referred to his home as our home. Again, I rolled my eyes, wishing I could just go inside. They could miss me with this extra shit, but I knew damn well he wasn't about to let me out of his sight while she was present.

"Serenity, this is my lady, Dakota. Baby, this is my ex, Serenity." The entire time he talked, his eyes were on me. "Now what can we do for you this evening?" he said, finally looking her way.

"Is there any chance we could talk in private?" she asked quietly.

"This bitch," I mumbled impatiently, causing Giannis to gently squeeze my hand. Ain't no fucking way the two of them speaking one-on-one was about to happen now that I knew her angle. This girl wanted Giannis, but there was only one problem. He was mine now, and I wasn't giving him up for shit. This bitch had another think coming if she thought it was going down like that.

"I tried calling your phone, but I see you had the number changed, and I left a few messages at Good Life. I'm sure they weren't relayed to you," she stated with attitude.

"Of course not. My staff was instructed long ago how to handle calls from anyone I dealt with in the past, so they're doing exactly what they've been paid to do. As far as us talking in private, that ain't gon' happen. We've been over for some time now, and as I just stated, I'm in a relationship with this beautiful lady beside me. I would never disrespect her like that," he informed her coolly. My man was becoming irritated, but the entire situation was comical to me at this point.

"You're right, I shouldn't have shown up here unannounced. And, Dallas?" She turned to me. "I didn't mean to disrespect you or your relationship. This visit was nothing more than me attempting to catch up with an old friend," she offered with fake sincerity. She was clearly trying to save face. Bitch was crushed by the way Giannis stood up for me, and it showed in the way her voice was damn near cracking and the fake smile she had plastered on her face. I wasn't going for it though.

"First of all, the name is Dakota, and trust me when I say that my man don't need no friends, old, new, or otherwise, so you can get the fuck on with that shit," I sassed while Giannis snickered. His ass always thought some shit was funny.

She just stood there looking like she couldn't believe that I'd spoken to her that way. As prissy and put together as she was, I was sure she was surprised that he was with a female as rough around the edges as myself. Then she had the nerve to look to Giannis as if he would come to her rescue. *Bitch, please. My nigga is about whatever I am about. Fuck you mean?*

"And with that said, you should get going," Giannis added for confirmation. We turned to walk up the sidewalk when he suddenly stopped to address her again. "Ay, Serenity, don't come by here like this again. Anything we needed to speak about was discussed when we ended whatever we had, so there's no need to talk or be friends. I ain't trying to be rude, but like I said, I don't disrespect my lady, and I won't allow anyone else to make her feel a way either. Got it?"

"Got it," she replied with a smirk.

"Good," Giannis and I replied at the same time then smiled at each other. I didn't know what that look was about, but that bitch could play with it if she wanted to. We entered the house and left her ass standing there looking stupid. I didn't know her true purpose for coming here tonight. I mean, I had an idea, but I definitely would be paying closer attention to my man from here on out.

Chapter 5

Could It Be

Rio

It was now day eight since Breelyn had been down, and I was slowly losing faith that she would ever wake up. I had only left the hospital once since the shit went down, and Giannis looking out for me was the only reason I had clean clothes and food, because I refused to leave her side. Dakota stayed put most times as well, only leaving to get food or go home to bathe. Rah was in and out because he just couldn't take seeing her like this. I wouldn't be leaving anytime soon because I had to be the first face Breelyn saw when she woke up. I knew for a fact that she would be looking for me, and I refused to disappoint her.

While taking a much-needed nap on the hard-ass couch in the room, I heard someone calling my name. The voice was low and strained, so I thought I was tripping. I was in a deep-ass sleep at the time and thought it was all in my head. Just a dream, ya know?

"DeMariooo."

The voice was still low as hell but louder the second time. The familiar tone caused me to immediately spring up out of my sleep. My heart was beating stupid crazy, like it was trying to force its way out of my chest. I almost busted my ass tripping over the thin sheet I had wrapped around me. Could it be? Damn, I sure hoped so. It was all I'd been praying for.

When I finally came into view, Breelyn's eyes bucked, and she proceeded to sob so violently that it made me drop a few tears myself. No guards existed between us, so it was nothing for me to get emotional in front of her.

"DeMario." She continued crying as she slowly lifted her arm to caress my cheek. I could tell it took a lot of strength just for that simple motion. I kissed away the tears as well as every scar and imperfection on her face like I'd done every day she'd been laid up in this bed. I'd talked to her nonstop, begging her to come back to me.

"Welcome back, love. Thank you for coming back to me," I whispered, still kissing her face. After having my time with her, I alerted the staff that she was awake.

"Ms. Waiters, I'm so glad you decided to wake up from that extremely long nap," her nurse stated with a big smile.

"So am I," my lady responded with a wide smile of her own before Nurse Ivy proceeded to assess her. Well, she performed the best assessment she could, because I was clearly in the way. Breelyn was hanging on to me much like she was the day I snatched her fine ass up from the zoo. She refused to let me go then, and she refused to let me go now.

Nurse Ivy was an attractive older lady who had been very helpful to us since Breelyn had been admitted. She had even taken my hand and made me bow my head as she prayed over Bree numerous times. I wasn't a saint by any means, but I did believe in the power of prayer. Despite being a believer, I was terrified thinking that this was going to be my karma for all the lives I'd taken over the years. I was sure that my punishment was going to be a life without Breelyn, and that was a life I just didn't want to live. In the time we'd known each other, she'd become my whole world, and without her existence, my so-called life didn't mean a damn thing to me.

After Breelyn was seen by the surgeon and informed of the injuries she'd sustained in the accident, I called her family to let them know she was awake. Before they got there, we had a small window of time to mourn, and I also took a moment to update her on everything that had occurred since she'd been out of it. She knew it all, and instead of being hurt about what David had done, she was furious. I had to calm her down several times because she was so angry. She'd only been out of the coma for a short time, and I didn't want her to get too worked up and set herself back.

After giving her her daily bed bath like I did every day, she felt much better. We only had about fifteen more minutes of alone time before Kota made it back with food and a change of clothes for me. I wanted to leave so that they could have a moment to themselves, but I was too scared to walk out the door. I was afraid that when I walked back in, all of this wouldn't be real, and I would still be waiting for her to open those pretty eyes for me.

"Bree, I was so fucking scared, man." Kota rushed over to her in tears. I was sure she was thinking back to the day of the accident when she passed out at the sight of her cousin on that stretcher.

"So was I." Breelyn nodded her head. "When that truck hit me, I just knew that was it for me."

Her voice was really hoarse as she talked, and hearing her speak about the accident made me clench my jaw and fist. On cue, the sounds I heard on the other end of the phone that day began to play again in my head. I leaned down to kiss her face, attempting to block that shit out while she continued to talk to Kota. They held hands, crying and laughing off and on for the longest time.

I knew this incident would only serve to bring them closer. This shit surely made me love her even more, not only for her strength but also because there were so many times when I was afraid that I would lose her. That was the worst feeling ever. Her fighting to stay here meant the world to me. Like Ms. Syl told me, my baby was a lot stronger than people thought. Lucky for us, her broken bones would heal, and the scars that she hated would eventually fade. As long as she was able to leave this place with me, that was all that mattered. The road to recovery would be a long one, but I would be there to make sure it was as painless as possible.

Now that she was back and I knew she would be okay, it was time to deal with the man responsible for hurting her, for hurting all of us. That nigga was gon' have to see me about this shit, and what I had planned for him was going to be nothing nice. Blocking my murderous thoughts, I tuned back into the conversation.

"When I was out, I could hear conversations going on around me, but as bad as I wanted to and as hard as I tried, I just couldn't wake up," Breelyn stated with a shake of her head.

"All that matters is that you're here now." Kota smiled, hugging her again.

"That's right," I concurred as Rah made his way into the room. For a moment, he and Breelyn just stared at one another without saying a word.

"Boy, come here and quit standing there like you scared or som'n," she joked while wiping a tear away.

"Hey, Greedy," Rah said, moving closer to her bed.

Just like when Kota first came, I knew he needed his time alone with his sister. I wouldn't admit it to him, but he was the only person I was comfortable leaving her alone with. He wouldn't let anyone harm her, and I believed that with all my heart. I kissed my girl for like the millionth time before stepping out of the room to give the siblings and cousin a few minutes to themselves.

When I entered the waiting area, I found a pissed-off Giannis seated in the back. Lately he'd been looking like he had a lot on his mind. I didn't know if it was because of what was going on with Breelyn or if something else was bothering him.

"My nigga, what's up with you? Yo' ass been sporting the screw face for the last week at least," I pointed out.

After shaking his head and remaining silent for a few seconds, he finally spoke. "Man, it's Kota. Her ass sitting up here pregnant and don't think I know. Been sitting back waiting for her to give me the news, but she still ain't said a word. Just trying to figure out why she keeping a nigga in the dark about it," he said with a frustrated sigh.

"What, you saw the test or something? I'm saying, how you know she's pregnant if she ain't said shit?"

G looked at me like I was crazy when I said that. "Man, I know my woman, and I know every inch of her body. I already had a feeling, and then she passed out that day, so I really got to thinking. I understood she was going through something at the time, but my gut kept telling me that she could possibly be carrying my baby. I just hope she ain't thinking about getting rid of my seed, mane. I love her ass to death, but I don't think I could rock with her if she did some shit like that. Especially without telling me? I mean, we talked about having babies or whatever but we wanted to wait a few years. For all I know, she done decided she's not ready yet."

"G, she may have a reason for not telling you. Look at all this shit we been dealing with concerning Breelyn. You know Kota loves yo' light-skinned ass to death, and I just can't see her doing some sneak shit like that. Stop jumping to conclusions and give sis a chance to come clean," I advised. I fucked with Dakota the long way, and I knew for a fact that she loved the shit out of Giannis's ass. There was no way that she would do some shit like that behind his back. There had to be a reasonable explanation for her holding back this information.

"You right. Gotta be a reason she hasn't said anything, and my baby has been pretty stressed lately," he replied thoughtfully. "She got one fucking week, and if she don't bring it up, by then I'm going the fuck off," he snapped.

How he go from being an understanding boyfriend to pissed the hell off that fast? Dakota needed to hurry up and let this crazy fool know what was up before he lost his fucking mind. He was already loony tunes when it came to her, and she knew that better than anyone. I guessed I'd be pretty pissed myself if Breelyn knew for weeks that she was pregnant with my baby and neglected to tell me.

Thinking about her carrying a baby for me caused my heart to ache a little, but I quickly shook it off. All I knew was that Dakota better have a good damn excuse for why she was keeping my homie in the dark, because his thoughts were on some deceitful shit. In the mind of a man, the only reasons a woman didn't tell her significant other that she was pregnant were she didn't think he would be happy about it, she didn't want to keep the baby, or the child she was carrying might not belong to him. Might sound crazy, but in the mind of a man, it was real.

Chapter 6

Harsh Reality

Breelyn

Seeing my brother teary-eyed shook me, and the next thing I knew, I was shedding some tears of my own. And of course, Dakota's punk ass was weeping as well. To be here with them, talking to them, and touching them meant everything to me. I seriously thought I was a goner. Hearing DeMario's prayers and words of encouragement during my involuntary hibernation was what made me fight my way through. I even heard my absentee father in my ear when I was out of it. I wanted to be happy that he was there and had plans to fix our broken relationship, but I honestly didn't think I was ready.

As a child, I felt rejected by that man, and the feeling followed me into adulthood. I'd always dreamed of being a daddy's girl like Kota, but my father denied me of that all my life. Now he all of a sudden wanted to do right? Nah. It was now my turn to hand him my ass to kiss just like he'd done to me for years. I couldn't lie and say I wasn't crying on the inside when he expressed his love for me. Never had he uttered those three words to me. I was touched, but I was also very angry. I figured he was only saying it now because he thought I was about to die. For that reason alone, I couldn't accept or believe those words coming from him. He'd probably be showing his face around here soon enough. Or maybe not. Didn't make a difference to me either way.

My focus was going to be on this extensive rehab that lay ahead. That and DeMario. I swore I loved that man with everything in me. I never believed finding someone who loved me the way he did was even possible, but he proved me wrong. I'd be forever grateful to him for that.

That other nigga though? The one responsible for my current condition? The reason my body was experiencing pains greater than anything I'd ever felt before and the cause of me having to learn to walk again? That fool was a dead man. *He'd better thank the good Lord for every second he has left on this earth, because his time is quickly winding down.* It had been over for us for some time, and because he refused to accept it and thought harming my cousin would get me back, he was about to be eliminated from this life. Completely and permanently.

"So, y'all haven't caught up with Dave yet?" I asked.

Both Kota and Rah turned to me in surprise. They probably didn't think I was aware that he was behind all this madness, but Rio and I didn't keep secrets from one another. He broke everything down for me soon after I was awake, and for more reasons than one, I was ready for David's ass to be handled.

"Was just waiting on you to wake up before I made any moves, sis. Now it's time to hit the ground running. Nigga is a week or so ahead of me, but trust me when I say that I will find him," Rah said confidently.

"I want him dead, Elijah!"

"I told you I have it under control, Greedy," he assured me.

"I wish I could be the one to end his worthless, miserable life," I spat.

"Baby, who you in here talking about murking?" Rio asked jokingly as he and Giannis entered my hospital room.

"Who else?" I smiled up at him.

"Didn't I tell you that we would take care of it?" he asked, and I nodded. "You just focus on healing and getting stronger for me," he said seriously before leaning down to plant sweet kisses on my face. "I love you, Breelyn." He wiped away the tears that fell. I couldn't help but cry every time he told me he loved me.

"I love you too, babe."

I looked up to see Kota staring at us, wearing a big, cheesy-ass grin with an angry Giannis posted up behind her with his arms folded across his chest. I wondered what that was all about. His ass was normally all smiles when he was in my cousin's presence, but that was not the case right now. Giannis looked like he was ready to take someone's head off.

Turning my attention to Rah, I found him with that same annoyed look he had whenever Rio and I got all lovey-dovey and expressed our feelings for one another. I loved my brother, but I loved DeMario as well, and they were going to have to find a way to squash this imaginary beef they had and get along. I refused to choose sides. Not this time. If asked, they probably couldn't even explain their dislike for one another without the response coming off extra childish. It was all so silly to me, and I refused to entertain either of them.

"My baby!" I heard my Aunt Syl squeal from the door.

I loved me some Sylvia Bibbs, and I was so happy to see her beautiful face. This was a woman who had always been there for me and tried to give me the love I felt I was missing by not having my own mother with me. Looking at her now and seeing that light in her eyes told me how deep her love for me ran. I seriously regretted not fully accepting what she and Uncle Kasey had been offering me all these years. On everything I loved, I was tired of crying, but today was emotional as hell. Despite the harsh reality I was facing with my new physical limitations, seeing my family again gave me an indescribable joy. It gave me hope that I could get past this. With their love and support, I felt I could overcome anything.

"What did I tell you, son? I told you she was strong." Auntie Syl grinned in Rio's direction after hugging and kissing on me for a few minutes.

"That you did," he acknowledged with a smile of his own.

"You really think I'm strong, Auntie?" I asked once we were alone. The rest of the family had gone down to the cafeteria to grab food. Rio had Auntie Syl sit with me while he ran home to check on things and take a nice long shower. It took everyone including myself to talk him into leaving, and he'd finally given in. He had been by my side the entire time, and I knew that because I felt him and heard his voice. There wasn't shit a person could tell me about his love and dedication to me. I'd experienced fake, and DeMario Taylor was far from it. He was the realest, hands down.

"Chile, hush. Did you or did you not just make it through something that would have taken the average person out? That alone should answer your question, Breelyn. I didn't doubt for one second that you would come out of this. You have a ways to go to get back to your normal state, but don't be discouraged, baby girl."

"It's hard not to be discouraged when I can't even get out of the bed without assistance, Auntie Syl," I complained.

"Clearly yo' ass is hard of hearing, Breelyn. I know your strength, but you have to recognize it as well. I've been watching you since you were a little girl. You remind me so much of my sister. Just like you and Kota, she was my family as well as my best friend. We did everything together, even married brothers."

She smiled thoughtfully. I loved when she would tell me stories about the things she and my mom would get into when they were younger. "Anyway, you're tough as nails just like her. As a child, you would hardly cry for anything, unlike Dakota. Her ass was a straight-up wimp," she reminisced, making me laugh. I swore Dakota's ass stayed crying when we were children, but she was the toughest chick on the block. "Even so, if you don't have faith and you don't put in the work, then you can't expect to do well during your rehabilitation. All I know is that you better put your best foot forward, because Rio won't let you get too down on yourself or give up. Get it together and get ready to do work, chile," she advised.

"I already know he's about to be on my case throughout this entire process," I groaned, already dreading him making me push through during those times I knew I'd want to say fuck it and give up. His pushiness came from a good place, so I vowed not to give him too hard a time.

"I love him for you, Breelyn. That other boy, he wasn't for you. His spirit ain't right, and I picked up on it the first time you brought him to see me. You were head over heels for him, and I refused to be the one to rain on your parade, so I kept quiet. But this one here? I can see that the love he has for you is real. It's the type of love that very few are lucky enough to experience."

She spoke words that I felt were some of the truest I'd ever heard in my life. I knew that what we had was some once-in-a-lifetime shit, and I planned to cherish it. I knew he was something special the moment we came into contact with each other.

"I know, Auntie Syl, and I love him for me too." I grinned.

"I know you don't want to hear this, but I want you to keep an open mind when Kenneth comes up here. Fix your damn face, Breelyn," she snapped when I rolled my eyes. I quickly got it together, because although Auntie Syl was a sweetheart, she played no games. When she spoke or gave an order, we listened and knew better than to question her.

I nodded in agreement and wiped the frown from my face directly. I listened as she went on and on about why it was important for me to forgive my father and try to establish a relationship and be cordial with him. The same man who basically abandoned me? It didn't quite happen that way, but that's how it felt to me sometimes. I listened and gave Auntie Syl the impression that I would do the right thing, but this was one time I didn't plan to take her advice. He had never been there when I needed him, and now I was supposed to be the bigger person and just forgive and forget. Fuck no! I loved him because he was my father, but I could do that shit from a distance. I'm talking real far away.

Chapter 7

Goons Lurkin'

Rio

"The fuck I tell you 'bout touching my shit?" Rah bitched, pushing my hand away from the aux cord.

"Well, turn on some music then! Ain't nobody trying to sit in here listening to your loud asthmatic breathing for the rest of the ride. Sound like a big ol' sloppy-ass nigga with sleep apnea or some shit," I clowned, causing G to snicker in the back. That was the first peep we'd heard out of his ass all night. My dawg was in his own little world.

Rah's punk ass was huffing and puffing because he didn't want us in the car with him. Ask me if I gave a fuck though. His bitch ass almost made me drop my brand-new iPhone when he snatched that aux, and it took a lot for me not to karate chop him across his fucking throat. He took the disrespect too far sometimes, but he had the right one tonight.

"Fuck you, ugly-ass nigga!" he spat.

"Naw, it's fuck you, ol' crybaby-ass li'l boy. Acting like you mad because I touched yo' shit. You really pissed that we insisted on coming along and shut yo' li'l solo mission down. Rather run up on this fool on your own than to have a couple solid ones by ya side. Fuck the fact that Breelyn is my lady, right? And what about G? That accident was supposed to happen to his woman, your cousin, so what sense does it make leaving us out? I don't understand that shit at all," I said, shaking my head at him in disgust.

Rah, Giannis, and I had been riding around and fucking shit up for hours and were now headed to see Montell. We happened to overhear the plans Rah was making on the phone at the hospital earlier. He tried to slip out unnoticed, but G and I followed him home. Imagine his surprise when he came back out dressed in all black to find us waiting by his ride. He'd been in a pissy mood ever since. Punk ass.

"It ain't for you to understand! I'on need yo' permission or supervision to do what I need to do. The fuck you gon' do that I can't? Can't stand yo' cocky ass," Rah griped as he pulled up to the gas pump at the corner store that Montell normally came to on his lunch break.

"And I don't give a fuck!" I argued back.

Apparently Rah had someone following Dakota's ex for the last week, but so far he hadn't led them to where David was laying his head. Tonight, we were just going to approach him straight up and force him to give up the info on his cousin.

Rah jumped his ass out of the car still talking shit. Of course, I followed suit ready to talk my shit too. G, as always, was quiet as his best friend and I went back and forth insulting one another.

"You can get up out my ride with all that bullshit," he ranted.

"Fuck that shit you talking. I'm in this bitch already, so I'm going any-fucking-way. The hell you think my girl gon' say if something were to happen to yo' stubborn, nappy-bearded ass while you running around acting off your emotions? Fuck nah! I don't want or need those problems. She's been through enough, so whatever the fuck I have to do to make sure we handle this nigga and make it home in one piece is what the fuck I'm going to do. I know Breelyn is your sister, but she's my woman, Rah!" I told him, slamming my palm to my chest. "My fucking life, and I plan to marry her one day, so you may as well get used to seeing my face, because I ain't going no-fucking-where." It had been a long time coming, but this was a conversation that needed to be had. I wished we could have had it after this kill mission, but it was what it was.

Rah paced back and forth in front of his ride for a good five minutes, glaring at me, before he calmed down.

Rah

I didn't take too kindly to folk talking to me the way Rio had. Had he been anyone else, I would have shot him between his fucking eyes and not given his strong-faced ass another thought. However, I was working on myself, the guy meant a lot to my sister, and he was right about everything he said, so I couldn't be too upset.

I was in my feelings about Greedy and felt it was up to me as her brother to seek vengeance on her behalf. Dakota's as well. I wasn't purposely leaving anyone out but simply acting on my emotions like he'd said. I had never been tried like this, and the mere possibility that I could have lost my sister was a hard pill to swallow. Then to know that David hated Kota so much that he wanted her dead was crazy to me. Was it really that deep, or was this nigga just out of his mind? Seemed to be some shit going on in his head that I had no clue about.

I should have deaded his ass when we had the chance, but we stupidly let him walk away. Because of that my sister was looking at months of physical therapy and possible low self-esteem due to the scars and temporary disabilities some of her injuries left behind. She seemed to be handling things like a champ, but there was no way to know the shit she actually felt and kept to herself to make us think everything was all good. For that reason alone, I planned to put an end to David Parrish so that her mind could be at ease.

After taking a moment to get my mind right, I faced Rio. "Look, I'm down with doing this with you. I'd do anything to make sure my sis and cousin are safe, and I also agree with a lot of what you said, with the exception of that crybaby shit you keep screaming. I'm a grown-ass man, *DeMario*," I stressed, putting emphasis on his name. "So the only thing I ask is that you talk to me like you got some gotdamn sense. You ain't gon' keep trying to De-Bo a nigga. I'm just as thorough as you are, so you gon' have to respect my gangsta," I commanded.

"You got that. Respect my mind, and you'll get the same in return. I only come at you like that because yo' ass been disrespectful as fuck since day one and I wasn't feeling that. Ol' crybaby ass," he mumbled before hopping back in the passenger seat.

I just chuckled and shook my head before following suit. "Ain't nobody fucking crying! I just wasn't about to let another nigga run game on my sister. And for the record, I still don't like yo' crazy ass."

"And I still don't give a fuck. One thing you don't ever have to worry about is me doing your sister wrong. I love Breelyn on some real shit, so like I said before, whatever issue you got with me, work that shit out on your own time, because I ain't going nowhere. We both have the same goal, and that is to dead this pussy so that he can't come for Breelyn or Dakota again, right?"

"Yeah, man," I agreed.

"A'ight, so let's do this shit . . . together," Rio proposed, holding a fist out for me to pound.

"A'ight."

Top, bottom, then fist to fist and the beef was no more. Now it was time to find David and get his mama ready to purchase that black dress. Rio picked up my aux cord and played Plies's first album, *The Real Testament,* and skipped to "Goons Lurkin" before relaxing back into his seat with his eyes closed.

"Yo' ass is lucky this mu'fucka bump, or I would have knocked you the fuck out for fucking with my shit," I snapped with a serious mean mug. I knew we just squashed shit, but I really felt a way about people touching shit in my car. His ass didn't seem to care. He didn't do shit but laugh, making me shake my head in annoyance. Finally, Giannis spoke up.

Giannis

"Now that you ladies have kissed and made up, can we please get this show on the road? I'm ready to make a mu'fucka bleed," I said from the back seat. My voice held not one lick of humor, and I didn't even crack a smile when my homies flipped me off in response to the jab I took at their petty arguing. They stayed going at it about a whole bunch of nothing, and tonight was not the night for that shit.

"There that buster go right there." I nodded toward Montell as he entered the store. "I'ma let y'all holla at him because I don't want to say some shit that makes him not want to give up his kinfolk. Might even end up whipping his ass on GP," I seethed from the back seat.

Rio and Rah nodded to my words before exiting the vehicle once again. The shock of seeing the two men

approach him as he walked out with his purchases was
evident on dude's face. He already knew what was up,
and the fear he displayed was comical.

By now the entire hood was aware that Breelyn was
the one who had been injured in that wreck, and that
was most likely the reason David's ho ass had been missing in action. Fool thought he was hurting my lady, but it
didn't turn out like he planned. Either way, he'd fucked
up royally. We'd kicked in his mother's door, ransacked
his home, and searched every other spot we could think
of and came up empty. David knew we were hunting his
ass, so he was on the move. Running out of options, we
decided to pull up on this fool Montell to see what he
could tell us. Hopefully he did the right thing and gave us
what we needed.

Right now though? A brother was cool, calm, and
collected. Just waiting and ready to fuck shit up. Dakota
had been going through it with Breelyn being down, and
that had been fucking with me tough. She had some other
shit going on too, but I was just waiting for her to come
to me and let me know what was up. Usually anything my
woman needed me to make right for her I could handle
with no problem, but in this instance, I couldn't do a
damn thing. That right there was something I couldn't
fuck with.

To make matters worse, if things had gone the way that
ol' boy planned, it would have been Dakota laid up in the
hospital unable to walk and banged the fuck up. It was
hard enough seeing sweet Breelyn in that condition, but
my baby? My Dakota? Nah, bruh, I wouldn't have been
able to handle that.

I was mad about a lot of things right now. Mad because
we didn't kill that nigga the night of the party and low-key
pissed that Rah had planned to go see about him without
including us. Rio was giving him such a hard time that I

decided to fall back for now. I would definitely be talking to his ass about that shit later though. No matter if it was Dakota or Breelyn, I still would have wanted to be at his side to handle this shit.

Montell's ho ass was lucky he came through with that information that day at Kota's office or else I would have been ready to do him in too. He didn't even do shit, but fuck it. I was just that angry, and when I was angry, I got quiet. And when I got quiet . . . Let's just say y'all don't want to see me. All that pretty-boy shit was out the window, and the beast that dwelled within me was unleashed. Shit was ten times worse now that I had Dakota and a possible shorty to look out for. Mu'fuckas would feel the heat behind anything to do with those two.

My phone vibrated in my pocket, and I already knew who was hitting me up. I didn't have time to talk to her ass right now though.

BabyMama: Be careful tonight. I love you Giannis (Heart emoji)

Me: Fa sho.

My response was weak as hell, and I felt bad for not telling her I loved her back, but a nigga was in his feelings for real. I'd been real standoffish with my girl, and I was sure she'd picked up on it. If she hadn't before, I was sure she would after reading my text. I stayed on some lovey-dovey shit with Dakota. "I love you" texts and calls for no reason at all. Never ended a call or text without expressing my feelings for her, but tonight I wasn't on that.

BabyMama: ???

See, my lady didn't miss shit, but I left her hanging, silenced the phone, and placed it back into my pocket. I would deal with her when I made it back to the house. Hopefully she had some news for me when I got there.

Focusing back on the task at hand, I glanced over to my boys as they jammed up a scared Montell. I had no clue what my lady ever saw in a nigga like him, but whatever.

Rio

With the headlights turned off, Rah made a quick U-turn in front of a shotgun house located on an isolated street in south Dallas. Parking two streets over from our destination, we quickly made our way back on foot before the nigga had a chance to move around.

"Oh, how the mighty have fallen," I mumbled as we moved closer to the house.

This shit here looked nothing like that mini mansion of his that we tore up. Talk about a fucking downgrade. From what I could see, all but one of the windows had boards on them and the yard was a cluttered, fucked-up mess. It was littered with beer cans and other trash while David's Phantom sat parked on the grass directly in front of the dilapidated porch. This man wasn't doing a very good job of hiding out doing shit like that. How the fuck you gon' park a luxury vehicle in front of what could only be described as a low-level crack house? He was the lowest of the low.

Glancing around, I noticed that there were two other homes that seemed to be occupied in the cul-de-sac, with the one that David occupied situated at the back of the dead end. Its location was perfect for what we had planned. Only one light was on in a room all the way toward the back, so that's where G headed to cut him off should he try making a run for it. Rah hit the front, and I took the back.

Just for the fuck of it, I turned the knob to see if the door was unlocked, and to my surprise, it opened right up. *How the hell his dumb ass call himself hiding out only to do stupid shit like this, giving us easy access to the house?* A foul-ass smell assaulted my nose as soon as I crossed the threshold of the back door. Nigga was living in a fucking pig sty.

Multiple takeout boxes with week-old food in them were all over the counter, stove, and table. Needles, pills, and other drug paraphernalia sat atop the filthy table, showing just how far from grace his ass had fallen. I was met at the junction of the living room and kitchen by Rah, whose face was just as screwed up as mine had been, eyes questioning what that smell was. I just shrugged, ready to find the person we came for and get the fuck up out of here.

Nodding toward the hall, I motioned for Rah to take the lead. After clearing out the smaller of the two bedrooms and the restroom, we made our way to the room at the end of the hall. The light shining from the bottom of the door illuminated the hallway floor and alerted us that this was the room we were looking for. The man we all hated with a passion was on the other side of the door, only moments from meeting his Maker, and he didn't even realize it. His coming death was inevitable. There was no escaping it, because Giannis would be right outside if he somehow made it past the two of us, and there was no way we were letting that happen.

Guns in hand, Rah motioned for me to proceed. Taking two steps forward, I used my right leg to kick the door in. Felt like I barely used any strength to kick it but that bitch flew clean off the hinges. The anger and animosity I had toward this dude had my adrenaline pumping. Plus knowing that the stress I'd been dealing with was finally about to be released on this mu'fucka had me on one.

Surprisingly, Rah and I moved in sync like we'd done this shit together many times before. As soon as the door flew open, he was moving in with that Desert Eagle drawn with me close behind, sweeping the room.

"Ain't this a bitch!" we both shouted when we looked across the small space at the sight before us. All hope of making David die a slow, tortuous death went down the drain just like that. Severely beaten, tied, and bound, ol' boy's body was in terrible shape. Someone had whooped his ass something serious, and his throat looked to have been cut or some shit. I couldn't tell with all the blood. From this angle, it appeared that his shit was damn near sliding off his shoulders. When I got closer, I saw that that wasn't the case at all. He'd definitely been fucked up though. I swore I wished I would have been the one responsible for doing that shit to his ho ass, but I guessed it just wasn't meant to be.

While I took on the task of making a few calls to have this mess cleaned up, Rah pulled out his cell phone to text Giannis. About thirty seconds later he appeared in the doorway, wearing the same perplexed expression as us.

"I wonder who got a hold of his ass," G questioned.

"Mane, it ain't no telling. This nigga swore he was a kingpin but was forever owing somebody or kicking in doors taking from the next man to pay off debts. The list of mu'fuckas itching to get at this fool was a mile long," Rah informed us with a shake of his head.

"Well, let's get a move on then. I assume we're moving on with plan B?" G questioned as he stared at David with that fire still burning in his eyes. Just like it was me, it was pissing him off that we didn't get the chance to get our hands on him first.

"Yup. I already got my people on the way," I replied, and Rah nodded his agreement as he texted away on his burner phone. Things hadn't worked out like we wanted, but it was all good. Someone was going to have to answer for this shit . . . eventually.

Chapter 8

You Gets No Love

Kenneth Waiters

"Afternoon, baby girl. How you doing today?" I asked as I entered Breelyn's hospital room.

"Same as I was yesterday, Kenneth," she muttered, causing my jaw to clench in irritation.

It was the same thing every day I came up here to see her. I would ask her a question, and she'd either give me a short, smart-aleck response or she wouldn't say shit at all. I knew I deserved the cold shoulder she was giving me, but knowing that didn't make it hurt any less or make it any easier to deal with. I was getting nowhere with her, and I'd admit I was about ready to give up. Practicing patience was key because quitting was not an option. I'd quit on her before, and I was trying to do things differently this time around.

"Have you had your therapy session yet?" I ignored her attitude and took a seat in the recliner beside her bed. I wanted to be around to help her out because I knew Rio would be out handling some business with my son for the day. This would be the only time I would get alone with her, and I wanted to take advantage, maybe plan some things for us to do once she was out of the hospital. I just needed her to be more open to the idea of us forming some type of bond.

"Nope, I declined therapy today," she said, causing me to look over at her in surprise. Her ass was steadily flipping through the channels like I didn't exist.

"Breelyn, I don't think skipping therapy is a good idea. I'm sure you're trying to get out of here soon, and getting the necessary treatment will help move that process along," I offered in the least pushy way I possibly could.

"So now I'm supposed to take advice from you? Now you want to be a dad and tell me what's best for me? That's laughable, Kenneth," she chuckled sarcastically.

"Wasn't shit funny about what I just said, Breelyn. I know you feel a way about me but you being disrespectful has to stop. At the end of the day, I'm still your father and will be treated as such," I said sternly.

"If you don't like what I'm saying, you can always leave. You already know you gets no love over this way!" she barked.

"Don't raise your voice to me, Breelyn Waiters! You want to talk to me crazy and yell at me? You don't fuck with me? Tell me something I don't know. I just find it funny that you feel that way about me but you don't have an issue spending that money I drop into your account weekly," I countered.

Was it right to bring up what I did for her financially at a time like this? No, it probably wasn't, but her gotdamn mouth was getting out of hand. I would rather she not say shit to me at all than handle me the way she was right now. And although I was trying to be nice, she had me all the way fucked up. The pissed-off look on her face didn't move me in the least. She remained quiet, so I continued.

"I know I messed up bad, and I probably don't deserve another chance, but I'm asking for one anyway, just like I did with your brother. Whether you believe it or not, I love you, li'l girl, and no matter how shitty you treat me, I'll never stop trying to make it right," I told her.

I was a poor excuse for a father and I knew it, but I was here, and I was trying. Kasey had done more than enough, and I owed him my life for everything he'd been to my children. He'd been that way since we were younger, always picking up our slack and handling shit for us. Herb and I had a different father than he did, but you'd never know it with how close we were. He stayed on my ass over the years about improving my relationship with my children, and I was finally taking his advice. I would always be thankful to my brother for the way he stepped up when it came to Rah and Breelyn, but now it was my time to take over.

I watched as my only daughter hurriedly wiped a tear from her face and looked away from me. I could tell she didn't want me to see her cry. She could act hard all she wanted, but I feel like she needed me just as much as I needed her. I'd have to practice tough love to get through to her because it was clear she wasn't responding to the nice guy routine.

"Breelyn, at the end of the day I'm a grown-ass man, so I refuse to let you talk to me any kind of way. And best believe you're about to get your ass up and do therapy whether you want to or not," I informed her. I wasn't about to let her slack off. If she thought she was getting out of some shit just because I was the one sitting with her today, she had another think coming. I politely walked over to her bed, snatched the call light from her hand, and pressed the button for the nurse.

"How may we help you?" the female over the speaker asked.

"I was hoping you could have the physical therapist come back in. My daughter wasn't feeling well earlier, but now she's ready for her session."

"Of course, we'll send a page and have someone come back down right away, sir," the nurse said nicely.

"What the fuck? Who the hell do you think you are? They can come in here all they want to, but you can't force me to get up and work with them. I'm not about to do shit," she spat angrily.

I didn't know what the hell had happened to my sweet girl. I'd never known her to curse this much or be so mean. I guessed I'd have to spend time getting to know the new Breelyn.

"You sure about that?" I laughed, pulling out my cell phone and dialing a number before turning my back to her. I made sure to speak in a low tone so that she couldn't hear me.

"Wh . . . what are you doing? Who are you calling?" she wanted to know. Judging by the shakiness in her tone, I could tell she had an idea of who I was speaking with. He had instructed me to call him if Breelyn gave me any problems. I hadn't planned on soliciting him for help with my own daughter, but if he was the one person she would listen to, then I had no choice.

"She's right here. Hold on," I said before extending the phone to her. Reluctantly, she took the phone from my hand.

"Hello," she mumbled lowly. "But, babeee, I'm tired and I'm hurting. Of course I do, DeMario. Okay fine. Are you on your way back? But what if I need your help? I don't want his old ass. I want you," she whined, releasing a single tear from her eye. She was just being dramatic for no damn reason. He seemed to have her ass spoiled just like the rest of us.

Listening to only one side of their conversation was a trip. She was no longer crying, and I honestly didn't think it was possible for her to smile any harder. I couldn't imagine what he was saying to her, but whatever it was, he seemed to be getting through. It was something special to witness my daughter experience a loving, meaningful relationship. That last nigga she was with wasn't worth shit. I wasn't around much, but even I knew that. Shit was doomed from the beginning, and everyone seemed to see it but her. I was so glad when I heard that it was over and done with and now she had someone thorough by her side.

When I was approached by Rio a few weeks ago, I didn't know how to take him at first, but after sitting down to lunch with him in the hospital cafeteria, I learned a lot about him and found that he was very much in love with my daughter. He reminded me so much of my own son that it was crazy. He didn't bite his tongue about his feelings on my situation with my children. He voiced his opinion and moved on like it wasn't shit. He said he wanted to make sure that if I came back into Breelyn's life, it was for good, and not just something to do for the time being. Anyone else would have gotten busted in their shit for thinking they could check me about my child, but I knew that what he was saying was coming from a good place and he only wanted what was best for Breelyn.

Breelyn ended the call with a dreamy sigh. However, when she handed me back my phone, I was met with the most evil glare she could muster up. I just laughed at her childishness. Before I could spark up a conversation like I planned to, her nurse, Ms. Ivy, entered the room. If this had been a different time and situation, I would have wasted no time spitting game to the woman. Her chocolate ass was fine as hell, and I was mesmerized by the way those blue scrub bottoms hugged her big booty.

My eyes followed her around the room as she talked and laughed with Breelyn. Every now and then she would glance my way, offering that cute, professional smile of hers, and my ass was smiling right back. Maybe a woman

my age was what I needed. I'd spent years fucking around
with women half my age mostly because they didn't
expect much from me. That and the fact that the sex was
out of this world. All I had to do was toss them a couple of
bucks, fuck them right, and I was set. I didn't have much
more than dick and money to give a female anyhow, so it
was a win-win situation for all parties involved.

My heart they couldn't have because it was still with
my wife. After all the years of grieving the loss of Layne,
I was feeling like it was finally time for me to move on. I
knew she would have wanted me to be happy, but I didn't
think I could do that if my happiness didn't include her.
She meant everything to me, and I just never thought
another woman could take her place. I guessed it was
time to find out if there was enough space for someone
new to dwell where she'd reigned supreme for so long.

Nurse Ivy's voice brought me out of the thoughts of my
deceased wife. "We'll give that medication some time to
take effect and then I'll send the therapist in, Ms. Waiters.
That should definitely help you get through your session.
Is there anything I can do for you before I go?" she asked.

"If you could ban this ugly elderly man from my room
or this hospital altogether, I would appreciate it greatly,"
Breelyn answered sarcastically.

"Keep on and watch me call Rio back," I threatened.

"Snitch," she grumbled with an eye roll while Nurse Ivy
just laughed at our back-and-forth.

Even though Breelyn was still giving me a hard time,
I was thankful just to be talking with her and spending
time with her. It made me feel good the few times I saw
her smile during our argument. I was taking whatever I
could get at this point.

About twenty minutes later, the physical therapist
and his assistant arrived. It was hard work, but my baby
girl pushed herself to the max throughout the entire

hour they worked with her. They started with the upper body and other exercises she could do in bed, and then they moved to the hard part, which was the walking. When she wanted to quit, the messages I intermittently received from Rio and relayed to her gave her the get up and go that she needed to get through it.

I was happier than she was when she reached that milestone today by walking farther than she ever had since she started therapy. She made it all the way down the hall before she asked to be taken back to her room. Nurse Ivy and a few others who had cared for her at some point during her lengthy stay all cheered her on. It felt so good to see my baby progressing and not giving up on herself. She definitely got that tough shit from her mama. She reminded me of Layne in so many ways, and I hated that I hadn't taken the time out before now to get to know my own daughter. Even her laugh was the same, and every time I heard it, my heart skipped a beat. Layne had left me with these two amazing children, and I was so grief-stricken that I'd missed out on being a part of their lives. If I would have done right by them, I was sure we all would have healed a little better after her death. You live and you learn, though, and from now on it was all about my children. They were grown, but I didn't care. I planned to take advantage of whatever time I had left with them.

The annoying laugh of the therapist began grating on my last fucking nerve. His tall Lance Gross–looking ass was really starting to piss me off. Breelyn was probably clueless, but he was clearly taken with her, and the low-key flirting he was doing was unprofessional. As he helped her back in bed, he was unnecessarily holding on to her, and I just couldn't stand a second more of it. I knew his ass wouldn't be doing all the extra shit and cracking these corny-ass jokes had Rio been the one up in here instead of me.

"I got it," I announced, taking over the task of lifting both of Breelyn's legs from the floor and slowly placing them in the bed. I used a little force to move him out of the way when I saw he was still standing behind me. He and Breelyn shared a quizzical look, but I knew I wasn't overreacting. Dude was doing the most when he needed to be focused on his job and not putting his game down on my baby.

"You did great today, Breelyn. I'm so proud of you," he offered while his assistant looked on like she was ready to move to the next patient. They'd been here way longer than any other time they came to work with Breelyn.

"Thank you, Carter. I appreciate you working with me. You're very good at what you do," Breelyn replied with a genuine smile. On her end, it was all innocent, but I sat there and watched as he ate up every word she spoke. Grown-ass nigga was sitting up here blushing and shit. I had officially seen enough.

"Man, don't you have another patient you should be tending to? Your job is done here, so now you're just overstaying your welcome."

"Kenneth!" Breelyn shouted in shock. Dude looked just as taken aback as she was.

"Breelyn!" I countered.

"Well, I'm going to go, and I'll see you at the same time tomorrow. Make sure you don't decline our session. We need to get at this thing every day in order to get you back to your previous level of functioning," he stated, suddenly turning on the professionalism.

"I'll be ready," Breelyn responded with a nod before glowering at me. With that, they grabbed up their equipment and exited the room. As soon as they dotted the door, she was going off on me again. "What the hell was that? Did you have to be so rude to him?" she fussed.

"I damn sure did. How could you not tell that that man was flirting with you?" I asked in disbelief. There was no way that a child of mine was that fucking clueless.

"He was not! At least I don't think he was," she added thoughtfully. "I would never entertain no mess like that, so even if he was, you didn't have to be so mean about it."

"You lucky that's all I did. I started to call DeMario and have him come up here and knock his butt out. I still might, hell. Keep being mean to me, and I bet I dial that number and put my boy up on game," I teased.

She couldn't help but laugh. "You ain't shit for that," she giggled. "Please don't do that though. I swear that boy will be missing by tomorrow if you told Rio that."

"Told me what?" Rio said, entering the room on the tail end of our conversation. My son was right behind him carrying multiple bags of food and drinks from Big Shucks.

"About me not wanting to do therapy, baby," she said, not missing a beat. She shot me a look that told me to keep quiet, and I just laughed at her scary ass. We were joking on one hand, but I had no doubt that what she said was true. Looking into his eyes, one could tell that Rio was a killer. He was one of the kindest people you would ever meet until you crossed him or someone he loved. At that point, you would meet the savage he truly was. So yeah, I planned to keep the information about the flirting therapist to myself unless he continued to overstep those boundaries.

"Umm-hmm." Rio smirked before kissing her forehead. He then proceeded to set her food up in front of her, and Breelyn, being Breelyn, tore that shit down like a 250-pound linebacker. I just didn't understand how she could eat so much and still be so small. She'd always been greedy like that, so her nickname was very fitting. Rio just stood at the bedside and watched her the entire time she ate.

"So therapy was good?" Rio asked, taking her spoon and eating some of her gumbo.

"It was great actually." She beamed. It seemed she was proud of the work she'd done today. I was proud of her too. "Made it all the way to the second nurses' station before turning around."

"That's good, babe. I knew you could do it," he said before kissing her again.

I noticed that he kissed her a lot. It was nothing like Giannis and my niece Dakota's display of affection though, and for that I was glad. They would look like they were about to rip each other's clothes off and start fucking right there in front of everyone with how hard they kissed and groped. I was happy they were in love and all, but damn, I didn't need to see all that.

"So when were you going to tell me about that lame-ass therapist who be smiling all up in your face, Breelyn?" Rio calmly asked.

Of course she looked right at me like I was the one who had dropped a dime on her. She looked like she was ready to wring my neck, but she had the wrong one. I hadn't told Rio a damn thing.

"Nah, don't look at him. I'm asking the questions here," he said, pointing to his chest.

"He wasn't smiling in my face, DeMario," she lied to him with that sweet, innocent face of hers.

I could only suck my teeth like, "Yeah, right."

"Well, that ain't the story I got," Rio replied.

"Snitches get stitches," she mumbled, referring to me.

"He didn't tell me. I have other sources, wifey." He winked before I could defend myself against her accusation.

On cue, the door opened and in walked Nurse Ivy with a bouquet of flowers. Her ass was just a-humming and sniffing those flowers like she didn't have a care in the world. Right then we all knew who the real snitch was. Rio, Rah, and I all fell out laughing. Even Breelyn's slow ass caught on.

"Ms. Ivy, I can't believe you!" Breelyn admonished.

"Child, I have no idea what you're talking about," she said after placing the flowers on the windowsill with the others. She walked over and kissed Breelyn's temple then winked at Rio. Yeah, she was the damn snitch, and I wasn't mad at her. I'd been tempted to tell him my-damn-self.

"Don't be having people spying on me, DeMario," she said once Nurse Ivy left the room. "You know I'm not thinking about him or any other man."

"Oh, I know damn well you ain't, but it's not you I'm worried about. It's him. And now that muthafucka needs to be worried about me," Rio said coolly.

"Babe, don't. It's not even that deep," Breelyn sighed.

"When it comes to you, it's always that deep, love," was his response. To that, my daughter had nothing else to say.

Today started out rocky for Breelyn and me, but I felt that we made some progress. Only time would tell though. I was liable to walk in here tomorrow and have her treat me like shit all over again. It might have sounded crazy, but I don't even care anymore. For right now, being in her presence was enough for me even if she cursed me out the entire time.

Chapter 9

The Hell You Say

Giannis

"Sup, G. You wanted to see me?" Tyson, the assistant manager at my club Sensations, asked, pulling the door to my office closed behind himself.

"Yeah, I did. Have a seat," I ordered, and he did. "How long have we known each other, Ty?"

"Shit, since our college years, man," he answered with a smile that didn't quite reach his eyes. Thinking back, it was the same smile he always gave me, but for the first time, I was noticing how fake the shit was.

"Right, college years. Those were the damn days. Since then your family has become like mine and vice versa," I pointed out as he shifted uncomfortably in his seat.

Tyson and I went way back like he said, and he was my friend, or so I thought. We were nowhere near as close as Rah and I, but I considered this man my friend, and he'd played the fuck out of me while putting my business in jeopardy at the same time. I had trusted this man with assisting in running my club, which meant he had access to my bread.

Good thing I was hands-on despite having him and Margo run my spot, so I knew that every dime that came in or went out was accounted for. Well, except for the money he was making on the side, but I wanted nothing to do with that. Most might think I'd be happy about bringing in more dough, but I didn't want to make my shit like that. The club money was looking better than ever before. And just because the money was right and he wasn't stealing from me didn't mean we didn't have a serious problem on our hands. More so I had the problem because I was the owner. Before this shit came out, I was actually thinking of giving him more responsibility and adding him to the team at Good Life, but now all of that was dead just like his ass.

"So what's up, G? I know you didn't call me up here to reminisce on old times on our busiest night of the week. Talking about all the shit we used to get into back in the day will have me cooped up in here all damn night." He chuckled at his own weak-ass attempt at a joke. I didn't see a damn thing funny though.

"Shiidd, lately yo' ass stay busy up in here no matter what day of the week it is," I stated.

"Ah yeah, you know how I do it," he stupidly boasted.

"Nah, I thought I knew how you got down, but boy, was I wrong. All I want to know is, why?"

"Why what, man? The hell you on tonight, my nigga?" Ty asked, leaning forward in his chair to study me. It seemed he was slightly annoyed with my evasiveness and stale attitude.

"What am I on? I need to be asking you that shit. What I want to know is why you thought it was cool to do the shit you been doing in my fucking establishment like I wasn't gon' find out?" my voice boomed, causing his eyes to widen in surprise.

"I'on have a clue what the fuck you talking about," he lied.

"Nigga, you know exactly what the hell I'm talking about. You got my girls selling more than just fantasies and lap dances up in this bitch. Those who weren't down with your cause from the beginning have been threatened and all other types of shit. Now I know why I lost two of my best moneymakers a few months back. You scared the other ones into keeping the shit from me, but those two weren't having it and decided to just leave. How could you be so fucking stupid, fool? Now I'm in the middle of this bullshit. There's no telling what them females are saying about me and my business to other dancers and club owners. Guess that part didn't matter to you though. You know, the fact that this shit could fall back on me?" I fumed.

"Aww hell nah, Giannis, man. If them hoes are doing anything extra, I had no knowledge of that shit. That shit is on them. Had I known, you already know I would have dealt with they asses. You know me better than that, folk. We go way back, and I wouldn't do no foul shit like that to you," he responded very convincingly. I could see right through his ass though.

"So you just gon' sit in my face and continue lying, man? Just like I know you, you're familiar enough with me to know that I did my research before even approaching you about the shit. Videos, phone calls, pictures, and damn near all the dancers who were involved done spilled the fucking beans," I informed him, throwing a folder of stills from videos and pictures of what was going on behind closed doors in here.

After looking over a few of them, he just fell back into his chair, head dropped down with his eyes focused on his lap. His ass had been caught red-handed, and there was no way out of it. After a moment of silence, he spoke.

"G, man, look. I'm sorry about this shit, and I'm even sorrier for lying about it and not coming to you when the idea was brought my way by ol' girl. I let the money cloud my judgment, but I can assure you that I'll fix this and you'll never have to worry about anything like this happening again. I truly didn't mean to put you in the cross like that. You gotta believe me. We been friends for too long to let som—"

"You're exactly right. We've been friends for too long for you to try fucking me over like this. Get the fuck up out my office and my club altogether, Ty. We are no longer cool, and I'll let you explain to your people why I don't fuck with your shiesty ass no more. Your belongings have already been packed up and are waiting on the hood of that clean-ass Range yo' bitch ass just copped last week with money I'm sure you made off your bootleg-ass pimping scheme," I spat and nodded toward the screen on the wall to my left. Camera views showed two big-ass boxes placed on the hood of his new whip, which sat shining and pretty in the space designated for the assistant manager. I'd already had his name removed from the space this morning, and his ass clearly hadn't noticed.

"Come on, G! We can work this out, man. Shit ain't even that serious," he pleaded.

"The fact that you don't think so proves to me that we were never as cool as I thought we were. It's taking everything in me not to murder your ass right here and right now, so I suggest you heed my warning and get the fuck up out of here. Be thankful that I have too much love for your folks to do you dirty like I really want to," I said, standing up.

"G," he started but thought better of it when I removed the gun from the open drawer on my right and placed it on top of my desk. Another word from his mouth and my love for his family would no longer matter to me. Tyson knew how I got down, so he began his slow retreat toward the door with his eyes on my piece the entire time.

"And make sure you tell that bitch you're in cahoots with that me and mine are on her muthafuckin' ass!" I shouted before he was all the way out of my office.

Picking up my phone, I dialed a number. "Yeah, he's on the way out now," I said before hanging up. I let him leave thinking he was safe, but I planned to handle his ass just like I was going to handle that janky bitch he was fucking with. Rio's men had orders to follow him and only make a move on him when we gave the word, which would be very soon.

On top of the shit going on down at my club, this baby thing with Dakota was adding to my stress level. I'd just picked her up from visiting Breelyn at the hospital, and we were now on our way to the house. I couldn't even get happy about us finally moving in together last weekend because of the building tension between us. She was extremely chipper and talkative while I sat simmering mad on the driver's side. Her happy disposition was pissing me off, and it was taking everything I had not to snap on her gorgeous, bubbly ass.

I didn't understand how the hell she could be so giddy knowing she was sitting over there harboring secrets and shit. See, before I was only speculating, but I now knew for certain that she was pregnant. I knew because I overheard her non-whispering ass closed up in the restroom making a doctor's appointment. I even knew how many weeks she was. I just hoped that the appointment was to see an ob-gyn and not at an abortion clinic. I was going to lose my fucking mind if it was the latter.

I swore to God that if Dakota killed my kid, I wasn't fucking with her ass anymore. As much as I loved her and needed her in my life, that shit right there was all it would take for me to walk away from her and this relationship. I loved this girl on an insane level, and to think that she would carelessly get rid of something so precious? Something that was created out of our love for one another? That would fuck me up for life. And if she did it without consulting me, I would consider that the ultimate betrayal. It would be nothing for me to get to the bottom of things by coming right out and asking her about it, but a nigga was scared. Scared that she would either lie or tell me some shit that I didn't want to hear. Some shit I knew for a fact would tear us apart.

"Giannis, are you even listening to me?" she inquired, sporting that cute smirk of hers. There wasn't shit cute about her ass right now. I had no idea how long she'd been talking or what the hell she was even talking about.

"Nah," I answered nonchalantly.

"Damn, like that?" she chuckled. When I didn't join in on the laughter, she got quiet, and a serious look took over her face. "What's going on with you? What's with the attitude?"

"Ain't shit going on with me. I just wasn't listening to what you were saying." I shrugged. I could tell she was taken aback by my attitude. Maybe even a little hurt. Seeing the look on her face made me feel bad. Only a little bit though. "My bad, ma. Now tell me what you were saying," I backtracked, but I couldn't help sounding uninterested. Fuck that shit she was talking about. All I wanted to know about was my damn seed.

"Nah, it's cool. Fuck whatever I was saying, and fuck you too," she snapped, shocking the hell out of me. She'd never talked to me that way, and she wasn't about to start now.

"Watch your fucking mouth, Dakota," I demanded firmly, sitting up straight in the driver's seat.

"No, you watch yours! You're saying one thing, but your actions are telling me something different. I feel the distance between us, and that shit is hella suspect. Something is going on with you, and it better not have anything to do with that chickenhead ho who popped up at your crib not too long ago. I know the signs. I'm not some dumb bitch, Giannis!" she screamed before bursting into a fit of tears.

What the fuck had just happened? I swore I had no idea where the hell all of this was coming from, and I surely had no idea why she was bringing up Serenity. I hadn't seen or talked to that girl since her pop-up visit, so I had no clue what Dakota was accusing me of. All I knew was that I wanted her to stop crying. I hated being the cause of her tears. I promised Rio and told myself that I was going to give her some time to come to me about the baby, but I hadn't kept my word. I had unintentionally upset my girlfriend, who I now knew was carrying my baby. I felt horrible for all of two seconds because as soon as she opened her mouth to speak, all the shit I was just thinking and the apology I was about to offer her flew straight out the fucking window.

"I should just hook back up with Montell's dog ass! Why I need to be with you if I'm still going to have to deal with this cheating shit!" she cried hysterically.

"Man, what the fuck did you just say?" I barked, slamming down on the brakes. How the hell you gon' talk big shit but be crying at the same time? If I weren't so pissed, I would have laughed.

"I—"

Her words got stuck in her throat when I suddenly swerved over three lanes like a madman, causing several cars to smash their brakes to avoid hitting us. Pissed off to the point of no return, I ignored her calling my name and her terrified screams. By the time I threw the car into park on the shoulder of the busy road, all the tears she'd had in her eyes before had dried the fuck up, and she sat

there in stunned silence. Her hands were still attached
to her chest like she was about to have a heart attack or
some shit.

"The hell you say to me? Do you want to repeat that
fuck shit you just spit out yo' mouth, Dakota Layne?" I
got in her face so that I could hear her loud and clear.
That was, if she was bold enough to actually say it again. I
could have just heard her wrong. There was no way she'd
really said what I thought she did.

"Oh, now you don't have anything to say. You testing
the fuck out of me right now. I'ma tell yo' ass like this.
There ain't a muthafucka in life you're supposed to be
with other than Giannis Zion Williams. I'm it for you,
baby girl, and you better get that through your pretty
little head. You got me fucked all the way up! And let that
be the last time you ever accuse me of fucking around
on you, Dakota. Just like I'm it for you, there's no other
female out there for me. You are the be-all and end-all,
and the sooner you realize that, the better off you'll
be. Don't let the bullshit from your past relationship
interfere with what we have going ever again," I barked
before pulling back out into traffic. The entire time I
talked, she sat there looking stupid with tears streaming
down her face.

"Honey, I'm so—"

"I'on wanna hear a mu'fuckin' thing you gotta say right
now, Kota." I was pissed the hell off, and I didn't need her
popping off and making things worse. I refused to even
look her way because I didn't want to see the tears or hurt
I was sure my words were causing.

Chapter 10

Congratulations, Daddy

Dakota

I was trying hard to complete the final chapter in the finale of my book, but I couldn't concentrate for shit. I'd rewritten the same paragraph at least twelve times, getting nowhere fast. I needed to get it together because this book was scheduled to drop in a little under two weeks and I wasn't even done with it.

I'd been in bed pouting since we made it home because I really couldn't take it when Giannis was upset with me. I just knew that he would have come to make up with me by now, but he hadn't, which caused fresh tears to surface. He had completely shut me out, and I didn't like this feeling. I was used to him fawning all over me, so this was all too much for my sensitive ass to deal with. I could tell I hurt him just by the way he glared at me as he spoke, and I swore that wasn't my intention.

Giannis had never handled me the way that he had in the car, and I couldn't front, my feelings were so bruised. I didn't mean to let that stupid shit come out of my mouth, and I regretted it the moment I said it. Instead of letting me apologize, my honey went slap the fuck off on me. My insecurities were beginning to get the best of me, and I had no clue why. Giannis didn't play games with me or do things to intentionally hurt me, and I knew for a fact that he loved me.

I also knew that he wouldn't cheat on me. People may have thought I was crazy or naïve for believing that, but I did. Some women assumed that all men cheated, but I didn't give a damn about what they thought or what they had going on with their men. I felt in my heart that Giannis was faithful and wouldn't do me dirty. Seeing that girl at his home that night threw me off though, and I was allowing unfounded doubts to invade my mind and make me question what I knew to be true.

Another issue I was having was revealing the news to him about the baby. I'd set up a cute little way to tell him he was going to be a father, but he still hadn't discovered my surprise. Today when we were in the car, I was trying to drop hints so that he would go into his office and stumble upon the gift I'd left for him, but he hadn't been listening to a word I was saying.

Since this shit popped off with Breelyn, his time was spent with me going to and from the hospital. The running of his businesses had been placed in the hands of his employees. He'd been acting strange, and I had no idea what was going on. I completely jumped to conclusions when I brought up Serenity, but I couldn't think of another reason for him to be behaving the way he had been toward me. According to Breelyn, they'd already found David's ass dead as a doorknob in that crack house, and I thought after that he'd be back to his old self, but it seemed to me that his attitude had only become worse since then.

Maybe he knows, I thought, sitting up straight in bed. He'd made several slick comments over the last few weeks that were now starting to make sense to me. I had no idea how he could have found out, but I had a strong feeling that that was what his issue was with me. I knew how Giannis's mind worked, and because I'd yet to give him the news about the baby, he was most likely thinking that I didn't plan on keeping it.

Fuck being cute or creative about it. This shit had gone on long enough, and it was time for us to straighten things out. I'd already rescheduled my doctor's appointment twice because I hadn't told him about the baby yet, and there was no way I could miss the next one. Setting my laptop to the side, I tossed the plush blanket off of my lower body and got out of bed. I was just going to get it over with and tell him about this kid right damn now.

I jumped back in surprise when I opened the door to find him standing there with an apologetic look gracing his handsome face. "Baby . . ."

"I'm sorry, Giannis."

We spoke simultaneously before I burst out crying like the big baby I had become in recent weeks. I swore this soft shit was pissing me off, but I just couldn't help myself. It was like I was no longer in control of my emotions or these fuck-ass tears. Despite the waterworks, I was able to breathe a sigh of relief after Giannis wrapped his strong arms around me. And, Lawd, when he began kissing me, I damn near melted. The sensual pecks were nice, but my body heated all over as soon as his tongue parted my lips and slid into my mouth. Next thing I knew we were moaning, caressing, and kissing fervently. As bad as I wanted to continue down this path, a path that would surely lead to some of the best lovemaking of my life, there was a more pressing issue that needed to be discussed first.

"Dakota, what the fuck you doing, babe?" he groaned in aggravation when I ended our make-out session and pulled back from him.

His eyes were ablaze with love and lust, and I almost laughed out loud when I noticed that his nasty ass

already had his dick out, slowly stroking it from the base
to the tip, where he gently ran his thumb over the fat
mushroom. I swore that motion had my mouth juiced the
fuck up. This sexy-ass man of mine had me losing focus,
but I was determined to stay on task. Trust me, I wanted
him just as badly as he wanted me, but we would get to
that part shortly. With everything that had been going on,
we hadn't been getting it in lately, and I couldn't wait to
put this pussy on him.

"That can wait, honey. I need to show you something."

"Nah, fuck tha—" he started to protest before I ended
all talk with a soft kiss to his lips. He even had the nerve
to smack his teeth like a child. He always claimed that I
was spoiled, but his ass was too, sitting up here pouting
like a big kid just because he couldn't get no pussy. Shit
was funny as hell to me.

"Trust me, you need to see this. I know why you've been
moody, honey. Let me ease your mind first, and then I'll
handle this," I whispered while I took over the task of
stroking him.

"Stop playing with me, Dakota," he groaned desperately as his mouth latched on to my exposed collarbone,
kissing and sucking gently. He was so out of it that
I didn't believe he realized what I was saying. I was
basically telling him that I was aware that he knew I
was pregnant with his baby, but the thought of sliding
inside my body clearly had him delirious. I loved having
that effect on him, and I won't sit here and tell no lies.
He had the same power over me. My yoni was so damn
slippery right now that I could feel my juices gathering
between my damn thighs. It was time to have this
conversation so that we could move on to this bomb-ass
makeup sex. I planned to fuck him so good that he
would be apologizing for the way he spoke to me earlier
for the next few days at the very least.

Breaking away once more, I grabbed his hand and led him down the hall to his home office. After taking a deep breath, I finally opened the door, revealing my surprise. Too bad my horny-ass man was too busy staring at my butt cheeks peeking out from underneath this small-ass tee I was wearing to pay attention to the balloons and surprise that sat at his desk.

"Focus, Giannis," I whined while walking him farther into the room.

"I'm trying to, but shit, Kota. That ass is poking, mama," he said, giving it an appreciative squeeze and tap.

After removing his hand from my butt, I forced him down into his desk chair then typed in the password to his laptop, which just so happened to be my birthday. I pressed play on the video that was already pulled up. A slideshow of pictures of us began to play with "Forever My Lady" by Jodeci playing in the background. He watched with a broad smile as flicks from every single date, family gathering, or ones of us lounging around the house flashed on the screen. K-Ci and 'em sang their hearts out while we took a stroll down memory lane. Shit, my punk ass was about to cry watching the slideshow like I hadn't already seen it before. The final photo was a picture of the three home pregnancy tests that I took just for show and the ultrasound that I received from the hospital. Congratulations, Daddy was displayed in bold letters at the top. I wanted to give him the actual tests with his gift but thought that was kind of gross considering I'd pissed on them. In the end, I decided that a picture would suffice.

"You really having my baby, Dakota?" he asked, still not looking my way. He hadn't taken his eyes off the computer screen, but his palm was now pressed against my stomach.

"I am, and I can't put into words how excited I am about it," I said, beaming. That prompted him to finally raise his head. When our tear-rimmed eyes met, mine released the tears I'd been trying hard to hold in, and my heart nearly burst in two. My honey was happy, and that made me happy. "You know, it just dawned on me after you spazzed on me in the car why you've been acting so strange lately. I've been trying to get you in here to see this for a while now, but realizing what you were probably thinking made me say, 'Fuck a surprise.' I would never do that to you, Giannis, and I'm sure you know that. I could never get rid of something so precious, especially since it's with you." My voice cracked. I hated that he even thought something like that about me, but I couldn't really blame him.

"I know, Dakota, but you were taking entirely too long to tell me, so my mind started to play fucking tricks on me," he admitted, caressing my face. "I'm sorry, love."

"I'm sorry too. I don't know what my problem is, but I didn't mean that shit I said in the car. I know you, and I trust you. I don't know if it's the baby or what, but I've been hella emotional and paranoid. I don't want anyone but you. You have my word that I won't say anything like that ever again," I vowed.

"Please don't, Dakota, because when you say shit like that, it makes me feel like I'm not doing my part where you're concerned. My goal has always been to love you in a way that made you feel secure and trust that I would always be true to you. You have no idea how good it makes me feel knowing that you have confidence in me and what we share. You will never have to question my loyalty to you, Kota. I apologize for blowing up on you earlier, but I meant every single word I said. There is no one out there for you other than me, and it's the same on my end." His words were stern, and I knew not to

question them. "Now you're about to give me a baby."
His words seemed to get stuck in his throat as he pressed
his forehead into my stomach.

Standing between his legs, I softly stroked his back as I
let reality set in for him. Before, he was only speculating,
but me confirming my pregnancy made it real. I could
feel the tension leave his body as well as the few sniffles
he tried his best to mask. I swore his ass had me up in
here about to break all the way down. To others, Giannis
may have come off rough, but with me, he let that guard
down. He never had a problem telling me how much he
loved me, and I needed that. I needed that shit so bad.
The thing about Giannis that separated him from anyone
else I'd been with was that he didn't mind showing as
well as telling. His actions were just as powerful as the
words that left his mouth, and that made me trust and
believe in him like I had no other. Like I always told him,
his love gave me life. Never again would I let the words
or actions of others influence me or make me doubt my
man.

"Ahhh," I yelped when I felt myself being lifted into the
air. I was so deep in thought that I hadn't even felt his ass
move. My stomach was now level to his face as he planted
kiss after kiss on my still-flat belly, making my body
shiver. Finally, he looked up, and our eyes met.

"I love you so fucking much, Dakota."

"I know you do. I love you, Giannis."

"You ready to let me find out if what they say is true?
You know, see what the hype is all about?" he asked,
licking his lips.

"What are you talking about, Giannis?" I grinned imp-
ishly, pretending I had no idea what he was getting at.
He grinned back before nibbling on that sensitive area
right above my pussy. His mouth on me caused my lower
abdomen to quiver and my yoni to leak in response. The

gush of fluid made me feel like I'd pissed on myself. I was more than ready for him to go a little lower to lick, suck, and kiss the flesh that really counted.

"Quit playing crazy, Dakota. I'm trying to see what this pregnant pussy do," he replied before removing my shirt and laying me down on the leather sofa near the window.

For a moment he stood there, eyes perusing my naked body hungrily. This was the only man who could look at me in a way that made me feel like I was the baddest bitch walking. In reality, I knew I wasn't perfect and my body was far from flawless, but there was just something about the look in his eyes that said otherwise. Nigga looked at me like I was a fucking superstar, and I loved it.

"I mean, it's already been established that your shit is A1, but is it really possible for this pussy to be even better since you're carrying my baby?" he taunted, placing kisses on my inner thighs and stomach. His damn lips were still touching everywhere but the place I wanted them to. "To taste or not to taste," his cocky ass teased.

Giannis got off on this shit. His ass wanted me to beg for it, but I refused. The only reason I wouldn't was that he would show out, going above and beyond, doing everything in his power to make me cry mercy. And the orgasms that were sure to follow the prolonged foreplay would be indescribable. Called himself punishing me. Yeah, right. My ass would be in heaven the entire time. Just thinking about that had me grinding and pushing my pussy into his face even more. At this point, he had me so gone that I was like fuck it.

"Please, Giannis!" I begged.

"I guess I can go ahead and taste since you asked nicely." He nodded before going the fuck in.

My goodness, I couldn't even put into words how he was making me feel right now. My mouth involuntarily uttered his name over and over again. With every lick, it continued to roll off my tongue. "Giannis, Giannis, Giannissss!" I cried out breathlessly as real tears spilled down my cheeks. Long, drawn-out cries erupted from my throat. Ask me if I gave a damn! Didn't care how ridiculous or crazy I sounded calling out like a madwoman. I wasn't at all surprised when he began poking fun at me. Even during our sexual escapades, his ass was still cocky as ever.

"Dakota, Dakota, Dakotaaa," my honey mocked in between licks, making me smile while throwing my pussy in his face even harder to shut him up.

With a mouthful, his arrogant ass just chuckled and continued on his mission to please. I just didn't think it could get much better than this, but I was wrong. As soon as I had that thought, I'd be gotdamned if he didn't suck and slurp me into another powerful orgasm. In my whole life, I'd never experienced anything like this, and it might sound crazy, but there was no doubt in my mind that I would murder him if he ever tried to leave me. If he ever blessed another with his golden tongue or gave his bomb-ass pipe away to some undeserving broad, it was over for his ass. Giannis had me all the way fucked up in the head. I would legit sit down and do that time for taking him out if he ever tried to play me for another bitch. And that's on my muthafuckin' mama!

After making me cum, I didn't know how many times, he grabbed my ankles and spread my legs as wide as they could go. My pussy was like a magnet, drawing that mini baseball bat to me with no real assistance on his part or mine. That dick knew its rightful place was between my thighs, so he found his way home with no problem. My shit was super tight, so it took some doing for him to gain entry, but when that connection was finally made? No words! We simply paused and savored the sensation like always.

By now, I'd lost count of the number of times we'd made love, but the feeling was brand new each and every time. There was just something about his initial entry into my body that had me gone. Every. Single. Time. Magical was the only word that came close enough to describe it. He must have felt it too, because all that shit talking he was doing had suddenly ceased.

"Gotdamn that shit is true," he groaned in surprise with a hint of desperation in his tone. "It's tighter . . . and wetter. Damn, you feel that gushy shit right there? Shit, how the fuck you do that, babe?"

Hell yeah, I felt it, and damn, if he kept hitting that spot as expertly as he was, I was going to blow like a geyser. His ass was doing all that teasing a moment ago, and now the tables had turned. This pregnant pussy had him coming undone. If I weren't so close to releasing, I would have laughed at the sight of his bucked eyes. Nigga couldn't focus on anything but his stroke. His eyes were glued to my pussy, watching himself move in and out in awe.

"Swear I'm getting your ass pregnant again right after you have this baby," he growled.

"Shut up and make me cum, Giannis!" I cried on the verge of delirium. I was sure all that could be seen were the whites of my eyes, because they were rolled so far back as the movement of my hips mirrored his. "Ahhhh!"

"I'ma get you that nut, but you have to make me a promise first . . . shit, shit, shit!"

"Yes to whatever it is . . . just please!" I begged.

"Promise me you'll marry me, baby," he said, shocking the fuck out of me.

"That's not fair, Giannis. You can't ask me that right now," I pouted but continued meeting each and every one of his strokes.

"I'll be more romantic later, but right now I need you to give me what I want if you want that nut. Don't you want that shit, Dakota? Ahh, shit, that feels amazing!" he called out while going as deep as my body would allow.

"Yes, baby, yes! I'll marry you!" I wailed as my body went into convulsions. At that point he could have asked me to be his slave, promising to wait on him hand and foot for the rest of my days and I would have agreed. Every cell in my body was lit as I came harder than I ever had in my life. Giannis was right behind me, pumping his seeds into my body. My wetness and his semen made for one hell of a mess on this leather sofa. This shit was ruined, but I was too out of it to give a damn. I knew that if I weren't already pregnant, I surely would have been after that episode.

"And if you try to renege on the promise you just made, I'm fucking yo' ass up, Dakota," he threatened before proceeding to plant kisses all over my damp body.

"You just worry about the fat-ass ring you're about to put on my finger!" I joked. It really didn't matter to me what that shit looked like as long as I was marrying his fine ass.

Picking me up from my sprawled-out position on the couch, Giannis placed my legs around his waist. I needed his assistance because my shit felt like linguine right about now. It took all my strength to keep them in position and not slide down his body, but his hand resting under my ass helped me out a great deal. Despite being spent, the kisses he placed on my neck and collarbone were slowing causing my body to heat up once again. And what came next nearly took my breath away.

"Oh, don't you worry about that ring, baby girl. I got you covered. I promise you earned that. Shit, you earned it, Dakota!" he groaned loudly, sliding his thick muscle inside my dripping honey pot for the second time tonight.

I was also sure that it wouldn't be the last time this evening, and I was ready to receive all the dick my baby daddy had for me tonight.

Chapter 11

You Make Me Better

Montell Mathis

"Babe, what's going on with you? You've been locked in this room all weekend. Please talk to me," Erica pleaded, wearing a worried expression.

I hated that she was so worked up about what was up with me, but the truth was I was worried sick about my cousin. I was shocked as shit when Rah and his boy ran up on me at the Chevron. I was embarrassed to admit that I was extremely close to ratting David's ass out, but I stood my ground. He'd been in South Dallas since they'd been tearing the streets apart looking for him. He thought that was the last place they would expect him to be. Since they were having such a hard time locating him, I figured he was right. That was until he stopped responding to my calls and text messages.

I can't even lie. I was shook. It was obvious that someone had given up my cousin's location, and it was weighing heavily on me not knowing his fate. Since birth, it had always been me and Dave. I was closer to him than I was to my own brothers. They always acted like they were better than me anyway. I was also feeling bad about warning them about the plans he had for Dakota. Without that bit of information, they may not have figured out that he was involved in any way. In a sense, I'd given him up to the enemy. They weren't enemies of mine per se, but if a nigga had beef with David, then they had beef with me. It was just like that with us.

Despite what a fucked-up person he was, I didn't want my cousin to die, and I knew that's exactly what happened if Rah and those other two crazy fools had run up on him in that house. I'd gone by there that night after they approached me, hoping to at least warn him of what was to come, but I hadn't made it there in time. The front of the place was trashed as usual, but that back room that he'd been holed up in was uncharacteristically clean, and David was nowhere to be found. I'd been calling, texting, and stopping by there for days and nothing.

I felt in my heart that my cousin was dead and it was at the hands of three psycho-ass individuals I wouldn't want coming for me. Although I knew I couldn't win going up against them, everything in me wanted to go get some answers from them. I was sure they wouldn't tell me shit, but I needed to know what was up.

Sometimes I questioned whether David even deserved my loyalty, but at the end of the day, he was family and we'd always been down for one another. He was dead-ass wrong for what he'd done, and if they had caught up with him, then he got what he deserved. Shit didn't make me feel any better though.

My aunt Millie had been blowing me up, asking if I'd heard from him, and I was honest with her when I told her that I hadn't. It bugged me to see her so crazy with worry, and I had to fight the urge to tell her to stop looking because in my heart of hearts I knew her son was no longer among the living.

My only peace over the last few weeks came from being with my girl and my children. It was hard, but I knew I needed to shake this depression shit quick. I couldn't take my girl looking at me the way she was right now. Our emotions were tied together, and I didn't want my stress to add to hers.

I pulled her from her position on the edge of the bed to my chest and planted a kiss to her temple. "I'm good, E," I lied.

"You're not, and I know it, but I won't force you to talk about whatever it is that has your mind preoccupied. When you're ready, I'll be here for you," she offered sweetly. "And if you're worried about going to Dakota about David, I really believe that you did the right thing."

"I know, and I appreciate you. You done became my damn therapist over the last couple of months. Listening to all my problems without judging me or making me feel weak. Swear that means the world to me. I just don't want you to feel overwhelmed with all I have going on. If it ain't the kids, it's something with Ayesha or Dave. I don't want to become a burden to you," I spoke freely.

"You're not a burden at all, Montell. If you can't come to me and talk to me about the things you're dealing with, then who will you talk to? That's what I'm here for. Don't ever feel like you're putting too much on me. When you're down, it's my job as your woman to lift you up. Be your peace in the middle of the storms you face and help you dodge the curveballs life throws your way. Let me be that for you just like you are for me," she said, looking into my eyes.

It took everything I had not to tell her that I loved her right then. I mean I did, but for some reason, I was afraid to speak the words. It had been just a few short months since we decided to see if a relationship between us would work, and to be honest, things were going really well. Ever since I started opening up to her, it was like the dam broke and I was spilling my guts to her about everything: my insecurities, the abuse, and whatever else

I could think of. She got it all up out of me, man. I wasn't even kidding when I said she was like my therapist. Talking to her helped me deal with a lot of shit, and I was beginning to become too dependent on her. Not like how I was with Kota and the way I was dependent on her financially, but with Erica, I was dependent on her emotionally. I only prayed I could be to her what she was to me. Dreams of making things right with Dakota were no more, and Erica consumed my every thought when we were apart. I wanted to get this thing right this time. I'd failed with Dakota, but I grew from it, and I strived to be a better man for Erica. That's how she was able to convince me to contact Kota about David. She could get my ass to do anything.

"You don't have to say it, Montell. I know how you feel about me, and that's all that matters. And just so you know, I love you too, baby," she said before getting up and quietly leaving the room.

For a moment I just sat frozen, eyes fixed in the direction she'd just disappeared in. I'd always felt a strong connection to Erica, even when I was cheating on Dakota with her. I fought those feelings because I thought that Dakota and I were meant to be and that one day I would be the man she needed me to be. The truth was that I wasn't the man for Dakota and she wasn't the woman for me. Erica was that person, and it was good to finally realize that. Although our past dealings with one another were based on a lie, we were now building from a solid foundation, and this go-round, I was changing up. For Erica, I was going to be the man I was claiming to be in the beginning, not the nigga who was sneaking around on his girl and lying to her.

Getting up from the bed, I went through the house, searching for my lady. There was something important that I needed to tell her, and it couldn't wait another minute. After going all around our new apartment, I found her in the kids' playroom. The sight before me only confirmed the thoughts I was having.

Sitting on the floor Indian style with my daughter seated between her legs, Erica flipped through the pages of a book she was reading out loud to her. The voices she was using as she read caused Laysia to giggle, which in turn caused my smile to widen. Our son sat at her side, too young to really know what she was saying, but he was still quiet and attentive as she switched between characters and used expressions to tell the story. Sensing my presence, Erica stopped and looked up at me with a warm smile.

"I just wanted to thank you for everything that you do for us. You have made everything in my life better. You make me better." At hearing my words, she couldn't even speak, but I did notice her eyes gloss over as she swallowed real hard. "I love you, E."

Finding her voice, she finally spoke. "I know you do, and there's no need to thank me. Like I told you before, it's what I'm here for, babe," she replied before turning her attention back to the book, picking up where she left off in the story.

For some reason I didn't want to leave just yet. If I went back to the room, my mind was only going to travel back to David and every possible way he may have met his end. There was nothing I could do about it, and quite frankly I was tired of thinking about it.

Taking my place on the oversized bean bag that was next to Erica, I listened as she read. I wasn't at all interested in the kiddie book, but I just wanted to spend some time in the presence of my family. It only took a few minutes for Li'l Tell to lose interest in what his mother was saying and make his way over to me. We played around with some of his toys while Erica and Laysia did their own thing.

My phone was constantly buzzing as it lay facedown on the floor, but I refused to answer it. It was no one but Ayesha's bugaboo ass, and I didn't have time for her craziness right now. Ever since she found out that Erica and I were in a relationship and living together, her ass had been wilding out—blowing up my phone, showing up to my job, and even trying to keep me from seeing Laysia. We hadn't been together in forever, but she wanted to trip because I'd moved on.

One thing I wasn't going to play with her about was my child though. My mother had recommended a lawyer to me who helped out men who had custodial issues with their children, stand-up guys who were being fucked over by the system and bitter baby mamas. Months ago I put myself on child support to avoid the drama, and my lawyer, Meagan Sims, informed me that I was entitled to my visitation with my daughter. Ayesha could keep playing with me if she wanted to, and her ass was going to be the one with the weekend visits, and I'd be the full-time parent. That's the way I wanted it anyway, but I didn't want to be shady and keep Laysia away from her mother. Erica was more of a mother to her than Esha, but the fact remained that she didn't birth her, and my baby girl loved that hefty ho to death.

"Baby, just answer the phone. You know she won't quit calling until you do," Erica said, glancing over at me knowingly.

I knew she was right, but I wasn't ready to take Laysia back to her mother, and it was going to kill me to leave her behind while she kicked, screamed, and called out for me like she did when I dropped her off a few weeks ago. That episode was what triggered her mother to withhold my child from me for the last two weekends. Only reason I had her now was that something told me to stop by Ayesha's mother's house after getting off work the other day, and my baby girl happened to be there. I knew Esha was preparing for the turn up, and I was hoping she had dropped my baby off with her grandmother, and she had.

Laysia was so happy to see me, and it burned me up that she was telling my daughter lies about me not having time to pick her up and let her spend the weekend with me anymore. That girl was too damn loco, and I'd had enough. Bitch was running around telling anyone who would listen that Erica and I were turning her daughter against her and that we were poisoning her mind or some shit like that. Laysia loved her mother, but because of her ill feelings toward me, Ayesha lashed out at my baby often, so of course, she would rather be with me than with her.

Picking up my phone, I looked down at the screen and could do nothing but shake my head. I had at least fifteen missed calls and countless text messages. This sad ho was threatening to send the law to my apartment if I didn't return Laysia to her house within the next hour. Lord knows I couldn't afford to get caught up with these pigs and spend another day away from my girl and my children.

I was going to do what she was asking this time, but soon there wouldn't be shit she could say about how long my daughter stayed with me. Her ass would be lucky if she got Laysia once a month. I hated to do it, but I was tired of the games, and I was ready for my baby to have some stability in her life. When she was here with us, she didn't have accidents at night, and she just seemed like a happier child all around. I wanted her to stay that way, so if removing Ayesha from the picture for the time being was what it took to help my baby keep progressing, then that's exactly what I planned to do.

***

It had taken me two whole hours to make it to the store from dropping my daughter off. After leaving Esha's, I was supposed to stop by the store to pick up some things for Erica so that she could make us some tacos. My baby made the taco shells from scratch, and I couldn't wait to smash on them shits.

Only thing standing in the way of me getting my grub on was my retarded baby mama. I almost put hands on Esha for all the unnecessary clowning she was doing. As soon as the door to her place swung open, the drama began. All I could hear was "bitch-ass nigga" this, "broke-ass nigga" that. She called Erica and my mama every ungodly name she could think of. What my mama had to do with anything was beyond me, but she made sure to go in on us all.

Although it was hard, I remained quiet and didn't respond. Well, that was until she started yanking my daughter around by her arm and screaming at her. At that point, I had to intervene. It took everything I had not to knock her ugly ass out. Bitch was livid, and I had no idea why. What I wasn't about to do was let her take the frustrations she had with me out on my child.

It pissed her off that Laysia was crying for me and asking if she could live with me instead. I didn't want the bitch beating on my child, so I stayed long enough to bathe my daughter, read her another story, and tuck her in. Laysia was asleep when I left, so I felt she would be safe and Esha would have no reason to fuss at or spank her like she kept yelling she would do when we first arrived at the house.

I urged my baby not to say anything in front of her mother about living with me only because I didn't want to set her off and have her hitting on her when I wasn't around. I really didn't want to leave her there, but I didn't

know what other choice I had. The court system didn't
tend to side with fathers, and if I didn't have concrete evi-
dence that something bad was going on and that Laysia
was being neglected, there wasn't much they could do
anyway. Little did Ayesha know, I was slowly but surely
collecting the proof I needed to prove to the courts that I
was the fit parent out of the two of us. She'd find out soon
enough though. I just prayed things came together with
the quickness so I wouldn't spend so much time worried
about my baby girl.

"Did she say sharp or mild shredded cheese?" I questioned myself out loud. I wanted to call home to make
sure, but Erica was always making fun of me for claiming
I didn't need a grocery list but stayed forgetting items or
bringing home the wrong stuff. I refused to give her the
satisfaction of being right once again.

"Kinfolk!" I heard a little voice squeal from not too far
away.

Turning around, I spotted my little cousin Davy running toward me full speed. Seeing his happy face had my
mind once again on his father. David's twin stopped short
right in front of me, ready to do our signature handshake.
This was some shit I'd been doing with him since he was
like 2 years old.

"What's good, baby cuz? Where's ya mom?" I asked
looking around for Shawna. I was a little reluctant
to face her because I had nothing to tell her as far as
the whereabouts of her baby daddy. Now that I was
thinking about it, I didn't recall her reaching out and
asking any questions about him in the time he'd been
out of sight. That was strange, because when I tell you
this chick lived and breathed David Parrish, I tell you
no lies. If he was out fucking around and not answering
his phone, the next number she would dial would be
mine. Questioning me and venting about how she knew
he was out doing her wrong.

"Davy! Davy, baby, where are you?!" I heard my cousin's girl calling out. You know that panicked tone women have when they lose sight of their child in a public place? Yeah, that's how she sounded.

"Shawna!" I called, getting her attention. When her eyes landed on me and Davy, I could see her body and facial expression visibly relax.

"Davy, baby, you can't run off like that. You scared the mess out of me," she fussed as she walked up on us and pulled him into her chest.

"Come on, ma, I'm not a baby," my little cousin complained, making me laugh.

"You will always be my baby, Davy," she cooed, planting a juicy kiss on his cheek.

It was when she said baby that I looked down and realized she was no longer pregnant. The baby must have come early, but I was shocked that my cousin nor Shawna had mentioned anything or called me to come to the hospital. Shit, I didn't even recall Aunt Millie saying anything about the baby, and I had just talked to her the day before.

"I see you didn't have a problem snapping back," I observed as she gave a weak smile. I wasn't really into white girls, but Shawna was attractive and kept herself up really well. Her body was amazing and stacked up like a sister, so I could definitely see what my cousin saw in her. That was David's thing though. You had to be a ten or better to be on his team. It was just crazy to me that all these beautiful women put up with so much shit to be with him. I'd tried since we were teenagers to imitate his love life, but that shit never worked in my favor. My relationship with Dakota was a prime example. Now all I was trying to do was be myself and do right by my girl. With the exception of Ayesha's aggravating ass, that method was working out just fine for me. "So, where is she? When do I get to meet my baby cousin?"

"There is no baby, Tell," she answered, looking down at Davy sadly before bringing her watery eyes back up to meet mine.

"What the hell did I miss? What you mean there's no baby?" I was totally confused.

"My baby sister died, and she's not coming back. My mama said my daddy not ever coming back either, but I don't really care about that part," Davy answered before his mother could respond to me. I was shocked as shit that he spoke of never seeing his father again like it wasn't a big deal, but the conviction in his voice told me that he meant every word. I knew David was a jerk to most people, but he was a good-ass father to Davy, or at least that's the way things came off to me.

"Davy, what did I tell you about our business being our business?" she chastised him in a stern tone.

"I'm sorry, Mommy, I forgot," Davy replied sadly, feeling bad about breaking the promise he'd made to his mother to keep what she'd told him about his sister and father between the two of them.

"What he means is that I lost the baby, and as far as his father goes, he hasn't been around lately." She shrugged.

There was so much more that she wasn't saying, and that was evident by the uncaring expression she wore. Even her tone reflected the fucks she didn't give about David being missing in action. I decided not to press, but best believe I would be checking some shit out. His ass was probably hiding out somewhere that only she knew about, and it pissed me off that I was being kept out of the loop. I was thinking maybe he found out that I warned Dakota about his plans and wasn't fucking with me or something.

"I'm sorry to hear about the baby, and you know how David is. He probably just needed to get away for a minute. He'll pop back up soon, I'm sure. In the meantime, I'll check some things out," I assured her.

"If you say so, but if I were you, I would leave it alone. I won't say too much, but just know that your favorite cousin wasn't as down for you as you thought he was," she said while tossing a bag of mozzarella cheese in her basket.

"What the hell does that even mean? David is my best friend," I countered as my mind began working overtime. I was more confused than ever. No one was closer to me than David, so she didn't know what the hell she was talking about. He had my back when no one else did, so there was no way I was listening to this shit. David not down for me? There was no way that shit was true.

"If that's what you think, then I'll continue to allow you to believe it." She shook her head before grabbing her son's hand and walking away.

I didn't even know what had just transpired between Shawna and me. She was looking hella suspect in my eyes right now, and by the looks Davy shot his mother as she talked, it seemed he was privy to some tea but had clearly been sworn to secrecy.

Chapter 12

Blessings and Losses

Rio

It had been a long time coming, but I was finally taking Breelyn home today. Pulling up to the curb outside the hospital entrance, I was in awe as I admired my woman. Even seated in a wheelchair with noticeable scars on her face, she was still the prettiest girl in the world to me. At times, I could tell that she was still a bit self-conscious about her appearance, and it killed me to see her doubt herself. The marks on her face, arms, and legs were noticeable, but as her man, I did my best to reassure her that she was still gorgeous to me. And although she was a beautiful girl, I was more concerned about who she was on the inside anyhow. That's the woman I fell in love with. What she looked like before and what she looked like now didn't bother me at all.

I also understood that although my opinion somewhat mattered to her, my words could only do so much. Breelyn would have to regain confidence and accept her new self, flaws and all. That wasn't something I could do for her. I didn't understand how she couldn't see what I saw when I looked at her, but I guessed that was some female shit.

I was so caught up in staring at her pretty ass that Nurse Ivy had to practically shout my name to gain my attention. I immediately jumped out of the car and rushed to the passenger side when I realized that I was the one holding us up. I quickly opened the car door and helped my baby into her Charger. I'd driven it to pick her up because I didn't want her to struggle trying to get in and out of my truck.

"Sorry, baby. Looking at your fine ass had ya man sidetracked," I whispered to her as I buckled her seat belt. Like she always did when I complimented her, Breelyn just blushed.

"Stop being mannish, DeMario, and get this child home so that she can rest," Nurse Ivy admonished with a playful swat.

I wanted to tell her that it was about to be straight fucking and no rest up in that bitch for the next few days, but I didn't want to talk nasty in front of her. The woman had become like family to us in the time that we'd been here. Breelyn complained anytime she was assigned another nurse, and they accommodated her spoiled ass anytime Nurse Ivy worked. She took very good care of my baby, and for that, she would always be good with me. After saying our goodbyes, we were headed home.

Breelyn had no idea, but our home had been ready for some time, and with Dakota and Ms. Syl's help, it was now fully furnished and decorated. I just wanted her to be happy about something. I'd do anything to put that smile back on her face. Not only had the wreck fucked my baby up physically, but we'd taken another major loss as well, one that no one else but us knew about. It was one of the main reasons not being able to kill David still fucked with me on a daily basis. That fuck nigga had taken more from us than he'd ever know.

The look in Breelyn's eyes anytime we spoke on it broke my heart in two. I couldn't really deal with my own feelings because I was so worried about her and how she was coping. She played it off most times, but I knew she was dealing with a lot emotionally. The mood swings were a constant reminder of her true mental state. One minute she was cool, and the next she was going off on me for no fucking reason. For now, I would have to tuck my shit away and focus on helping her heal from this ordeal.

I looked over to find her passed out with her head facing the window. These days she tired easily, but I was sure she would be back to herself in no time. At least I hoped so. She'd excelled and surpassed all the goals set for her in rehab, so I prayed that she would continue to improve.

The fact that she was asleep right now worked out perfectly for the surprise I had in store for her. Had she been awake, she would have asked me 101 questions about where we were going by now. Pulling into our circular driveway, I couldn't help but feel proud of the job I'd done. Hopefully Breelyn would love the finished product as much as I did. I was nervous and happy at the same time because not once since her accident had Breelyn mentioned or questioned me about the progress on our home. Before shit went left, it was all she could talk about. Hopefully she hadn't changed her mind about moving in with a nigga.

"Bree, wake up. We're home, baby," I called out, gently shaking her from her sleep. Nervously, I watched her as she came to and began looking around. It took her a minute, but I could tell when she finally realized that I'd brought her to our brand-new home instead of the old one in North Richland Hills.

"DeMario," she whispered, looking over at me with her hands covering her mouth. "For real, babe?" she questioned before looking back and forth between me and the house. Our new ranch-style home sat on five acres with not one nosy-ass neighbor in sight. "Why didn't you tell me it was done?" she asked.

"I wanted it to be a surprise. Plus, you hadn't really said anything about the house. Honestly, I wasn't really sure you still wanted to move in with me," I admitted.

"Damn." She shook her head regretfully. "I know what I'm going through isn't easy to deal with, but you should know how I feel about you. Of course I still want us to live together. You hadn't mentioned anything to me, so I assumed all of this was on hold. Figured you wanted me to get better before we moved forward. And then my mind has been consumed with so many other things that I just . . . I don't know." She just shook her head, having a hard time finding the right words.

"I already know, Breelyn. But ay, before we go inside, there's something I wanted to talk with you about," I said, taking her hand in mine. I'd been meaning to talk with her about this for a cool little minute, but it never seemed to be the right time, and I could never quite find the words to say to her to make it go over easier. I knew she would be happy but also sad because of what had happened to her, but I needed her to be prepared when she got the news.

"What is it?" she asked, searching my eyes.

Before I could fix my mouth to answer her, our front door was being yanked open, and the surprise that I had prepared for her was now waiting on our front porch. Her brother, cousin, aunt, uncle, and countless other family members stood there. All were smiling and excited to see her out of that hospital bed and finally home. Even her father Kenneth was standing there grinning from ear to ear. It seemed we took just a little too long to come inside, so they'd brought the party outside. Seeing the smile on her face made me feel good, and just like that, I forgot all about what I was going to tell her. Not being able to wait another second, Dakota came and snatched Breelyn's door open, and of course she was talking shit.

"Bring y'all slow assess on. Your warden is only giving us a total of two hours to chill with you before he says we have to go home, so let's get this show on the road." She stuck her tongue out at me while Breelyn bit her bottom lip.

My baby already knew what time it was. As soon as they got the hell up out of here, I was diving in that pussy and planned to stay there until my energy was depleted. She could leave everything up to me, and she wouldn't have to lift one finger if she was too tired. I had no problem doing all the work. Sneaking and bending her over the sink in the bathroom of her hospital room was a thing of the past. So were all the quick oral sessions we got in hoping no one walked in on us. I was ready to really get down through there. I couldn't think of a better way to relieve this pent-up stress I'd been dealing with than making slow, sweet love to my lady.

"As much as I love y'all, if it were up to me it would be more like an hour," Breelyn countered, giving me a sly wink.

"Whatever, man. Bring your fass ass on," Dakota said with a smack of her teeth.

Getting out, I went to the passenger side to assist her in getting out of the car. Her eyes darted around, taking it all in, while she wore the brightest smile. Everything she had in mind or wanted for our home had been brought to life and made a reality. I was happy to be the one to give this to her. Sure, we had suffered a major loss, but we were also blessed. I had to remind myself of that every minute of every day. To be honest, praying daily and having Breelyn here with me were the only things getting me through.

"How are you, baby girl?" Kenneth beamed, looking down at his daughter once she reached the steps.

"I'm good, Kenneth." She nodded with a smile. I was glad to see their relationship progressing the way it was. It was a slow process, and I had to stay on her ass about that ugly attitude of hers, but it was getting better between them. I mean, she was still calling him by his first name, but I didn't think that was something that would change anytime soon.

"I'll give you an official tour and fuck you in each and every one of these rooms once everyone leaves," I said close to her ear where only she could hear me. I felt her ass shiver at my words, and that shit turned me on.

"You promise?" she asked, grabbing the front of my shirt and pulling me closer to her.

"I promise, love," I whispered to her with a soft smack on her ass. I didn't want to be too over the top with it in front of her people. I'd save that freaky shit for later when we were finally alone.

When we made it to the kitchen, the women in the family were all gathered around arranging the food. "Welcome home, baby girl." Ms. Syl started the greetings with a hug.

"Thanks, Auntie Syl." She kissed her cheek, and everyone else followed suit, getting their hugs in with Breelyn.

Like anytime we got together, there was a full spread of soul food, and I knew my girl was about to go ham. I wanted to laugh at her hungry ass when she licked her lips and patted her stomach at the sight of the food. Her love of food has always fascinated me. She could eat all she wanted and get fat as hell for all I cared. I'd be like those enabling-ass spouses and family members on *My 600-lb Life,* feeding her everything her heart desired while she laid her juicy ass in bed, unable to move. I was finding that love could have you doing some dumb shit, and I was fucking retarded for Breelyn Waiters.

"Move, Elijah!" she fussed, pushing her brother out of the way. Nigga had two plates in hand and was already digging in the mac and cheese, which was his favorite.

"Yeah, move, rude ass," I concurred with a light pop to the back of his head. It was just like his selfish ass to try to eat before the guest of honor.

"That's no way to treat someone who's a guest in your home," he stated, wagging a finger in our direction while everyone else just laughed.

"You ain't no damn guest. You're family. And nobody is eating before my lady, and that's all there is to it," I declared just in case anyone was confused as to how this welcome home celebration was supposed to go. I snatched the plates from his hand, causing him to flip me off.

"Whatever y'all gon' do, hurry up and do it so I can feed both my babies," Giannis chimed in, earning a smack to his arm from Dakota. "What?" He looked down at her, not realizing his mistake until all eyes were on him.

"What you mean babies?" Kasey, Dakota's father, spoke up. He had moved from his chair and was now standing in front of Giannis and Dakota with his arms folded across his chest.

"Damn, my bad." He offered an apologetic look in Kota's direction. She was standing there looking like she was afraid to speak up. They clearly hadn't talked over how they would share their good news with the family yet. Only reason I knew was because of that tantrum Giannis threw in the waiting area at the hospital weeks before. The other day he'd told me about the big blowup they'd had, which led to her telling him that he was going to be a father. This was what I tried to tell Breelyn in the car before we were interrupted. I swore this was not the way I wanted her to find out.

My eyes immediately went to her. Her expression was blank as she eyed Dakota, seemingly putting everything together in her mind. She suddenly pushed off the island in the kitchen and moved as fast as she could toward the back. I was right on her heels, no longer concerned with what was happening in the kitchen. I caught the bathroom door before she could close it. She placed the toilet lid down before taking a seat and dropping her head. After closing the door and locking it myself, I kneeled down in front of her.

"Breelyn, baby, you good?" I stupidly asked, already knowing the answer to my question.

"Yup, just peachy," she answered sarcastically without looking at me.

"Look, I know this is hard for you, but we're going to get through it. Maybe it just wasn't our time. That doesn't mean we can't be happy for Dakota and G."

The look she gave me let me know I may have said the wrong thing. "That's easy for you to say. You're not the one who lost a child!" she spat.

"Fuck you mean that's easy for me to say?" I jumped to my feet, no longer in the mood to comfort her. I was sick of her ass flipping on me. I was dealing with some heavy shit myself, but that didn't seem to mean anything to her. "Don't do that, Breelyn. Don't do that shit. I loved my seed just as much as you!"

"I just don't see how you can tell me to be happy for them when the same reason for their happiness was ripped away from me only days after we found out. How can I be happy about that?" she cried.

"Because she's your family, and I know for a fact she'd be happy for you if the shoe were on the other foot. You're being petty as fuck right now, and as much as I want to make things better for you, I can't support your attitude about all this. It's not right, and it's selfish as fuck," I spoke honestly, making her cry even harder. She knew I was right.

It was hard to walk away from her, but I did. I left her in the bathroom alone to think about the shit she just said. Hopefully she came out and rejoined us with a different mindset. I would never say this out loud, but this situation was starting to get the best of me.

Chapter 13

It Ain't Always All About You

Breelyn

"DeMario, where are you? Call me back as soon as you get this," I spoke softly into my phone. This was my second time calling his phone, and once again I was sent to voicemail. At first I thought I was tripping when the line rang only once and the voicemail suddenly picked up. I immediately dialed his number again only to get the same results, so I knew then that he was rejecting my calls. But why? Didn't he realize that I needed him here with me? He'd been gone a lot over the last week, and I was starting to wonder what was up with him. I felt abandoned in a sense, and I didn't see the point of having all this land and the big, beautiful home if I was going to be left here alone.

Things between us started changing after the news broke about Dakota and Giannis having a baby at my welcome home gathering. Rio had come chasing after me following my abrupt exit from the kitchen, and as always, he did his best to make me feel better. I hadn't been very receptive to his words and in turn said some things that rubbed him the wrong way. Luckily the family was so focused on what Dakota's answer was to the question her father posed that they didn't notice my hasty departure.

Don't get me wrong, I was happy for Dakota and Giannis. She deserved a baby with the man she was madly in love with. My cousin deserved happiness period point blank. I just wanted the same thing for myself, which made it a little hard to get excited about their good news. It was crazy how our love lives mirrored one another's in many ways, but it seemed as I was the one continuing to get the short end of the stick. We were both with fuck boys, got some sense and moved on to men who treated us like the queens we were. Then came the houses, cars, and babies. Only my child didn't make it. Kota, on the other hand, was living the dream while I slowly died on the inside.

Speak of the devil, I looked down at my phone and saw yet another text from my cousin. It was the third or fourth time she reached out to me today, but I wasn't in the mood to talk to anyone besides my man. Too bad he was nowhere to be found.

Kota B: If you don't call/text me back I'm coming by there. I know damn well you see me calling and texting. What the fuck is going on?

Kota B: Please call me back, Breelyn. I love you.

Auntie Syl: Call me, baby girl. I'm worried about you.

Yes, I saw each and every text message they sent, along with every call placed to me. I just chose to ignore them. Dakota had been trying to contact me for days about going to lunch and doing some shopping with my aunt for her and Uncle Kasey's anniversary party that was coming up. My depressed ass hadn't even been courteous enough to respond.

I felt really bad that I hadn't talked to Dakota since she was here that day. Hadn't even taken the time to congratulate her on the baby. What type of shitty person does that to their best friend? I wasn't upset with her per se. I was just pissed off at life in general. My cousin was having a baby while mine had been taken away before I ever had the pleasure of meeting him or her. All because of David Parrish.

I cursed the day I met his shiesty ass. Fuck that—I cursed the day he was born. He was dead and gone, and I still hated him with everything in me. I wished I could bring him back just to murder his ho ass all over again. He had ruined my life, and I would never be the same because of him. Rio promised that we could work on a baby as soon as I was well enough, but I didn't want a replacement baby. I wanted the one I lost. I knew that what I wanted was an impossibility, but I wanted it nonetheless.

My appearance was really fucking with me, too, especially the scar on my neck that was visible despite what shirt I wore. It looked like someone tried to slit my throat or something. Some glass from the windshield had sliced me there, and the scar tissue made the healed wound look gruesome. At least to me it did. The ones on my face were smaller and not as thick, but knowing they were there at all messed with my self-esteem. I kept telling myself my scars would eventually fade or that it didn't matter how I looked. I was blessed enough to have a man who loved me in spite of it, but at the same time, something was still missing.

I'd lost part of me in this whole mess, and I needed that piece of me back so that I could move on with my life. I was so angry because it seemed that the moment I found my true love and claimed my happiness, it was taken from me within the blink of an eye. All I could think was, *why me?* I knew better than to question God, but I was really waiting for Him to come through with an explanation for me on what exactly He was trying to do in my life. What lesson was I to learn from this? What could I possibly gain from going through something this heartbreaking? This shit hurt so bad that most days I didn't even want to go on living. My thoughts were becoming darker, and that wasn't a place I wanted to be. I wanted to be happy again, but I didn't know where to begin. I felt like Rio would eventually leave, because I knew my actions were pushing him further and further away. It wasn't intentional, but I was sure he would only put up with so much.

The ringing of the doorbell and heavy pounding at my door snatched my attention. At first I thought it was DeMario, but I quickly nixed that idea since he would have just come in with his key if it were. I let the ringing and knocking go on for a full minute before I threw back my thick green blanket and pulled myself from the couch. I'd been lying in that same spot for nearly twenty-four hours, not eating, drinking, or doing much of anything else. I only got up once to bathe, and that was it. It was like I was stuck. I couldn't even remember if I'd had to use the restroom in that time, and that was a damn shame.

Looking through the peephole, I was met with a worried-looking Kota and Rah, who I could tell was vexed. I didn't want to be bothered, but I know that they weren't going away until I let them in.

"Damn, could you knock any louder?" I sassed as I pulled the door open.

"Well, if you'd answer your fucking phone or return a text, we wouldn't have resorted to beating the fucking door down. What the hell is going on with you, Greedy?" Rah asked as he pushed past me and made his way inside.

Dakota just stood there, studying my face, trying to figure out what was up between us. I was feeling so conflicted about my behavior that I couldn't even make eye contact with her. I just stepped to the side, allowing her to enter my home. There was a definite disconnect between us, and I could feel it. To make matters worse, it was all on me. I had to fix this and fix it fast.

When I made it back to the den, they were both seated and looking my way, awaiting a response to Rah's question. "Look, I'm sorry I haven't hit y'all back, but I've just been a little down and didn't really feel like being around people."

"We're not just people, Breelyn. We're family, and we want to be there for you through whatever it is you're going through." Dakota's voice cracked, making me feel ten times worse than I already did.

"Exactly! Pushing us away ain't the move," Rah added.

"What y'all wanna be around me for?" I mumbled.

"What the fuck kind of question is that?" Rah answered for them both.

"Look at me!" I screamed at the top of my lungs. "I'm walking around here with a fucking limp! That shit ain't sexy, bro! Breathing all messed up since they took that tube out my chest. Got scars and marks all over my fucking face and body. And if that weren't enough, that nigga took my unborn child from me." I broke down, wrapping my arms around my midsection.

"Excuse the fuck out of me if I need a little time to myself! She gets to have her baby, but mine is gone. Why is my life so fucked up but you get everything?" I turned to face my cousin. "You've always gotten everything. A perfect fucking childhood, mom and dad included. What about me? Where's my perfection? What makes you so special?" I shouted, causing Kota's eyes to fill with water and spill over, while my brother just shook his head in disbelief.

I lost it. No longer did I have control of my emotions. Everything just began to spill out, all of it. There was nothing I could do to stop my tears or the confessions that spilled from my mouth.

"Greedy, cut this shit out! You outta line like a mu'fucka right now!" Rah snapped, standing up, but I continued. I knew my words were killing Dakota, but I didn't stop. I couldn't stop if I wanted to.

"David wanted you this whole time, Dakota! The entire time I was with him! All the shit I put up with! The beatings? The disrespect and the cheating? Damn near losing my brother? All I gave up just to be with him, and he didn't really want me. He wanted you." I sobbed uncontrollably.

Dakota sat silently throughout my entire rant with tears cascading down her face. Once I was done, she rose from her seated position on the couch, placed the strap of her Chanel bag over her shoulder, and exited the room without speaking one word. I hadn't meant to hurt her and was only speaking from anger. My problem wasn't with her. It was with David, but the way that shit came out made it seem like I was blaming her when that wasn't the case.

"Kota, wait!" I turned to follow her and was met with a hateful glare from the love of my life. There he was standing at the entrance to the den, looking like he was ready to fucking kill me.

"You still riding that nigga's dick, huh? What happened to you saying you were over him? That can't possibly be true if the fact that he wanted Dakota and not you upsets you like this. I thought your fucked-up attitude and mood swings were because of the baby we lost, but now you got me thinking you've been acting out because of him. Where the fuck does that leave me, huh? Where does that leave us, Breelyn? And just know that you're not the only one who lost a baby. I guess it's just fuck me. My feelings don't mean shit, right? I'ma tell you something your people should have told your rotten ass a long time ago. It ain't always all about you, baby girl."

The hurt showed all over his face and had me moving toward the door to be closer to him. Suddenly, going after Kota was the last thing on my mind. I couldn't have DeMario questioning my feelings for him. I couldn't care less about David. I was just hurt that I'd been through so much with a man who secretly wanted the closest person to me instead. Who wouldn't be upset about something like that? Was I tripping?

"Chill, bro. You know she didn't mean it like that," Rah said, stepping in on my behalf.

"That's not what I meant, DeMario. I love you, and I know that you know that," I tried to explain. When my hand went up to caress his face, he promptly stepped back and out of my reach. I swore that shit hurt me to my core. Through my pain, I'd caused pain to the ones I loved most. If I lost him and Dakota, that would indeed be all it took for me to completely lose my mind. I couldn't see my life without either of them in it, but I was doing everything in my power to distance myself from them. What the fuck was wrong with me?

"I'ma go. Rah, I'll talk to you later," he said with a nod before turning to leave.

"Rio, man, hol' up," Rah called out as he moved toward the front behind him. "Don't dip out on her like that," I could faintly hear my brother say.

I didn't attempt to stop him as he walked out. In my heart, I knew that sooner or later I would drive him away, and it seemed I'd been successful. I was a basket case, and it was getting to the point that I was actually contemplating taking the antidepressants that had been prescribed to me by my surgeon. I was hurting emotionally, not crazy, so up until now, I hadn't felt the need to take the medicine. My current state and the suicidal thoughts that ran rampant through my mind as I watched my life walk out of that door had me rethinking that.

Chapter 14

Don't Wanna Be Without You

Rah

"Rio, man, hol' up," I called out as he moved toward the front with me behind him. "Don't dip out on her like that," I said once I caught up with him.

"Man, I ain't leaving that girl, but I need to get away for a minute. I already told you how I felt about your sister, and that was the honest-to-God truth. I can't just sit around while she self-destructs. She's intentionally pushing me away, and there's only so much a person can take, bro."

"Just give her some time, man," I pleaded. I'd never thought the day would come where I would be begging this nigga to be with my sister. I felt bad for Breelyn, but my heart went out to my potnah as well. I knew for a fact that he loved my sister, but he was right. She was alienating the people who loved her, and it was getting to the point where it had us wanting to say fuck it. She wasn't even fucking with Auntie Syl, and my OG was hurt behind that. I wanted to shake the shit out of my sister so that she would somehow get it together, but I knew coming at her like that would only make things worse.

"Chill. I already told you I wasn't leaving. I'ma need a minute though. This shit too draining, and I haven't had a chance to process it myself. Nigga responsible for Breelyn losing my baby and it's got her down bad, but nothing I do or say seems to help. I'm just fucked up right now. Right after we handle this shit with Giannis, I'm going to New York. You got my address there, and you got the number. Just call me if anything happens or if she needs me. I'm coming back, I just need to get away, ya know?"

"Yeah, man, I understand. I got her until you get back. Her ass need to talk to a professional or something because what we're doing ain't cutting it."

"My nigga, I already suggested that and she bit my damn head off about it. Maybe you'll have better luck than I did. But check it, I'ma get up with you later. Don't hesitate to hit me up if some shit pops off before I make it back this way."

"I got you."

We chopped it up for a few more minutes about a little issue we'd been dealing with, and then he was gone. Blowing out a deep breath, I went back inside to check on my sister. It looked like I was going to be camping out at her place for the next few days. There was no way that I was leaving her ass alone right now. She was too damn unstable.

I wanted to call Dakota and have her come back, but I already knew her stubborn ass wasn't trying to hear that shit right now. Breelyn was way out of line for coming at Kota B like that, but she was just hurting and taking it out on others. It wasn't right though, and I refused to make excuses for her. I just knew her well enough to know that she acted out like this when her feelings were hurt. Dakota knew this as well, and hopefully she wouldn't take Breelyn's words to heart.

Back in the overly spacious den, I found my sister balled up in that spot on the couch, crying her eyes out. I walked over and sat down before pulling her crybaby ass up to sit next to me.

"I knew he would leave, I just knew it," she wailed.

"Mane, Greedy, come on. He coming back, sis," I said, wrapping my arm around her shoulder to bring her closer. I just held her as she rested her head against me and cried. I held her until that ugly cry became a soft whimper. I wanted to curse her ass out for fucking up my shirt with all that damn snot, but I chilled.

"You really think he's coming back, Elijah?" She sniffed.

"I know he is because he told me so. Just give him some time to cool off. In the meantime, you need to get at Dakota to apologize for that shit you said. I know you didn't mean it like that, but it came across real fucked up, so I know her feelings are hurt. As ruthless as her ass is, you know she's sensitive as fuck. Especially when it comes to one of us, so you need to make shit right with her, Greedy," I advised.

"I know I do and I will. I never meant to make it seem like I was blaming her for anything. I'm just so mad right now, Elijah. That's no excuse though, and I shouldn't have taken it out on her. I've been doing the same thing to DeMario, and he doesn't deserve that. Neither of them does." She sniffed again and wiped her face.

I nodded in agreement right as I heard her stomach growl loud as hell. "Damn, when was the last time you had something to eat?"

"I couldn't even tell you. I haven't had much of an appetite lately." She shrugged.

I knew then that she must have really been going through it because rarely did her hungry ass skip a meal. Maybe some nourishment would put her in a better mood. "Go and get cleaned up, and I'll take you to get something to eat. Looks like you couldn't tell me when you last washed yo' ass either. That ain't a good look, Greedy." I turned my nose up just to fuck with her.

"Don't even try to play me like that, Elijah Raheem. I washed my ass today, nigga," she laughed, pushing me lightly in the chest.

"Well, comb your hair then so I can take you out. Shit looking like a damn bird's nest right about now," I teased, making her chuckle some more. I was glad to see her with a smile on her face. I swore I hated to see her or Kota upset and crying. That shit did something to my damn soul. All I wanted was to take the pain away, but there were times, like right now, when I couldn't. I didn't like that. I had to get over trying to save them from everything. There would be certain things beyond my control, and there would be times that they would go through shit that I couldn't prevent or fix. All I could focus on was being there for them when they needed me most, just like I was doing for Breelyn right now.

I took my sister to Gloria's, which she was happy about because it was her favorite restaurant. She wasn't lying when she said she hadn't been eating, because she was tearing her enchiladas down. We'd ordered a shrimp cocktail to share, but her ass ate it all before I even had a chance to taste it. Normally I would have snapped on her for that, but I was just happy that she was in a better mood and was eating. I wasn't used to her looking so puny.

The only time she got down during our dinner date was when she tried calling Rio, and the nigga didn't pick up. I knew he needed his space, but he was gon' have to chill with the silent treatment. I don't think it was the best thing to do to her right now, and I planned to get in his ass about that shit. Hearing my baby sister say that she'd contemplated suicide during our lengthy conversation at the restaurant fucked me up. To be so low that you wanted to take yourself out was mind-boggling to me. I guessed that was because I'd never experienced depression.

"Greedy, have you considered talking to a doctor about what you're going through?" I was attempting to approach the subject cautiously because I didn't want to upset her or make her feel like I thought she was losing her mind.

"Like a shrink?"

"I don't think that's what folk call them anymore, but yeah."

She sighed deeply before answering. "DeMario suggested it a while back, and at the time I wasn't trying to hear it. Thought he was trying to say I was crazy or something. Now I'm thinking it might not be such a bad idea. Every time I try to express myself or talk to someone about how I feel, it comes off wrong and not at all the way I intended. That's why I've just been wanting to stay to myself."

"If you feel that way, then I definitely think you should talk to someone. Isolating yourself is the last thing you need to be doing," I advised.

This was a difficult time for my baby sister, and not having Rio here was going to make it that much harder. But just like she pulled herself up after shaking David's ho ass, I was positive that she could do the same if things didn't work out with DeMario. Having a man in her life should have been a bonus and added to her life, but her happiness and how she felt about herself couldn't be dependent on him or his presence in her life. Listen to me sounding like I knew something about life and love. Guess I retained a few gems from my back-porch conversations with Uncle Kasey.

"I think you're right. I'll look into it first thing in the morning," she agreed.

"Just know that whatever you need, I'm here for you. Anything, you hear me?"

"I hear you, and I love you," she said as she wiped the tears that fell from her eyes.

"I love you too, but you gon' have to chill with the waterworks, mane. You gon' have a nigga getting clowned for sitting up here shedding tears with your ass," I said, trying to lighten the mood. Of course she laughed, and I was happy to be the one to take away her pain even if it was only for a moment.

After our late lunch, we hit up the mall, and I cashed out on her. She seemed to be in good spirits as she spent up all my fucking money, and I was glad I didn't have Kota's ass with me too. Fucking with those two at the same time always put a hurting on my pockets. I had it though, so I wasn't really tripping. Anything I had to do to cheer her up, I was doing it without question.

Witnessing Breelyn and her dude go through what they were going through made me think of my situation with the lady in my life. Well, she wasn't really in my life per se, but I was realizing that I wanted her to be. I no longer wanted to go through life's trials on my own, and who better to be there by my side than the chick who'd been there for me in the background for a cool minute?

For so long I'd been afraid of the way she made me feel, but in recent months I'd started to embrace the idea of us being an official couple. No more sneaking around and keeping our shit on the low or worrying about what people would say about us being with each other. I didn't want to cause any static between her and Kota and Breelyn, but that was going to be hard to avoid. When everything came out, there was sure to be some smoke.

At this point, I was like fuck it. I wanted who I wanted and didn't care what people thought of it. Like I'd always said, if I was going to settle down with anyone, she was the one and only female I'd be doing that with. I'd been playing around long enough, and it seemed that she was finally giving up and moving on with someone else. That shit there made my fucking head pound just thinking about it. To have the chick I felt was meant for me living out the dream I had for us with the next nigga was something that I just couldn't let happen.

After three days with Breelyn, I was finally back home after she basically kicked me out, assuring me that she was well enough to be alone. I couldn't get my lady off my mind, so I picked up the phone and dialed her number before I could talk myself out of it. Hopefully her petty ass didn't have me blocked. She was notorious for doing shit like that. I was two seconds from hanging up, but she finally picked up on the fifth ring. Her ass probably sat there contemplating if she was going to answer at all.

"What is it, Rah?" she spoke softly.

"I need to see you."

"I can't do this with you right now," she whispered.

"You with yo' nigga?" I asked, although I really didn't give a fuck if she was. To hell with his ass.

"That's none of your business, sir. What you wanna see me for anyway? I thought we were officially done playing this game," she reminded me.

"I gotta have a reason to want to see you now?" I asked while avoiding the last part of her question.

"Umm, yeah, you do," she retorted.

"Why you acting like you don't want to see a nigga? That's not what you were saying when you showed up to the hospital," I reminded her.

"My showing up that day was just me being there for a dear friend. You said that you needed me, so I came through. That was it."

"Well, I need you again. Drop by and see about ya dear friend," I replied sarcastically. It pissed me off that she was trying to downplay our involvement, but I didn't want to go off on her and make her hang up on me.

"I can't do that. I'm not going there with you again. You made your choice, and you said you'd let me move on." Her voice was pleading with me to let this thing with us go, but I couldn't do it.

"I changed my mind," I stated real matter-of-factly. I knew it was crazy, but I wanted her to just say okay and give me what the fuck I was asking for. That would be too much like right, but I didn't want to fuss or fight with her anymore.

"What the fuck, Elijah?" She only called me by my name when she was pissed, so I prepared myself for whatever she had to say. "You can't just all of a sudden switch up and expect me to go with the flow. Years! Fucking years I've waited for you to choose me, but you refused. Got me hiding our relationship from your family because you never took me seriously, and I refused to look like a fool by claiming you as my nigga. You treated me like shit, like I meant nothing to you. Now what? Now that you think you're ready to be with me I'm just supposed to be down with that? Fuck no! It ain't even going down like that!" she argued.

"Do you still love me?" I asked, causing her to go silent on the other end for a few seconds.

"I'll always love you. Always. I just—"

"Just come over, man. All I want to do is talk," I pleaded, not letting her finish her sentence. All I needed to hear was that she still loved a nigga. I would fix the rest once she got here. She just needed to show up.

"Your ass never wants to just talk, boy, so cut it out. Please remember who you're talking to with your slick ass," she sassed.

I couldn't wait to fuck that little attitude up out of her. She was wrong this time, though, because I actually wanted to talk about our situation, and after we had that settled, then we could get to all that other shit. At this point I wasn't beyond getting my Keith Sweat on to get what I wanted, so I kept talking. "Look, babe, I'm stressed as fuck right now. Breelyn is dealing with some tough shit, and I'm trying to help her through it. She's beefing with Kota, and on top of all that, her nigga won't even talk to her. I just have a lot going on, and I need someone to talk to," I said, laying it on thick as hell, hoping to garner some sympathy from her. It was extra as fuck, but I was going to do or say whatever I had to to get her through my front door.

"Why are you doing this to me?" she whined into the receiver. I knew I had her just by the tone of her voice. Anytime her ass started talking like that, it meant she was close to giving in to me. There was a long pause before she spoke again. "I'm on my way," she said lowly before ending the call without waiting for my reply.

I could do nothing but shake my head. We'd been going back and forth for so long that I knew her well. She knew me too, but tonight I was going to surprise her ass by giving her what she'd been asking for for the longest. I was hoping it wasn't too late for us and she would forgive me for not making her my woman before now.

About twenty minutes later I heard that soft knock on the door. I couldn't believe that I was actually nervous right now. My heart was beating triple time and everything. It was crazy to me that once I admitted that I was in love with this girl, I was doing and saying shit that I never thought I would. Begging instead of demanding that she come see me. Sweet-talking her and shit. I swore that wasn't even my style and over time she'd become used to my brash ways. The switch up was quite humbling, but there was no doubt in my mind that she was the only one I would do any of this shit for. Settling down, apologizing for my actions over the years, or all the other gay shit I was willing to do to win her over. On my mama, there wasn't another chick alive who could make me do this shit.

"I'm here so talk," she said with an eye roll once I opened the door to let her in.

She was posted in the foyer like she had no plans to come all the way inside. Her arms were folded across her chest like there were a million and one places she would rather be than here with me right now. The rest of the body language though? It told an entirely different story, and trust me, I knew that body well. She was reacting to me even though she more than likely didn't want to be. Even her breathing pattern had changed and become more rapid. Yeah, she could pretend that with me wasn't where she wanted to be, but I wasn't buying it.

I purposely hadn't worn a shirt, and I stood there stone-faced as her eyes traveled over my chest and arms. I was giving her the once-over just like she was doing to me. Just the sight of her leaning against the wall, wearing those tight-ass jeans that looked painted on with a form fitting V-neck white tee had me bricking up in my baller shorts. It had been a minute since we'd been around each other, so we were both kind of stuck in a trance.

My eyes zeroed in on her breasts, and I watched her nipples sprout forward as soon as her gaze landed on my print. On her face, she'd just applied lip gloss, and I was loving the natural glow that her skin held. On her feet were some black Fenty Puma slides, and those pretty toes of hers were painted in her favorite snow-white color. Her curves were ridiculous, and I couldn't wait to get a sample of that treasure. The thought alone was driving me crazy. I normally didn't mind telling her the things I wanted to do to her body. Trust me, there was so much freak shit on the tip of my tongue waiting to come out, but I kept quiet. Because I didn't want to piss her off or make her leave before I said what needed to be said, I kept my nasty comments to myself.

"Come here," I requested.

"Don't do that, Rah. You promised that you just wanted to talk."

"And I do. I want a hug, too, though." I bit my bottom lip as I looked at her intensely. "Quit acting like I'm some regular nigga off the street. Fronting like yo' fat-booty ass don't love me," I teased. She was claiming that she knew me but was standing there acting brand new. She knew damn well I wanted to do more than talk before she drove her fine ass over to my spot.

"You get on my nerves, man. You do this to me every time," she fussed with a small smile before finally stepping into my embrace. This woman felt so fucking right in my arms, and we both breathed a sigh of relief when our bodies finally came into contact. I hated that it took me so long to give in to this thing we shared. Breelyn almost dying made me realize that life is too short not to spend it with the person you love the most. I'd taken her through so much shit and taken her for granted for far too long. Now it was time for me to step up and treat her the way she needed to be treated, and it was going to start with us coming out to my family as a couple. My sister and cousin were probably going to have something to say, but that was their problem, not mine.

"I'm ready, baby. Please tell me I'm not too late," I said after holding her for a long-ass time.

There was a long pause before she drew back and looked up at me. She didn't think I was being sincere, and I could tell by the way she searched my face. If she only knew how serious I was right now. I was finally ready, and I hoped with everything in me that she didn't reject me. If she did, I would be fucked up, and I felt sorry for any other female I came into contact after this. This was the one and only time I planned to put myself out there like this. If my efforts didn't pay off, I guessed I'd be dogging it out until death like Kenneth. I just hoped it didn't come to that. I'd done a lot to her and probably didn't deserve her, but I wanted what I wanted. I just needed her to come through for me and trust me this one last time.

"Please don't play games with me, Rah. What exactly do you mean when you say you're ready?" she finally asked.

Before I gave her an answer to her question, I kissed away the lone tear that fell from her eye. "I mean that I'm ready for us. You and me."

"Like us being together, together?" she asked in disbelief.

I felt like shit because from day one I told her that this was something that would never happen. I told her that my fuck buddy was all she would ever be. I meant that shit when I said it, but we'd grown close over time, and her ass grew on me. When I realized that she was trying to move on and didn't want to fuck with me anymore, I started admitting to myself what I'd always felt for her but was too hard or jaded on love to act on. It was way past time for me to quit playing games with her heart.

"Yes, us together. I don't wanna be without you. Just tell me what I gotta do. Tell me that I'm not too late," I begged, pulling her farther into me.

"I don't think . . . mmm," she moaned, unable to complete that statement.

I caught her off guard by covering her lips with mine. I wasn't prepared to hear her say anything opposite of what I wanted her to say, so I silenced her with a kiss. I figured she might have been about to tell me she no longer wanted me, so I planned to make love to her at least one more time before we parted ways.

Before she knew what was happening, I had that ass spread out over the back of the couch, tonging her ass down with her bottoms and panties on the ankle of only one of her legs. I was moving so fast I was shocking my damn self. I didn't want to give her time to back out or turn me down. I had to hit this shit right just one last time.

"Damn, Rah . . . shit . . . wait," she moaned and begged when I went low and propped one of her legs up on my shoulder and went to work feasting on that pussy.

"Nah, bae, I can't do that," I said before flicking my tongue repeatedly against her clit then sucking it into my mouth. I didn't know who was enjoying it more, her or me. Her ass was moaning loudly, and shit, so was I.

She'd always had this unique sweet-ass taste to her that I couldn't get enough of, so I was in heaven right now. I loved eating pussy, but I didn't get to indulge often because she wasn't fucking with me and there was no way I was putting my mouth on anyone but her. It took me only a few minutes to make her quiver and release her love.

I had to grip her leg and ass tightly to keep her from falling over headfirst into the couch cushions after cumming so hard. Just for kicks, I went back in to see how quickly I could make her cum a second time. I knew her body inside out, so it wasn't shit for me to have her shaking and swearing again in under five minutes.

By this time she wasn't able to move, so I picked her up and took her to my bedroom. We kissed passionately as we tore at each other's clothing. Everything about this episode seemed final, and it was fucking me up mentally but also drove me to give her my all. If this was going to be the end, I wanted to make sure that she never forgot Elijah Raheem Waiters. Any nigga who came after me would have to damn near perform magic tricks to even come close to doing to her body what I planned to do tonight.

"We don't work, Elijah," was all she said while staring up at me with lust-filled eyes.

When those same eyes glossed over with emotion, I bent down to kiss her hungrily. Every time she came at me with that shit, I was gon' shut her ass up. We worked just fine when I wasn't trying to convince her that she meant nothing to me. We kissed hungrily as I slid inside of her wet place raw, and the feeling caused me to bite down on her cheek harder than I meant to. The sexy-ass moan that she let slip out made my dick even stiffer. I'd been fucking for a long damn time, and she was the only chick I'd ever run up in without protection. I was like fuck it at this point. A nigga was determined to go out with a gotdamn bang and knock her ass up so she'd have no choice but to be with me. Fuck it, I'd be a trap king in more ways than one.

"Ughhh," she whimpered sexily.

"Gotdamn, girl," I called out, hitting her deep. I was trying to touch her fucking heart with the tip of my dick. Shit, anything to make her stay and not give up on me. Five strokes later, she was already squirting that good creamy shit on me. The feel of her pussy gripping my pole was better than having all the money in the world. I used to legit hate her when I found out she let another nigga sample what I thought to be mine. Now my goal was to reclaim it so that I would be the only man to have it for the rest of our lives.

"Daddyyyyy!" she cried just like I liked when another orgasm snuck up on her not long after she came down from the other.

"Daddy got you, baby. I'm right here. Ahh, fuck!" I groaned right as I let off inside of her.

It didn't stop there either. Round after fucking round we went at it while I begged and pleaded for her to consider me just one more time. Continuously, she refused, stating that we just weren't meant to be. I just kept right on fucking her the way I knew she liked to be fucked, hoping she would change her mind.

"You was for real when you said we don't work? You don't want to be with me, Judy?" I panted. Spent with our breathing well beyond normal limits, we lay in a position that didn't even have a name with my semi-hard dick still inside of her.

"What the hell I tell you about calling me that?" she muttered, swatting me with one of the throw pillows from my comforter set.

"You know you always gon' be Big Booty Judy to me," I laughed while dodging her punches.

Playful licks were passed back and forth, which quickly led to us feeling on and caressing one another. Leave it to us to be in bed naked and play fighting. We'd been doing it for the longest, and it would never get old. It made me think of the many times this exact scene would lead to stupid wild sex sessions in this very bed. As hard as my mans was getting and as bad as I wanted to drop this dick back off in her, I wanted to see where her head was at first. Was she rolling with me, or did she plan to keep it pushing? I was straight up grasping at straws at this point, trying to tap into something deep down inside of her. Anything to make her see that with me was where she belonged.

"Answer the question though. You gon' fuck with a nigga or nah?"

"Elijah, you know I want to be with you," she said, smiling the first genuine smile I'd seen on her face in a long ass time. "Can I trust that you won't play me this time? If shit goes left, I'm out for real. I can no longer do the back-and-forth with you. Either we doing this for real or we're not doing it at all," she stated firmly.

"Understood. With that being said, you know that boyfriend of yours gots to go. Whatever the fuck you and that square got going is over and done with now that you're my lady," I added for clarification. Leave it to me to waste no time claiming what was mine.

"I shared you for years with plenty of females, so I'm sure me having this one side nigga won't be a problem," she stated with a straight face. Her ass had to be shitting me. She knew damn well I wasn't going for no shit like that.

"If I just g'on and kill the nigga like I really want to, there won't be shit on the side for you to have. Now act like you ain't catch that," I warned.

"I love your violent ass." She fell over laughing. "Always threatening to shoot or kill someone."

I didn't see a muthafuckin' thing funny about what I'd said. I was serious as hell.

"Chill, man. There's no need to kill him. I broke things off with him nearly a month ago," she informed me before popping a quick kiss to my upturned lips. Her mouth on mine removed the frown from my face. Her black ass was always saying shit to get a rise out of me, and it worked every time. I was actually thinking in my head how I could sneak out tonight, off that nigga, and make it back before she woke up.

"Why did you keep saying you didn't want me when I was making love to you?" I asked out of the blue. She had a nigga thinking he didn't stand a chance.

"I was only saying no so that you would fuck me harder. You was doing the damn thing, bae," she laughed, making me rise up on my elbows to glare at her.

"Yo', you ain't shit! Stay playing with my emotions," I chuckled. I legit thought this was the end of us when she kept refusing me while I stroked her insides.

"But seriously though, are we really doing this?" she questioned as she mounted me, coming to rest that pussy on my lower abdomen. I wanted her to go lower and sit on my dick, but I could tell she wanted to talk.

"Hell yeah, we are," I said, palming her chocolate breasts. "And to prove to you how real it is on my end, I want you to come with me to my aunt and uncle's anniversary party in a few weeks. We gon' show up together and let mu'fuckas know what it is with us." I fondled her juicy titties the entire time I talked while she stared into my eyes. She bit her lip and scooted down a little when I began rolling her nipples with my thumbs and index fingers.

"What about your cousin and sister? They're going to fucking kill me," she said, suddenly stopping her grinding to place her hands over her face.

"Chill out and leave the worrying up to me. I got you, baby girl," I promised her.

"I don't know how all this is going to play out, but I trust you. One thing I can honestly say about you is that you've never given me your word on something and not come through. With that in mind, I'm leaving it in your hands. I'm just showing up, and hopefully everyone accepts and understands what we mean to each other."

It meant a lot to me to have her trust, and I meant what I said when I told her that I had her. No one would come for her in my presence. I loved Greedy and Kota B, but big bro had to have a life too. And she was it. It took me a minute to accept and realize it, but hey, better late than never.

"Damn, I almost forgot that there was something else I needed to tell you." I sat up with my back against the headboard and pulled her up with me to where she was still straddling me.

"What is it?"

"So, you remember that li'l situation we talked about when you came through after we saw each other at Good Life that night?"

"Yes, I remember," she answered but looked sad all of a sudden. When she went to drop her head, I quickly caught her chin and lifted that shit right back up.

"Come on, ma, don't do that. This shit was way before you, and you know that. If I would've known before now, you know I would have already told you."

"You're right, and I'm sorry. So tell me what happened. Y'all finally did the test?"

"We did." I nodded.

"And?" By the look on her face, she already knew the answer to her question. To hide her tears from me, she laid her head on my chest, while I gently stroked her back and broke things down for her.

Chapter 15

Put My Heart on the Line

Serenity

The day I'd been praying for had finally come, and I couldn't contain my excitement. I knew that sooner or later he would come around, even though he had me worried for a minute there. Despite his warning the night I popped up on him and his little girlfriend, I continued to call, trying to get him to meet up with me to talk. I had to call his businesses because I didn't have his personal number, and when I contacted his mother, she flat-out refused to give it to me. I didn't like her old white ass but was thankful that she'd at least passed the message on that I'd called.

Two days ago, he hit me up to arrange a meeting. I just knew that once I got him alone, I'd be able to convince him that with me was where he needed to be. He was acting like he didn't know me in front of his baby-face-ass bae, but I understood his position. I was sure he didn't want to hurt her feelings, so I decided to give him a pass for treating me the way he did that night.

"Damn, I wish his ass would stop calling me," I mumbled when I saw Tyson ringing my line for the fifth time today. I knew we had business to discuss, but ever since Giannis called to say he wanted to see me, he was all I could focus on. Tyson and I made good money together and even had exceptional sex from time to time, but that was all it was on my end. Good money and good sex. Besides, I could never get serious with a man who would sleep with an ex-girlfriend of one of his closest friends. I was out of line as well for fooling around with him, but I used sex with Tyson to get him to do certain things that I couldn't on my own, and I knew he wasn't dumb enough to ever tell Giannis about us.

Plus, I needed a fucking boss in my life, and he definitely wasn't one. His ass worked for the boss, and that's who I had my sights set on. The one I could build an empire with. Giannis tried locking me down some years back, but at the time I wasn't trying to hear it. I was too deep in the family business and focused on stacking my paper to be tied down back then.

Because I was always on the go, I'd convinced Giannis that I was a traveling nurse, but that was far from the truth. Now that I'd moved up in rank after the disappearance of my older brother, Chino, I didn't need to get my hands as dirty or spend so much time on the road. I no longer had to travel state to state recruiting girls or transporting them to our overseas contacts. I had pussy-whipped men like Tyson on payroll to do that shit for me. As a female, you'd think, I'd be against the trafficking of women and children, but it was all I'd ever known, so it just wasn't in me to feel bad about it. To me the shit was normal. Giannis was a good person at heart and would never agree with what I did for a living, so I planned to keep that part of my life separate from the one I planned to have with him.

"Tyson, why the fuck are you blowing my phone up like this? Obviously I'm busy if I'm not fucking picking up!" I snapped in irritation. I figured that if I went ahead and answered, he could say whatever the hell he needed to say quickly so that I could continue getting ready for my date with Giannis.

"If I'm calling you back-to-back like this, it should be obvious that what I need to talk to you about is important, Serenity! Fuck you got going on that you couldn't answer at least one of my calls!" he barked into the phone.

Damn, he was angry with me for real. I almost laughed but decided to try a softer approach. "Look, Ty, I think we should go back to things being strictly business between us. You can't be calling me and tripping on me when I don't answer a call or text. I'm a busy person, and I can't be at your beck and call like that. Besides, we're just fucking around anyway. It's not even that deep."

"But, ba—"

"No buts, Tyson. Let's just focus on getting this money and do away with the extra shit. Your feelings are clearly involved, but I'm just not feeling the same way you are," I interjected.

"Like that, Ren?" he said sadly.

"Yeah, straight like that." This man swore I was his woman and stayed trying to check me. It was past time that I burst his little bubble though.

"Don't do this right now, Ren. We got big problems. This nigga—"

"Tyson, don't make this harder than it has to be," I cut him off. "I'm not your chick, and you're not my man. I've been seeing other dudes the entire time, and I just assumed you entertained other females when we're not together," I told him.

"Nah, actually, I haven't been, but it's cool. Thanks for keeping it real with me though. My bad for tripping on you. Strictly business from now on, ma," he switched up quickly.

"Thanks for being so cool about this. How about we meet up for brunch to discuss the girls at Sensations this coming Sunday? I have some new things planned for them, which means more money for us, okay?" I attempted to butter him up.

"Yeah, just let me know when and where. Good luck with everything," he added before hanging up. That last part was weird to me, but I didn't have time to dwell on it because I had only twenty minutes to make it to Giannis's place.

Slicking down my pixie haircut in the back, I checked my face to make sure my beat was still on point before I exited my Beemer in front of Giannis's condo. He always loved my short hairdo, so I'd had it freshly done this morning. I also made sure to wear his favorite color, which was red. The skintight dress I wore left little to the imagination, and that was the exact look I was going for. Tonight I was getting my man back.

I made a mistake when I ended things with G years before, but I hoped that by the end of the night none of that would matter. After ringing the doorbell, I shifted my weight from side to side, trying to put on my sexiest face and pose for when he opened the door. I knew I was being extra as hell right now, but from the moment he first saw me up until when we were making love at the break of dawn, I wanted our encounter to be perfect. I wanted him to see the woman he was in love with before, not the one who walked away from him a few years before.

"Hey, baby." I smiled seductively once he opened up for me.

"Come on in." He kept it short as he stepped to the side so that I could pass him. His reaction to seeing me looking like I was looking wasn't exactly what I was hoping for, but I wasn't giving up. My baby was going to make me work for his forgiveness, and I didn't mind because I was the one who had messed up.

Walking in front of him, I put that extra sway in my hips just in case he was checking me out, which I knew nine times out of ten he was. Giannis had always been an ass man, and I had plenty for him to admire. "I thought you were cooking. I don't smell anything," I giggled but continued to move toward the back where I remembered the kitchen was located. Knowing Giannis, he had probably ordered out for us. I would have liked to have had a home-cooked meal, but I'd take what I could at this point. I was just happy to be in his presence again.

When I reached the kitchen to see that the counters were bare, I was confused. When I turned to question him about what was going on, I was met with an expression that put me on pause and halted anything I was planning to say. The way he looked at me said that he held absolutely no affection for me whatsoever. Not a single drop. I wanted to say there was even some hatred in his gaze, but I was hoping that I was mistaken. On the phone things were different, and he made it seem like he couldn't wait to see me. Right now? At this very moment? Not so much.

The clearing of someone's throat caught my attention, and like a dummy I made my way toward the sound. When I rounded the corner and entered the dining area, I was met with the scowling faces of his girlfriend and a gentleman I'd never seen before. Something about the look in the man's eyes scared the shit out of me. Shit was hella spooky.

"Baby, what's going on?" I looked to Giannis, who was now leaning against the doorjamb with his arms folded across his chest as he mean mugged the shit out of me. I had no idea where all of his hostility was coming from.

"Bitch, I know you better chill with that 'baby' shit. Giannis Williams ain't no baby of yours and never will be, trust that," Dallas, or whatever her name was, addressed me.

"Relax, love," Giannis spoke to her in a softened tone, causing her to fold her arms across her chest with a pout. I couldn't help but roll my eyes. "Serenity, I guess I didn't make myself clear when I told you to never contact me again, because you're still on that bullshit. I was at the point where I was just going to send some of my girl's family members over to beat that ass, but when I came across some information on what you been up to, I felt that more should be done," he said, confusing the hell out of me.

"Really, Giannis? You'd have someone put hands on me over something like this? Just for trying to talk to you and get you to realize that I'm the one for you? That's all I wanted, to get back what we had. You can't tell me that you no longer feel anything for me. You asked me to marry you, for goodness' sake." My voice cracked. I knew it was a big mistake coming here to put my heart on the line when everyone in the room fell out laughing except for me. The fact that Giannis was laughing harder than everyone else showed just how much he didn't care about me.

"Ho, you sound dumb as hell." Ol' girl continued chuckling it up at my expense. "Whatever hopes and dreams you had of having my nigga in your life will never come to fruition," she said with confidence before addressing Giannis. "Honey, I'm tired, so I'm going upstairs to lie down for a minute. Come get me when you're done here so that we can go home." She was trying her best not to continue laughing at me.

I had never been so embarrassed in my life. When Giannis saw that she was about to stand, he rushed over to help her up. Acting as if I weren't even in the room, he kissed her passionately while he caressed her stomach. I couldn't see a baby bump, but from the way he was acting, I assumed she was pregnant. My heart broke right then and there.

"Really, Giannis?" I asked on the verge of tears.

"Yeah, really! The fuck you thought? I wasn't supposed to move on with my life or som'n?" He looked at me like I was stupid while confirming my suspicions. "Come on, babe. Let me help get you settled," he told her in the most affectionate voice I'd ever heard him speak in.

That was supposed to be me he was catering to. Giannis was supposed to wait on me! As crazy as that sounded, I honestly believed that the love he had for me would over-shadow and outshine any female who thought she had a chance with him. I was wrong, and it seemed I'd come back too late. Now this bitch was living my life, and I wanted nothing more than to rid the world of her and that fucking baby she carried. I was already planning and plotting in my head ways to have her dealt with. She was pretty as hell, so she was someone Saldana's son Marc would be interested in for sure. He'd taken over for his father after he was killed, and I'd be contacting him as soon as I left here. Giannis would be singing a different tune about us being together if she weren't around, and that much I was sure of.

Before I could react or say anything further, the other man in the room finally spoke up. "Have a seat," he ordered as I watched the love of my life walk out of the room.

"No, I'd rather not," I said before turning to make my way back to the front, running smack dab into a hard chest. When I looked up, I met the eyes of a man I hadn't seen in a very long time.

"What up, Ren? How you?" he asked with a devious grin that sent chills throughout my entire body. I never did like his ass, and he never cared for me or my relationship with Giannis. I couldn't deny that the nigga was still fine as ever though.

"I'm just fine, Rah. Excuse me." I acknowledged his presence while trying to move past him, but he wasn't budging.

"Not so fast, pretty lady." He motioned with his head back toward the table, instructing me to sit down, but there was no way I was doing that.

I waltzed my ass in here thinking I would walk out with my relationship with Giannis back intact, but I had this sinking feeling that I wouldn't be leaving here at all. At least not alive. There was just something about the way they were glaring at me that told me so. Then something Tyson said on the phone stuck out to me all of a sudden, and the fact that he'd been blowing me up for days stood out in my mind, only adding to my suspicions. He was trying to tell me about some problem we had, but I wasn't trying to hear it. Giannis was the only thing on my mind at the time. Now I was in here, unprotected because I'd left my gun in the console of my ride. I didn't want any interruptions, so my phone was there, too. I couldn't even call for help, so I had no choice but to comply with Rah's request.

Setting my purse on the counter, I joined the quiet man at the table with G's right-hand man coming to stand directly behind my seat. I was trying not to show how scared I was, but it was hard. I was literally shaking in five-inch heels.

"Thank you, Ms. Clark," dude said, surprising the hell out of me. He knew my name but I had no clue who the hell he was.

"How do you know my name?" I stuttered.

"I'm familiar with your brother Pacino. Or let's say I was familiar with him when he was alive," he answered right as Giannis rejoined us.

"Wait, what? Did you just say, 'was,' as in past tense? You had something to do with his disappearance?" I asked in a shaky voice. I missed the hell out of my brother. My family had already come to the conclusion that he'd been killed, but I chose to believe he was out there somewhere and would come home to us one day soon. From what this man was saying, I was wrong.

"I did. I had everything to do with it, and I'm going to have everything to do with what happens to you as well," he answered like it wasn't shit.

"But why? You don't even know me," I asked after swallowing the big-ass lump in my throat.

"I know what you and your family do to make your money, and that's reason enough for me to do what I have to do."

"Bitch told me she was an only child and was brought up in a foster home. Can y'all believe that shit? Fraud ass really had me going," Giannis joked as the others laughed along.

Although Giannis laughed it off, I could see in his eyes that my lies had hurt him because I wasn't who he thought me to be. I also knew that if he knew about the family business, then it was more than likely that he was aware of the shit I had going on in his club. Come to think of it, my cousin Kiara had been blowing me up before she went missing a week ago, and like a fool I'd blown her off as well. My family and I assumed she'd run off with some dude like she had many times in the past, but now I wasn't so sure about that. Now I wished that I would have taken a few moments to hear her and Ty out when they called. It was clear that my team was trying to warn me about Giannis discovering the shit we had going on right under his nose.

"Told you a long time ago that her fake fancy ass wasn't about shit," Rah threw in his two cents. "Pussy whipped ass ain't wanna listen to ya boy though."

"Chill, nigga. Yo' cousin the only chick ever had me pussy whipped," he teased, prompting Rah to toss one of the place mats from the table at him. They continued cracking on each other like I wasn't even in the room. With nothing but pure fear in my heart, my eyes darted back and forth between them as they spoke. I didn't know what the quiet one meant when he said he knew enough about me to do what he had to do, so I interrupted their bickering to ask.

"What's going to happen to me? You're going to turn me in to the police? You do know that we have enough of them on payroll to make all this go away, right?" I smirked, gaining some confidence all of a sudden. I remembered that Giannis was in the room with me, and I knew there was no way that he would let them hurt me, so my heart rate decreased tremendously. There was also no need for me to be concerned about the law. We'd been in business for a long-ass time, and it was because of them turning a blind eye to our dealings that we'd made as much money as we had over the years.

"Nah, ma. I don't deal with the law. I take care of shit on my own and in my own way." He nodded, his voice cold and serious. That statement alone shut me the fuck up. "At first I wasn't sure what to do with you. Kill you? Maybe inflict some slow torture on you? That shit is kinda my specialty." He smiled like what he was saying was normal. "Thought about selling you into the same life of sex and violence that you promote on a daily basis, but after much thought I figured we'd go with two out of the three. I have a soft spot for women and children, so selling you into the life would make me no better than you, so we'll forgo that option. Just like the torture and agony the people you exploit to make money endure, I'm going to torture you, then I'm going to kill yo' ass," he informed me as tears fell from my eyes.

I wanted to respond, but all the shit I planned to talk just moments before became lodged in my throat. My sins and the sins of my family had caught up with me, and just like my brother, I was about to die for it.

"Giannis, please don't let him do this! Please!" I begged my former lover, finally finding my voice.

Ignoring me, he picked up his phone and dialed a number. "Yeah, we have her. Take him to the new spot and wait for us," he ordered before hanging up. "Looks like you and your li'l boy toy will be reunited soon." He smirked.

I assumed he was referring to Ty, and I almost felt bad for getting him mixed up in this. I couldn't believe I was going out like this, but what hurt more was that the man I loved didn't even give a damn. In response to my pleas, Giannis shot me the middle finger with both hands before giving Rah the go-ahead with a quick nod. The next thing I knew I was being placed in a tight sleeper hold as I clawed away at the beefy forearm around my neck. I didn't even get a chance to scream before I blacked out.

Chapter 16

Closure

Dakota

"Come on, Kota, smile for ya man. You're supposed to be happy right now, baby," Giannis groaned.

"I am happy, honey," I replied with the most sincere smile I could manage. I was sure he knew that shit was fake though. He had to be tired of me and my pouting but I couldn't seem to shake this funk I'd been in. Breelyn and I had never had a disagreement like this and it was eating me up. Her being angry at me and ignoring me for days at a time? We just didn't do that shit. Back in the day we'd fuss and fight over who stole whose clothes, or her borrowing makeup or other things of mine and never bothering to return them. Typical teenage bickering was as far as it went, but this shit was much more extreme. She was basically mad at me because she lost her child and I hadn't. Her ass had me thinking she wished I had been the one in the car instead of her, and that was fucked up because I could never think that way. Since she'd been hurt, and before I found out I was even pregnant, all I kept saying was that I would take her place in a heartbeat. Did she really mean that, or were my emotions getting the best of me again?

"I'm sure she wants to apologize. If your stubborn ass would answer the phone when she calls, you would know that. Don't shut her out when she's going through it," Giannis reasoned, making perfect sense.

I knew he was right, but I was still upset with Breelyn. I'd been in a pissy mood ever since she went in on me at her spot. I really wanted to clap back at her bipolar ass, but I understood she wasn't exactly in her right mind. I never knew about her losing her baby because she didn't tell me, and she normally told me everything.

I thought that was part of the reason I was so hurt. I guessed it just made me feel a way for her to be going through something and not trust me enough to be there for her. It was like she didn't have plans to tell me what happened to her at all, and that just wasn't the way we got down. Thinking about it now though, I was sure that losing a baby was a hard thing to go through and probably something she wanted to keep to herself for a while. Even so, it hurt. She was the first person I planned to tell about my pregnancy before Giannis blew up my spot at her welcome home dinner. If I could have had things my way, I would have had Breelyn right there along with Giannis for my first appointment. I wanted her to share in this time of my life with me just like we'd shared in every other big moment we'd experienced throughout the years. Now I felt that asking her to tag along or talking to her about the baby was like pouring salt into her wounds or bragging about my happiness while she silently suffered.

"I'm going to call her as soon as we're done here," I told Giannis as we pulled up to the doctor's office. My hurt feelings didn't mean as much to me when I really sat back and thought about everything she'd been through.

"Good, babe. I'm proud of you for being the bigger person. Know yo' ass like to stay mad at folk for a long-ass time," he pointed out.

"Quit bringing up old shit, Giannis," I snickered.

"Old shit my ass, ma," he muttered, making me laugh even harder as we entered the office.

Last week I didn't talk to his ass for two whole days when I went to the freezer to grab my rainbow sherbet only to discover that his ass had eaten it already. Him going to the store to buy me five new containers didn't move me or make me talk to him. I sat my ass there tearing that sherbet up while mean mugging him as he apologized over and over. It wasn't until I was awakened with a bad case of heartburn and morning sickness the following day and needed to be comforted and cared for that I finally talked to him. He took excellent care of me, so I had no choice but to forgive him. I knew he had better not fuck with my ice cream again though. Next time I would go a whole week. I needed that sherbet in my life on a daily basis. Baby girl or baby boy Williams absolutely loved it.

"We have an eleven thirty appointment. Last name is Bibbs," Giannis said to the receptionist as he checked us in at the front desk.

"Here you go, sir. If you'd fill out this new patient paperwork, we'll get you and Mom checked in. We'll also need her ID and insurance card so that we can make a copy."

"Here, baby mama. I refuse to fill out this damn booklet. I'ma leave that shit to you," Giannis said, handing the paperwork over to me.

Seated in the back, filling out the papers, I couldn't help but notice that Giannis couldn't sit still or stop smiling. He went from picking up magazines and placing them back down after flipping a few pages to staring a hole in the side of my face, wearing that big, stupid-ass grin. Although I was down about the fallout with my cousin, I couldn't help but be excited knowing that he was this happy about the baby. He was sitting here looking like a big ol' hyperactive-ass child, and it was funny to me.

When I was done, he insisted on taking the forms back up even though I was more than capable. That was another thing that I found super cute about him. He waited on me hand and foot, not letting me lift a finger to do anything. I had to cuss his ass out the other day for following me to the restroom. I had no clue what he thought could possibly happen if I went in alone, but it was a trip to see him that way. I mean, did I actually think he could piss for me or something? I didn't understand his thought process, but it was sweet nonetheless. I was so into my thoughts of him that I hadn't realized that he hadn't returned to his seat beside me.

When I looked up, I saw that he was still talking to the cute little receptionist, and whatever he was saying had her smiling from ear to ear. That was one thing about having an attractive man, especially one like Giannis. He possessed that natural charm that drew women in, and they would become caught up just having a regular conversation with him. He could be talking about the weather and they'd sit starstruck and hanging on to his every word. I'd seen it happen many times since we'd been together, and at this point I was used to it.

Only time it pissed me off was when women openly flirted with my man right in my face. My honey was respectful of my feelings and never hesitated to put a bold female in her place. For disrespecting me, baby would disrespect the fuck out of you. I never had to say anything unless they couldn't take the hint, and y'all already know I was definitely the one to get a bitch told. If this heffa at the desk didn't stop with the touching on his arm as she laughed, she was about two seconds away from getting some of that action.

Giannis turned to look at me and could only shake his head at the obvious scowl I wore. He said a few more words to the chick then made his way back over to me. "Why you sitting here mugging and shit with your mean ass?" he laughed while lightly popping my exposed thigh.

"Because that bitch was a little too touchy-feely for my liking, and she was kee-keeing with you a li'l too hard. And I'm not mean, Giannis. I'm just territorial," I clarified.

"Nah, you mean as shit, but I love yo' ornery ass anyway. Sitting here looking like you was about to drag ol' girl."

"I wish I would swing on her ass while I'm pregnant. I got Chubb on speed dial though. She handling all my light work while I'm out on injured reserve," I said, causing him to fall out laughing.

"It wasn't even like that, so please don't sic Chubb's heavy-handed ass on her. I still got that fucking bruise on my arm from where she punched me last week. All behind that li'l-ass piece of chicken I took off her plate. Remind me not to ever fuck with her food again," Giannis said while rolling his shoulder as if he were really hurt.

My cousin Chase, better known as Chubb, was a fool with her hands. We'd paid her tons of money over the years to kick ass when we couldn't. Giannis had planned to have her get at that ho Serenity until he found out she was involved with strong-arming his dancers into selling their bodies. Then after finding out the shit her family had going on, the guys felt that more drastic measures were required. Anyway, I didn't know what it was about Chubb, but her tomboy ass lived for shit like that. As I laughed, all I could envision were images of Chubb chasing my honey around my parents' dining room table after she discovered that he'd taken her food. Shit was hella funny.

"Long as her smiling ass keeps her hands to herself, she'll be just fine," I told Giannis before kissing his cheek. I went to turn my head to look down at my phone, but he grabbed my face with both hands and pressed his lips to mine once more. I wanted to stop him, but his kisses felt so good that I became lost in them. We were putting on a show in front of the other expectant moms and dads, but of course we didn't give a damn.

"Bibbs," the nurse called, grabbing our attention.

His nasty butt sucked my bottom lip and pecked me at least six more times before releasing me. I swayed slightly when I finally stood, and he quickly placed his hand at the small of my back to steady me.

Leaning down, he spoke lowly into my ear. "Them kisses be having yo' ass dizzy, huh?"

"Shut the hell up, Giannis. Cocky ass," I mumbled as we moved toward the nurse. I couldn't deny that his words were true. His kisses had me dizzy, dumb, and discombobulated. All that good shit. I couldn't wait to get home and lie up with him for the remainder of the day.

Our first stop was for a urine sample in the restroom, where Giannis insisted on coming in with me. I didn't know how the hell I was supposed to put up with this type of shit for the duration of my pregnancy. I thought he was bossy and overprotective before, but it was even worse now. Had we been at home, I probably would have snapped on him, but here I acted like I had some sense. Who was I kidding though? I loved that his obsessed ass loved me so much.

When I was done in the restroom, Giannis led me to a room in the back. I found it weird that he knew where to go, but whatever. Knowing him, he'd probably toured the facility beforehand to make sure it was up to par. His ass stayed trying to run some shit. We'd argued at length on choosing a physician, but when he saw I wasn't budging, he gave in. I followed his lead in every other aspect of our relationship, so he didn't mind giving in to me this one time.

Upon entering the room, I stopped short when I spotted Breelyn sitting in one of the chairs. She looked so pretty today, and I could tell she'd put on a little makeup. Her scars were barely visible, and she was looking a lot more like the old Breelyn. I was just hoping she was feeling more like herself as well. Her countenance and the way she was fidgeting displayed the apprehension she felt as she reluctantly stood up. I tried not to, but of course my hormones got the best of me, and tears fell from my eyes when she reached out for a hug. We'd never gone so long without talking, so seeing her right now meant everything to me.

"I'm so sorry, Kota. Please forgive me. I can't take you being angry with me," she pouted with a few tears of her own.

"Shh, I'm just glad you're here. We'll talk about everything else later," I assured her. Offering no verbal response, she only nodded and hugged me tighter.

I looked back to find my man and the chick from the front desk smiling in our direction. Now I knew what the hell they'd been talking about that whole time. It was clear that she was in on this little surprise judging by her accomplished facial expression. I'd jumped to conclusions, and the good deed she'd performed on my behalf saved her from an unnecessary beat down.

After thanking her and showing my honey some love for his continuous efforts to keep me happy, he helped me get undressed while Breelyn waited anxiously for my doctor to come in. Just as Giannis helped me up on the table, Dr. Salaam entered the room. Dr. Salaam was a friend of the family and the only person I trusted to look after me and my unborn child.

"Good afternoon, everyone," she greeted us. "Looks like we have a full house for your first exam today. I just can't believe that Ms. Kota B is having a baby. I'm so excited for you, sweetheart." She beamed while hugging me tightly. "And it's nice to see you, young lady. How are you, Breelyn?" she asked, bending down to hug her.

"I'm well, and you?" Breelyn smiled.

"Just fine, sweetie. And you, sir, must be Giannis," she said, shaking her head from side to side.

"I am." He grinned with his hand extended to her.

"I can't express to you how glad I am that this day has finally arrived, because you had one more time to call this office asking a million and one questions. You were driving my staff crazy, and you came very close to forcing me to remove one of my favorite patients from my roster," she teased. Breelyn and I died laughing. Giannis was being his usual extra self, constantly calling after the appointment had already been scheduled, asking questions that he could have waited until today to ask. I understood his excitement and nervousness, so I didn't give him a hard time, but I knew that Dr. Salaam would let him have it once we made it here today.

"My bad, doc. A nigga just excited," he stated like only he could.

"I see. Go ahead and have a seat and we'll get started."

"If it's okay with you, I'd rather stand right here," he replied, coming to my side. I knew then that this was going to be a long-ass appointment.

"Child, what are you going to do with this one?" she laughed.

"Just love him," I answered with a broad smile.

"Gotdamn right you are," Giannis concurred with a kiss to my temple.

"I bet you better quit that cursing in my office, young man," Dr. Salaam chastised my honey.

"Yes, ma'am," Giannis spoke lowly. One thing about my man, he was always respectful to his elders, and I thanked God for that. Had that been Rah, he would have gone off on Dr. Salaam for trying to check him. They stayed into it whenever they were around each other.

Minutes into the exam, Breelyn came to stand on the other side of me. I was so happy to have the support of my best friend and man today. Everything went well, and by the time we heard the heartbeat and saw the baby on ultrasound, all of us, including Dr. Salaam's mean behind, were emotional. She'd delivered me, along with a slew of my cousins and other family members, Breelyn and Elijah Raheem included. She'd definitely earned her a spot in the family for life.

"Breelyn, dear, I would like to speak with you before you go," she said, pulling Breelyn to the side before she could walk out of the room. I told Bree we would wait for her outside.

After making my next appointment, Giannis and I walked outside to find Rah standing in front of his old-school Chevy SS, waiting for us. At the sight of him, my day had officially been made. I wasn't expecting to see him today, but I was glad he was here.

"Where is the final member of Three the Hard Way?" I joked as my cousin looked behind me to Giannis and looked away just as quick.

"Rio flew back to New York for a minute," Giannis answered, wrapping his arms around me from behind.

"Congratulations again, Kota B. Can't believe you let yourself get knocked up by this buster," Rah said, changing the subject. "I'on know what you see in his pretty boy ass, but to each his own." He shrugged.

"Fuck you, bitch. At least I got somebody. Who yo' lonely, irate ass got?" Giannis clapped back.

"Don't worry about who the fuck I got, but trust a nigga like me ain't ever lonely." Rah smirked.

All I could think of was when ol' girl burst into the hospital ER and ran into his arms that day. That was some shit straight up out of a romance novel. Talking about he ain't ever lonely. I bet he wasn't, and I couldn't wait to tell Breelyn about that shit. She was gon' be hot as fish grease when she found out. *What about yo' gotdamn friends?* I'd never made good choices when it came to choosing them, which was why I normally just stuck with Bree. Couldn't go wrong with that one. Despite our little hiccup, I still felt that way about her.

"So, y'all really doing this right now?" Breelyn walked up, interrupting the men who continued hurling insults at each other. "I don't see how you two have been friends for so long, because all y'all do is fuss and score on each other," she pointed out. They both just waved her off.

"What you doing here anyway?" I asked Rah.

"I came to pick G up so that you two could have some time alone," Rah replied, looking between his sister and me.

"Oohh, let's hit Gloria's!" Breelyn and I squealed excitedly at the same time. And just like that, we were back like we never left.

"So, I know we're cool and we called ourselves making up or whatever, but what happened the other day is not something I want us to just sweep under the rug like it never occurred and just move on. The things I said . . . I didn't mean that shit. Wait, let me reword that," Breelyn said, taking a deep breath.

"I'll admit that I have always felt a way about your relationship with your father in comparison to the one I have with mine. Doesn't mean I blame you. Just means it bothered me because it's something I've always wished to have for myself. That exact relationship with Kenneth. Daddy's little girl like you, ya know. Was even jealous of your bond with Auntie Syl if I'm being completely honest. Even though she tried to establish that same connection with me, I acted as if that weren't good enough. Not truly expressing myself to you or anyone else on my true feelings regarding my childhood has led to me holding this stuff in, and the other day it just came out. Came out on you, the last person in the world I'd ever want to hurt. You didn't deserve that. So I want to start off by apologizing to you for my reaction that day and the hateful words I spoke. I was in a very bad space at the time. And since then my nigga walked out on me so it got even worse for a minute. Still haven't talked to him." Her voice trailed off as she wiped a single tear from her cheek.

"What do you mean he walked out?" I asked, placing my hand on top of hers on the table. This was news to me. I couldn't even see Rio doing something like that, plus I'd just seen him when the fellas handled that business with Serenity, Ty, and Kiara. On top of all that, his ass was crazy about my cousin, so something serious must have happened for him to just walk away. Just like Giannis was with me, Rio didn't like being away from her for too long. I should have known some shit was up by the look Rah and Giannis shot one another when I questioned his whereabouts.

"I pushed him away, and he left. I mean, he's sent a few text messages checking on me and told me that he went home to New York to visit for a minute. Said he was coming back, but we haven't actually talked." She shook away the tears, refusing to let another fall.

"See, this was why I was so pissed about us not talking. I'm not even tripping on that shit from the other day. Like you said, my parents have always tried to be there for you, but I've never been in your shoes, so I can't judge you for feeling the way you do. All my life I've had the both of them to lean on. It breaks my heart that you feel you didn't get the same, but feel free to borrow their asses anytime you want," I said, making her laugh a little.

"I just hate that you were going through all of this alone. You didn't reach out to me once, Breelyn. I'm feeling like I'm no longer your go-to person. I realize things have changed with us both getting into relationships or whatever, but I don't want that to affect our bond. We never let it happen before so we're not going to start now. Fuck a cousin. You're my damn sister," I stressed.

"I know and I'm sorry. I'm trying to learn to deal with certain shit on my own for a change. I love that you and Rah are always there for me, I promise I do. You've always gone above and beyond for me, and you're right, we're sisters. Even when my brother and I fell out and weren't speaking, he was still there for me in some form. Even though you never said it, I'm sure he had you keeping tabs and reporting back to him about me. That coupled with him dropping that money into my account faithfully assured me that one day we would work things out, and we did. I feel like I'm too dependent on you two at times. Overly dependent on DeMario too, and that can't possibly be a good thing. Hopefully I'll get him back, but if I don't, it's time I become okay with being on my own. I miss him, but my life still has to go on, you know?"

"Maybe you should go up there to see him. Fuck the maybe. You should. Don't let a love like the one you've found slip away. Just like you're hurting, I'm sure he is too. That man loves you, and it's obvious to anyone who's around y'all. David is dead and gone, and it's time for you to start living again. Go get your man, Greedy," I encouraged her. I loved seeing her be so strong and optimistic, but I hated that she was separated from the man she loved and needed. Rio was my nigga and all, but I planned to kick him in his gotdamn shin for leaving my cousin here, alone, questioning his love for her.

"I thought about flying out to see him, but I just wouldn't be able to take it if he decided that being with me is something he no longer wants. I think I'll just wait to talk to him until he comes home."

"Whatever you want to do I'm with you, but at some point, you have to let him know that you're willing to fight for him. Quit being so stubborn and spoiled, Bree. He can't be the only one always trying to make it work. Show that man that you care as much as he does. What man wants to go through the storm with a female who, in the end, isn't as committed to making it work as he is? If you want Rio, go get him. That or give the next bitch an opportunity to stand in your place," I told her, giving her advice my mother had given me years before.

"Damn, your ass sounds just like Auntie Syl," she said, letting my words soak in her mind.

I didn't know why some women thought men were the only ones who should do the apologizing and fixing in a relationship. Shit, if you fuck up, own up to it and make that shit right, sis. Show your man with actions that although you can live without him, you choose not to. Just some knowledge my mama dropped on me, but it was gospel. Seeing as how she was about to celebrate twenty-nine years of being married, I trusted her advice and applied it to my life.

"So what you gonna do?"

"I'm going to New York to get my man." She smiled brightly. That beautiful smile that she was known for and the same one I'd missed so much.

"That's what the fuck I'm talking about!" I twerked in my seat while she doubled over in laughter. "I would go with you, but you already know my overseer ain't about to let me out of his sight." I was sitting here thinking of ways to convince him to let me fly out with Bree. Giannis could tag along for all I cared. I just wanted a quick change of scenery. We'd been talking about taking a trip for a minute, and before long I'd be big and pregnant and not allowed to travel, so this was the perfect time to dip off for a minute.

For hours Breelyn and I talked and ate like old times. I sat there with her as she booked her flight and helped her come up with a game plan for getting her man back once she made it to New York. Giannis was blowing me up by this time, so after stopping at Target for a few items we needed for the house, I planned to head home before his ass lost what was left of his mind.

"Dakota."

I stopped walking at the sound of my name. I already recognized the voice. It used to make my heart skip a beat when I heard it, but today there was nothing. Didn't move me in the least. I turned to find him standing there hand in hand with baby mama number two along with his children. They were the cutest little family. I offered his woman a genuine smile because I had no beef with her at all, and of course Kota B loved the kids. Erica seemed like a pretty cool chick, and I'd have to give a fuck about this man to have any ill feelings toward the person he was dealing with now that we were no longer an item.

"What's up, Tell. Hey, Erica," I acknowledged as I placed a couple packs of Pampers in my basket. There was no annoyance or attitude present in my tone. My heart no longer held any animosity for him. I had no more energy to give in his direction.

"Hey, umm, I didn't mean to bother you, but there is something I wanted to talk to you about," he said while nervously looking to Erica as if he needed reassurance.

"I'll give you a minute. You know where to find us when you're done. Come on, babies," she told the kids.

"Okay, Mommy," they said in unison and followed along obediently toward the toy section.

"They're getting so big, Montell," I observed with a smile.

"I know, right? They bad tails are a handful, too." He smirked while admiring his family.

"So what did you want to talk to me about?" I asked, getting to the point. In my opinion, there was nothing for us to discuss, but I felt like we could legit be cordial at this point. That was, as long as he kept shit cool and didn't question me about his ho-ass cousin. A while back he'd reached out to me, seeking info on David and questioning if Rah and the fellas had anything to do with his sudden disappearance. I, of course, played crazy, telling him that at this point we were all just trying to move on with our lives and he should focus on doing the same. Like I would really disclose that information to him.

"This is hard for me, Kota, but it's something that needs to be said." He sighed dramatically like what he was preparing to tell me was serious.

"Montell, if this has anything to do with us and our former relationship, let's just move on. We're in a good place. No beef on my end, and there shouldn't be any on yours. I've moved on, and so have you," I offered, looking in Erica's direction as she interacted with the kids. She clearly had no problem with her man standing here talking to his ex, and to me, that meant she trusted him.

"I mean, it does have something to do with us, but probably not what you're thinking. Just something that's been eating at me that I want to get off my chest. If you don't hate me already, this is something that could potentially make you feel that way. Something that's been bothering me for a minute and—"

"Montell, just spit it out. I'm tired, and I need to get home before this crazy man has a heart attack," I said as I felt my phone vibrate for the third time since I'd been standing here talking to him. Giannis was going to be on ten by the time I made it home, and I didn't have time for the extra shit tonight.

"My bad. So umm, you remember when I told you that Jada tried throwing the pussy at me the night we were at Rah's birthday party?"

"Yes, I remember," I answered.

"Yeah, so that wasn't the way it happened exactly," he finally said after taking another deep breath.

"Well what the fuck really happened, Tell?" I snapped, feeling myself getting amped up.

"It was kinda the other way around."

"Kinda? What the hell does that even mean? Quit beating around the bush and say what you have to say!" I was getting irritated because I knew where he was going with this shit, and it pissed me off that he hadn't come clean before now. Fuck that. I was mad that he had even lied about it in the first place.

"I knew Jada was intoxicated. Shit, we both were. I pushed up on her and she took the bait. I'm sorry for not being honest with you about us being intimate with each other. It was just that one time, but I've felt like shit ever since then. As soon as we were done, she felt bad and threatened to tell you what went down, and I couldn't have that. I convinced her that you wouldn't believe I'd come on to her first because of her reputation, but I wasn't one hundred percent sure she'd keep quiet. So that very next morning before she had the chance to get to you, I made up that bullshit story about her trying to fuck with me. It was wrong, and it may not mean much now, but I—"

"How could you do that, Montell? You were my man and that girl was one of my best friends! What type of person does that?" I shouted, looking his way with nothing but pure hatred. It wasn't like I didn't know this shit already, but to have him admit it to my face was crushing. I had no love for him, but it hurt to know that two people I'd at one point held near and dear to my heart would so carelessly hurt me. As much as I'd done for the both of them, I was repaid in the worst way possible. Fuck who made the first move or that it only happened once. Shit was fucked up no matter how you sliced it. I felt dumb as hell for even believing him in the first place.

"A fucked-up person does that, Dakota. I was fucked up inside at the time, and I know that my apology doesn't mean much right now, but I am sorry. I'm very sorry for everything I've done to you. Sorry for abusing your trust and ruining that friendship. I swear I'm a different man now. A better man. That's why it was so important for me to come clean about this. I'm hoping that some way somehow you can forgive me." He looked down at his feet, clearly ashamed of all the fucked-up things he'd done.

"I can't believe this shit." I shook my head, not really able to look him in his eyes. He was sad and remorseful, and I didn't want to see that. I didn't want to feel sorry for him. How could I? Every time I turned around, I was hit with more bull crap, and he tended to be in the mix each and every time. A childhood friendship was ruined because he was a cheating, low-down dog. And Jada's bitch ass wasn't any better.

"Like I said before, it might not mean much, but that's one thing I've always regretted doing. I mean, I regret a lot of shit where you're concerned, but that there used to keep me up at night. I know how close you were with her, and I hate being the reason that you are no longer friends. You were right when you said that I wasn't the man for you. I tried like hell to convince you otherwise, but you were right. If I truly loved you the way I should have, I would never have done half the things I did to you. Not to take anything from you, because you were the best woman a man could ever ask for. I just think our paths crossed at the wrong damn time. In hindsight, it was kind of the right time. We went through our shit, it ended, then that led us to the people we are truly meant to be with. I'm glad that you're happy, and for the first time in a long-ass time, so am I," he said, glancing down the aisle at his girlfriend who was shopping away, still not paying us any mind.

"Oh, so I didn't make you happy, Tell?" I nodded my head, slightly offended. The way he looked at her, he'd never looked at me that way before. I didn't know why that shit stung. I didn't have any feelings toward him whatsoever, but to hear him say that he was just as unhappy with me as I was with him hurt my feelings a little. I guessed that went back to the selfish person I used to be in relationships. I was always concerned with the wrong that was being done to me. Thinking back, I could admit that I rarely took the time to really hear him out when he tried expressing certain things to me. Childhood things. Insecurities and whatnot. I was always on him about manning up, but every time he fucked up, I used words to attack his manhood. I would never try something like that with Giannis, and that just showed how much more respect I had for him over Montell. Giannis's crazy ass demanded respect, and from day one I didn't mind giving it to him.

"That's not what I said, Dakota. At the time, I couldn't be happy with you because I wasn't happy with myself. Was thinking running through numerous women would make me feel better about myself and the things I went through as a child. There's so much that you don't know about me, man. So much that I didn't get to tell you. Maybe if I had, you could understand me better, but I guess that's not too important now that we're with other people. I just wanted to tell you that and apologize for everything in person."

"Did you know that your cousin tried hitting on me, Montell?" I asked out of nowhere. Shit, since he was getting some things off his chest, I figured I would do the same. "Turned him down every time he came at me, but since you're offering me closure, I figured I would offer you some as well." The look on his face right now spoke volumes.

"Dave?" he asked in disbelief.

"Yep, and it happened on numerous occasions during our relationship. Actually, it started before we hooked up, but any chance he got me alone after you and I made things official, he was telling me how he was a much better match for me than you were. How you were too weak to handle someone like me. How he knew you weren't fucking me right. Why do you think we could never get along? I hated him for being a backstabbing-ass nigga and also for the way he played my cousin. He despised me for being one of the only females to reject his advances." I nodded with pursed lips.

Nigga was standing before me shocked into silence as those good ol' wheels in his mind began turning. He was probably recalling all the slick comments, the lustful glares, as well as the unnecessary anger directed my way from David.

"I never told you before because me fucking with him is something that would never happen no matter how hard he tried or how bad you treated me. I also wanted to spare your feelings, but hey, we're clearing our consciences, right? Spilling hurtful secrets, so to speak, so I thought that might be something you'd want to know. The next time you see me and feel the need to speak, don't. Have a good life, Montell," I stated before pushing my basket away from him and moving on with my damn life. That man wouldn't get another thought from me for as long as I lived if I could help it. Now all I could think of was what the hell I was going to do about my former best friend. That bitch had it coming.

Chapter 17

On My New York Shit

Rio

"So you mean to tell me that she was going through all that and you chose to leave her behind and come here?" my cousin Valencia asked.

When she said it that way, I couldn't help but be ashamed of myself. The look she was giving me told me she thought I was one of the dumbest niggas in the world. There was just so much going on back home that if I didn't get away when I did, I was sure to lose my fucking mind. I was now realizing that that wasn't a good enough excuse to walk out on my baby though. At the time I just didn't know what else to do to make her better. Then to hear the pain in her voice when she was going in on Kota about David was too much. I was so pissed off I felt as if I would spontaneously combust at any given moment. No lie, that hurt me a little. No, fuck that, that shit hurt me deeply. No use fronting about it. That was what really made me get the fuck out of dodge. She was talking like she still had feelings for that man or something.

"It ain't like I wasn't planning to go back, Val. I just needed a minute to get my mind right. No way in the world I would end things with Breelyn. Especially like that," I assured her. I said that last part more for myself than for her.

"Well, you better start acting like it, DeMario. There's no telling what she's thinking right now, and I can't imagine how she felt after you left. I haven't even met her in person, but I love her for you. She's softened your crazy ass up a lot," she laughed.

"Yeah, she fucking up my rep on the real. I'm crazy about her though," I admitted. Talking with my family reminded me of what I had in Breelyn, and I realized it was time for me to take my black ass home. I was thinking a break from her depression was what I needed, but I was finding myself slipping into depression my damn self just from not talking to her or seeing her face daily. This shit was tough, but we would get through it someway, somehow. Together.

"I'm about to get up out of here before my husband starts ringing this damn phone," Valencia announced while glancing down at her cell.

"A'ight, yo. Let me walk you out."

We were chilling at my huge-ass loft in Tribeca. This was where I stayed anytime I came home to visit. I received this place as payment for a job I completed years ago, and I loved it. Murder for hire brought me tons of money and came with some nice-ass perks as well.

"When are you taking yo' butt back to Dallas to see about my girl?"

"Shit, I'm thinking about getting up out of here tomorrow if I can get a flight out," I answered.

"Good! I'm sure she's missing you just as much as you're missing her, cuz. Have her call me when she gets a minute. Been trying to hit her up, but she's dodging me. Make sure you tell my girl that what you two have going on has nothing to do with me," Val fussed.

"I'll be sure to tell her that as soon as I see her." I smiled, bringing my favorite cousin in for a tight hug as she continued fussing at me. I hadn't seen her in forever, so coming home hadn't been a total waste since I got to spend some much-needed time with her. She was more annoyed with me than she was with Breelyn about the fact that she wasn't answering the phone for her.

Although they'd never met, they'd become cool as hell through phone calls and text messages. Since the passing of my mother, Valencia was the only family member I kept in contact with. Because of that, I wanted my girl to get to know her just in case something happened to me, and she'd know who to give the other half of my dough to. Thinking back, instead of leaving Breelyn in Dallas to be looked after by her family, I should have just brought her with me to New York. The change in scenery alone probably would have improved her mood a great deal. I was kicking myself for not thinking things through and making such a rushed decision.

"Shit, it looks like I might get to relay the message my damn self," Valencia stated with a hint of humor in her voice. I had no clue what the hell she was talking about until I heard that voice, and from the tone, I could tell she wasn't happy.

"DeMario, what the hell do you think you're doing?" she popped off, causing my eyes to widen in surprise.

Quickly, I released Valencia and turned to find a scowling Breelyn standing with her hand on her ample hip. Ignoring her mean mug, I stepped to her and hugged her so tight that her body was lifted from the ground. She was stiff for the first few seconds, but soon she relaxed and wrapped her arms around my neck, placing her forehead against my chest. No words were spoken. We just held each other, forgetting all about poor Valencia standing there until she cleared her throat to snap us out of our moment. I released my lady but took her hand in mine.

"Damn, I'm sorry. Baby, this is my cousin Valencia. Val, this is my baby, Breelyn," I introduced them, smiling like I'd just been told I won the fucking Powerball lottery. All the shit we'd been going through didn't even matter at the moment. I was just glad her ass was here. What the hell was she doing here right now? Shit had me grinning like a fool.

"Valencia?" Breelyn's demeanor softened. It had just dawned on me that my girl thought she'd walked up on me locked in an embrace with some bird. Breelyn didn't know how Valencia looked, but Val had seen plenty of pictures of her since I'd been here. Every time I thought of her I pulled out my phone and went through my camera roll to see her pretty-ass face. The more provocative ones made my dick hard, so I only looked at those in private.

"The one and only," Val laughed. "It's nice to finally meet you, Breelyn." They hugged like long-lost friends. "Yo, I legit thought your ass was about to swing on me when you walked up on us," she teased as we all laughed.

"My bad. All I saw was a woman with my man's arms around her. Things were about to go left real quick," Breelyn threatened, looking my way. Her jealousy was cute and all, but me dipping off with the next bitch was something she would never need to worry about no matter what we were going through.

"As much as I would like to stay and talk to you some more, I have to go. My crazy-ass husband is threatening to come find me if I don't make my way home right this moment," Val said, looking down at her phone again. "I'm sure you two have a lot to talk about anyway."

"That we do, but hopefully we can link up before I head back to Dallas," Breelyn replied with a parting hug. Talking about when she went back to Dallas. Little did she know, when she left, I was going to be right there with her.

"Definitely."

Once alone, Breelyn and I kind of just stood out in the hallway, staring at one another like it had been months instead of weeks since we'd last seen each other.

"I can't believe that you flew out here," I said, taking her small hands into mine.

"I had to, DeMario. I wanted to tell you how sorry I was, and a phone call just wasn't going to cut it. I'm ready for you to come home. The distance? Just texting and not talking to you or seeing you physically is killing me, babe," she expressed with cloudy eyes. "I know I pushed you away, but I was being stupid. I need you. Please come home. I—" She didn't get another word out before I crashed my lips into hers, devouring them like a famished man. It had been too long since I'd felt them, since I'd felt her, and I needed this moment like I needed air to breathe. "Mmm," she moaned when I backed her into the wall.

Suddenly remembering where we were, I broke off the kiss and began placing soft pecks all over her face and neck. Taking her hand, I opened the door and led her inside. As soon as we crossed the threshold and the door to my loft was closed and locked, she attacked. She was on me like a fucking magnet, lifting my shirt to get it off while kissing and licking all over my chest. My dick was hard as Chinese arithmetic right about now.

"Damn, baby, slow down. Don't you want to talk first?" I stalled. She had me feeling like I was about to prematurely nut in my fucking boxers with the way she was rubbing my dick and sucking all on me and shit.

"We can talk later, DeMario," she responded before quickly dropping to her knees and freeing my dick. I didn't even remember at what point she got my damn pants down, but sure enough, they were at my ankles.

"Aww fuck!" I whimpered like a little bitch when I felt my dick hit the back of her throat. "Breelyn, what the fuck, man!"

That was all I could say. This girl had never blown me down like she was right now, and I was in heaven. Heaven I say! Maybe a nigga needed to take trips out of town more often. You know, accept a few out-of-town jobs or some shit after we made it back home. Being away from her for a week or so would be well worth it if I could come home to head like this every time. One twirl of her warm, wet tongue around the head of my pipe, followed by a few taps on her tonsils later, was all it took for her to rob me of my nut. The biggest fucking nut I'd busted in a long while. Shit almost brought me to my knees, but I was a G so I held it down. And not one to be outdone, I yanked her freak ass from the floor, turned her around, and pushed her into the wall forcefully. When I lifted her dress to find that she wore no panties, I smacked her ass hard, making it jiggle like crazy. Her ass knew exactly what she was doing wearing this little-ass dress here, and I was glad she did. My baby came here to get fucked, and I planned to give her exactly what she wanted.

"Ouch, babeee," she whimpered as I hiked her leg up while placing featherlight kisses to her neck.

"Damn, I'm sorry, Breelyn. Did I hurt you?" I freaked and attempted to place her leg back down. I knew she liked that rough shit, but I also knew there were some positions that had become uncomfortable for her since the accident. The last thing I wanted to do was hurt her.

"I'm fine, Rio. Just keep going, please," she demanded while placing her hand on mine to keep it in place. I quickly proceeded on my mission.

"I love you, DeMariooo," she let out loudly as I filled her up with every single inch I'd been blessed with. Her pussy was so fucking wet that the smacking sound could be heard throughout my home. Shit was like music to my ears.

"Damn, Bree. I love you. I swear I do," I grunted, on the verge of busting already as I held her tightly from the back while continuously ramming my dick into her.

Baby was just going to have to forgive me. Her pussy was smacking and gripping me too tight for me to hold back any longer. It was over for me the moment I felt her slick walls convulse and release a flood of juices on me. A millisecond later I was painting her womb with my babies. This fucking against the wall business was the gotdamn truth. Holding on to her, I kind of just slid down to the floor, energy depleted, as we both just lay there panting like wild boars.

"I'm happy as fuck to see you right now, Breelyn. I don't think you understand what you coming here means to me." I turned to face her once I could talk without feeling like I was having an asthma exacerbation.

"I missed you so much, and I just couldn't be away from you another day," she said, looking into my eyes as she spoke. "Please come home," she requested again.

"I was already planning to go back tomorrow, baby. Even if you hadn't come here. You do know that I'd never leave you on some never to return type shit, right?" I asked, and she just shrugged her shoulders innocently. It killed me that she didn't feel like she could trust me. Leaving for good was never my plan, but I needed her to know that she could always count on me. "I just needed to regroup. I've done that, and I'm ready to come home, baby."

"Good. I was miserable without you, daddy," she pouted, moving closer to snuggle her face into my neck as she inhaled me.

"I was miserable too, baby. I haven't slept right since I've been away from you," I said, squeezing her tighter. "Come on. Let's get cleaned up then lay up for the rest of the day. Tomorrow I'll take you to see my city and maybe hook up with Valencia and Nyijah. Friday we're going home."

"Okay." She grinned. For a moment I could only stare at her pretty ass. Looking at her at times almost brought tears to my eyes. Not on no weak shit, but I really needed someone to explain to me how a murdering-ass, rough-neck ass, "couldn't get the hoes to pay him a lick of attention in high school"–ass nigga like me ended up with her. It was all still a mystery to me.

"What?" she asked bashfully.

"Nothing, it's just . . . You're so beautiful, baby, and sometimes I wonder how someone like you can love someone like me. Whatever the reason, I'm happy that you do," I answered, turning those cheeks of hers a bright shade of red. She opened her mouth to respond, and nothing came out. Instead of saying anything, she mounted me, bringing that out-of-this-world pussy down on my already-erect dick. After another round of love-making right there on the hardwood floor in front of the door, we finally retired to the bedroom for a shower and many more rounds of hot, buck-naked sex.

Because I knew my baby had a thing for good sushi, I asked Val and her man to meet us at this sushi bar in SoHo the following night. The place was nice and cozy, and I just knew Breelyn would love it. We'd done some sightseeing earlier today, and this dinner was our last stop before heading back home tomorrow. As much as we wanted to, there was no way to extend our visit, because she had to get back to help her family prepare for Dakota's parents' anniversary party, which was taking place the following Saturday.

"So, Rio, when do you plan to move back home?" Nyijah, Valencia's husband, asked.

"To New York?" I questioned, and he nodded like, "Duh, nigga."

"Shit, I'm not," I replied quickly. It had always been my plan to move back eventually, but now that I had Breelyn, the plan had been revised. Stunned by my admission, my long-time friend kind of just sat there staring at me like I was crazy as he used chopsticks to pick up the raw tuna from his tray and stuff it into his mouth. I didn't see how the hell they ate this shit. No fucking way was I putting no raw fish in my damn mouth. And they had the nerve to dip the shit in soy sauce like that made a damn difference.

"I know you not trying to make bunk-ass Texas your home, yo," he scoffed. In his opinion, Texas was just too slow for those of us born and bred up North. "Home is where your heart is, nigga, and I know for a fact your shit beats for this here concrete jungle," he said, quoting some shit I'd told him years ago.

"Nah, you got it all wrong, my man. Normally I stay on my New York shit, but things in the game have changed. My home is wherever her heart is," I replied, nodding in Breelyn's direction. "If that shit is in Texas, Timbuktu, or on the muthafuckin' moon, then that's where the hell I'm gon' be, my nigga." I looked over at my lady to find her gazing at me with stars in her eyes. There was nothing in the world like having the woman you love look at you that way. It had me feeling like I was the fucking man, and I meant what I said. Wherever she was was where a nigga like me needed to be.

"Miss me with that romantic shit. Nigga done fell in love and got soft as hell. Trying to kick knowledge," he joked but was serious at the same time. I knew Nyijah well, and he was heated at hearing me say I didn't plan to return to New York. Valencia felt a way too, but she knew what Breelyn meant to me, so she understood.

"You need to be taking notes, Nyi, with your romance-challenged ass," Val stepped in, playfully calling her husband out.

"The fuck? I'm romantic as hell, Valencia! Did I or did I not have you stuttering and speaking in tongues last night?" he asked seriously. "'N . . . Nyijahhhh,'" he moaned, imitating her sex sounds.

"Just shut up talking while you're ahead, bruh," I leaned over to say to him. It was funny as hell that the nigga saw nothing wrong with what he was saying.

"Hell nah! You even talking like them hicks down there now. The hell is a bruh?" he asked, making Breelyn and me laugh out loud.

"Now I'm going to have to agree with my husband on that one. You've picked up an entirely new accent and set of vocabulary words since you've been out there. You called me 'mane,' 'bro,' or 'bruh' so many times when I was at your spot yesterday that I lost count," Val laughed.

"And if I hear 'fuck what you heard' one more time, I'm going to lose it," Nyijah added.

"Fuck y'all!" I laughed. "I'm not gon' lie though, I love it out there. Been telling y'all to come visit us. Probably won't want to come back this way for a minute."

"I doubt that shit very seriously, but we might come out soon. I'm trying to see what them strip clubs do down there," his nasty ass said while rubbing his hands together like Birdman.

"Oooh, me too, babe. I bet them females down there are thick as hell," Valencia concurred with her equally nasty ass.

"Nigga, your wife is gay as hell," I teased Nyijah, who only grinned harder.

"I know, and I love the fuck out of her fruity ass," he said before leaning over to deliver a nasty wet kiss to Valencia that had her moaning out loud.

It was way too much for the public eye, but those two were into some freaky shit, and I wanted no part of it. I loved the shake joints as much as the next man, but these two niggas always went in with ulterior motives. They would end up taking some bitch home then turn her out only for the ho to catch feelings for one of them. Then it would lead to them fussing and fighting if one continued to smash said stalker bitch beyond the threesome that was agreed upon in the beginning. I didn't want anyone but me getting up close and personal with Breelyn's pussy, females included. No one was allowed to touch her shit but me. Her ob-gyn got a pass, but even her ass was skating on thin ice, and she was like family.

"Well, Valencia, you stand corrected. I guess Nyijah can be romantic," Breelyn observed, causing everyone at the table to laugh.

"I do what I can do when I can do it." He smirked, feeling himself after Breelyn's compliment.

"This nigga," I chuckled lightly, amused by the fact that he really thought the shit that he said and did was considered romance. His clueless ass had no idea, and it was funny as hell to me.

The remainder of the night entailed more drinks, laughter, and catching up. We even spent a few hours at the booty club, making it rain on the voluptuous strippers in the lineup tonight. We had a great time, but it felt so good to go home and make love to a woman who belonged to me and me only, bum leg and all.

We were now showered and lying in bed after going at it like animals for the last hour or so. One thing that accident hadn't affected was her sex drive, and I was thankful for that. Our lovemaking was even more intense now and caused me to get chills anytime the thought of being intimate with her crossed my mind. My ass was on the brink of passing out when I heard her soft voice.

"Babe, you asleep?"

"Nah, ma. What's up? You good?" I asked on a long yawn. My ass was tired as hell.

"I'm fine, but I wanted to ask you something. You don't really believe that I'm not over Dave, do you?" she asked, following a long-ass pause.

"Nah," I quickly replied. Did I really mean that shit though? I honestly didn't know what to think after hearing her cry about that nigga wanting Dakota and not her. I just didn't think it would matter who he was choosing on if I was the one she truly wanted.

"Look at me," she demanded, and I did. She was on her side, arm propped at the elbow with her palm holding her head up. "Even if David were alive, I wouldn't be thinking about him—"

"About that," I attempted to interject, but she held up her hand to silence me so that she could continue.

"I hadn't wanted him around since before you and I even got together. Trust me, DeMario, you're the only one I want. At the house that day I was just pissed that I put in so much time with him only to find that he wished he could have her all along. That shit made me feel like I wasted so much of my life, but after you left that day, I had a chance to sit back and think about things. That day I decided that, if I had to, I would go through it all over again," she confessed.

"Why you say that?" I asked, not catching on to what she was saying.

"Because if I wouldn't have gone through that, if he hadn't run me out of town with his mess and his lies, I would have never met you."

I smiled when I realized what she was trying to say. Even in the dark room with only the moonlight shining through the curtain-free windows, I could still see her beautiful face and that smile that I adored.

"And although I'm very hurt about the baby we lost, I trust that we'll get the opportunity to be parents when the time is right. I'm realizing that it just wasn't in God's plan for it to happen for us right then, but we'll have that experience one day. That much I'm sure of."

"I'm sure we will too," was all I said about that. The baby situation still fucked with me, and I had a hard time talking about it, so I decided to leave that conversation for when we made it back to Dallas. I had something in store for her that would hopefully ease her pain and mine as well. "So basically what you're saying is that your man is worth all you went through with that fuck boy?" I asked, now fully awake.

"Yes, baby. Having you in the end was worth it all. I wish I could wake David's ho ass up from the dead to shake his hand and thank him. I love you with all I have, DeMario, and I never want you to second-guess that. When I was in that hospital bed asleep, struggling to wake up, you were all I thought of. I'm here because of you. Without you I would have had no reason to go on. Thank you for praying for me every day, baby. For keeping me clean, kissing my scars, and staying by my side. For that you'll always have my love and loyalty. My whole heart belongs to you, because it was dead before and you are responsible for bringing it and me back to life," she concluded with a sweet kiss to my lips.

She then turned on her side with her back to me, prepared to go to sleep. My damn heart beat out of control the entire time she talked, and in that moment my love for her increased tenfold. I didn't even know that was possible. Shit, I thought I already loved her as much as I could, but I was wrong. What she didn't understand was that her love brought me back to life as well. And now she gon' turn her back and go to sleep like that shit was cool? Nah, it wasn't even going down like that.

"Ma, what you doing?"

"I'm going to sleep, baby. You should be trying to get some rest too. We have an early flight in the morning," she yawned, pulling the cover up to her neck, getting even more comfortable. I swore I heard teasing in her voice, so I hoped that she was just fucking with me.

"Hell nah, Breelyn. You can't just turn over and go to sleep after saying some real shit like that to a nigga."

"I can't?" She smirked while flipping over on her back.

"No, you can't. Not before allowing me to tell you how sorry I am for walking out on you. For leaving you all alone. That should have never happened. This love shit can get complicated at times, but what I've learned since you woke up from that coma is that it's my job as your man to be present and to love you through whatever trials you face. Even during those times when you're treating me as if living without me ain't a big deal. I'm making a promise to you here and now that walking away will never again be the solution." I came at her straight from the heart, and I hoped she believed me. Scooting closer, she wrapped her arms around me.

"Thank you. I really needed to hear that, DeMario," she whispered against the side of my face.

"I know you did, baby, and I promise I meant every word," I assured her before kissing her deeply. I know she could feel how hard she had me, so I decided to go ahead and try my luck. "Ay, you still sleepy?" I felt her smile as she nodded. "Let ya man put you to sleep with this dick then," I said, biting down on my bottom lip cockily.

"You sure you can do that?" she questioned.

"I know I can, and yo' ass knows it too," I told her with confidence as I reached down and trailed my index finger down her slippery slit. Pussy was already crazy wet.

"Babeee!" she whined while grinding against my hand.

"Breelyn, a minute ago you told me that your heart belongs to me, but what about this? This belong to me too, bae?" I asked as I began drawing circles on her swollen clit.

"Yes, Rio," she panted heavily.

"Yes, what?" Just to fuck with me, she remained silent, only throwing me a lustful glare in response. To give her some motivation, I moved between her legs and traveled down south to put her legs on my shoulders. Once my mouth connected to her pussy, I began feasting like a savage. After a few minutes of French kissing her pussy, I asked again, "Yes what, Breelyn?"

"My pussy and my heart belong to you, DeMario!" she cried out as I licked her into a quick release.

Her confession had me on one, and there was no way she would be getting any sleep tonight. She had better get that shit on the flight home tomorrow like I planned to.

The following morning, we made our way back to the Lone Star State. Back to where her heart was and ultimately the place mine would always be . . . with Breelyn Layne Waiters.

Chapter 18

Nervous

Anonymous

Man, I was shaking like a hooker in church on Sunday as we emerged from the back of the shiny new Jaguar we'd been escorted to the party in. My date and I were exuding all types of black excellence this evening, but I couldn't even enjoy it because my nerves were shot to shit. Why he chose this particular event for us to make our debut as a couple was beyond me. Whatever his reasoning, I was behind him 100 percent. One thing that he continued to stress to me that I agreed with him on most was this being our time. Time for us to acknowledge the bond we had and just be with one another. All the hiding and secrecy was a thing of the past. We couldn't keep concerning ourselves with the thoughts and opinions of others.

"I got it, big dog." Rah stepped up when the handsome, burly driver went to grab the mini train of my dress that was caught up on the door. Once baby got me right, he took my hand into his, interlocking our fingers. "You gotta relax, baby girl. I told you that I had you and I meant that," he said, pulling me closer to his side as we moved through the lobby and toward the elevators hand in hand.

Although I was still a bit uneasy, trust, I had no regrets or second thoughts about us being together, and I hoped that he didn't either. It had taken a minute, but he had finally gotten his shit together. His ass didn't have much longer to make our shit right or I would have been done and over the entire situation. The back and forth had gone on way too long, but like the lovesick fool I was, I'd stuck it out, and now look at us.

Him confessing his feelings to me was the last thing I was expecting when I made it to his place that night. Not even gon' lie, I knew his ass wanted to fuck, which was the driving force behind me showing up in the first place. That was one of the only things we always got right. Sex with us was fucking sensational and just got even better over time. Us together like this though? Walking into an event where a majority of his family would be in attendance was not something I ever saw happening for us. It was new and exciting. I was happy as hell, and he seemed to be as well. At the end of the day, that was all that mattered.

Stepping off the elevator and into the beautifully decorated ballroom, I was in awe. Dakota's parents had gone all out for their anniversary. I had never had the privilege of being invited before today, but I was glad to be arriving on the arm of the only man I had ever loved. According to Rah, it was something his aunt and uncle kicked off a couple years back to celebrate their union and love for one another. That huge celebration had turned into an annual event for them, and they spared no expense.

I wasn't expecting it to be as fancy and upscale as it was, but I now understood why my man insisted on buying me a brand new dress, shoes, and accessories. He even dropped money for my hair and makeup. I was shocked as shit, because when I say that this fool rarely ever spent money on me, I tell no lies. Cold thing was he had plenty to spend. He just chose not to break bread to prove that I was nothing more than a jump off.

I didn't want or need him for his dough, but he was known to do some petty shit, and he seemed to go out of his way to make me feel like I wasn't shit to him. At least that's how I saw it. He wanted me to believe he didn't care, but I had always known that his feelings for me ran way deeper than he would ever admit. I wasn't at all concerned about what he could do for me financially, so I never tripped on it. All I wanted was his fucking heart, and he'd finally placed it smack dab in the palm my hand.

Did he deserve to have me after all he'd done? Hell no, but it was what it was. I was his and he was mine, plain and simple. No fucking takebacks. Rah could fuck with me if he wanted to. I would leave his ass for his fucking daddy if he played me for a fool this time. Fuck what you heard. We stayed on some tit-for-tat shit, which was one of the reasons he didn't want to be with me exclusively. Nigga could see other bitches and I was just supposed to be cool with it, but when I did the same shit that he did to me I was the bad guy. He could dish it out, but he damn sure couldn't take it when I got his ass back way worse. At the time I thought I was really doing something by hooking up with other dudes. When it came down to it, all I was really doing was adding mileage to my body, all because he'd hurt me. I was over that shit now and had actually slowed down and tried to be in a real relationship with someone else, but it didn't work because the man walking beside me at this very second was the one I wanted. He was the only one for me.

The stares and whispers began as soon as we crossed that threshold, but my man's confident stride and tight grip on my hand put my troubled mind at ease. With him by my side, I was prepared to deal with anyone who came for us. That included the dynamic duo, who I was sure would have plenty to say about this here union. Soon as I heard a loud smack of some teeth followed by, "No he fucking didn't," I knew it was time for me to put on the full armor of God and get ready for whatever these pit bulls in fancy dresses had for me.

"What up, family?" Rah greeted them cheerfully, clearly taking on an unbothered attitude. He hugged his cousin first, acting as if me being here on his arm was the norm.

"Hey, cousin," Dakota replied, earning her a sharp glare from Breelyn. Hell, even I was shocked that she was being pleasant. She didn't seem to be upset about me being here with him. She hugged Rah and continued bobbing her head to the music. I had no fucking clue what that was all about or why she was being so chill, but I was glad to only have to face one of them in a showdown. It was clear that Kota B had no beef with me at the moment. Her feisty ass could have been fronting, but I was sure hoping she kept it chill. Breelyn, on the other hand, looked as if she could backhand the fuck out of both Elijah and me at any moment.

Chapter 19

The Family:
Anniversary Party Shenanigans

Breelyn

"Elijah, you can't be serious. What the hell are you doing with her?"

"Look, I didn't come here to cause problems. Just trying to enjoy a night out with my man and celebrate Mr. and Mrs. Bibbs's anniversary like everyone else here," ol' girl said.

"Mel, shut up talking about you not trying to cause problems. So you really thought showing up here with your so-called friends' cousin wouldn't cause problems? Get the hell outta here with that! You knew damn well we'd feel a way about this shit. You bitches got big fucking balls these days," I spat. I couldn't help but notice how quiet Kota was right now.

"Yo, Breelyn, you need to chill with that disrespectful shit!" Rah stepped up with his hand extended toward me.

"Really, Elijah? I need to chill?" My head spun so fast in his direction it almost caused whiplash.

"Yes, Breelyn, you do. If anyone is causing problems as you put it, it's you. Auntie n'em are already aware of who would be my date tonight, and they ain't tripping so neither should you. Tonight is about them, not me and who I choose to—"

"Come on, y'all. This is not the time or place," Kota interrupted before Rah had a chance to finish his sentence.

"Wait, hold up! Why aren't you more pissed about this?" I eyed my cousin suspiciously. When it came to shit like this, once I got going, her ass was jumping in right behind me, talking just as reckless. Even more so because she was way more gutter than I was. I was new to it but Ms. Kota B was true to it so her reaction right now was throwing me off. "This is the second fucking friend to do some shady shit like this behind your back, and if I didn't know any better, I'd think you already knew about this," I accused. I knew Dakota like the back of my hand, so I knew something was amiss.

"It's not even like that, Breelyn. I just think there's a time and place for everything. And right this moment, at my parents' anniversary party? This ain't it, boo. Tell me again why we're even worried about who this nigga fucking?" she hissed lowly as she glanced around at the few guests now looking our way.

"Because that's what we do. As much as his ass stay in our business? The hell are you even talking about right now?" I looked at her like she was stupid for even asking me that shit.

"Excuse me, but we're not just fucking. We're together now," Mel interjected at the wrong damn time.

"Girl, you had a whole other gotdamn boyfriend last week, so chill with that staking your claim shit," Kota laughed as Rah and I joined in. Shit was funny as hell because her butt was damn near married to another dude not too long ago, but I guessed we were supposed to overlook that. Shocking the hell out of me, Mel cut her eyes at my brother and the nigga actually straightened up.

"My bad, baby," he apologized after clearing his throat. Seeing her check him threw me for a loop, and I couldn't help smirking.

"Let's just step outside and squash this shit right now," Kota suggested as she grabbed my hand along with Mel's, pulling us toward the exit.

"Aww hell nah! Y'all ain't taking my baby out there to jump her or some shit! I love y'all, but I can't let that happen." Rah stepped in, grabbing Mel's other arm and pulling her back.

"I'll be fine. Just go hang with the fellas and let us work this out on our own," she pleaded with him.

"I'on know 'bout that shit, Judy." He reluctantly looked from the two of us back to Mel.

"I'm not going to let anything like that happen, so back up, Rah. I got this," Kota assured him.

"I ain't making no promises," I threw his way just to fuck with him before snatching away from Dakota and leading the way out of the ballroom. "A'ight, spill it. It's clear that you know something that I don't." Her ass had barely stepped out of the door and I was already going in.

"Breelyn, relax. I only recently found out that they were dealing with one another. It was when you were in the hospital. I promise I wasn't trying to keep it from you, but my mind has been all over the place. You being the main focus."

"That's cool and all, but my real question for you is, why are you so nonchalant about this mess?" I questioned.

"Honestly, I did feel a way when I found out, but at this point I no longer give a fuck. I have my own shit to deal with. And what mess are you referring to, Breelyn? Rah finally settling down? Rah actually claiming someone as his girlfriend? How can I be mad at that? And let's be thankful that it's Melanie and not Jada's funky ass. Girl, I didn't even get a chance to tell you that Montell finally confessed to me that they slept together." She switched subjects like Mel wasn't standing there looking nervous as hell. "Nigga talking about it only happened once, but I'on really believe his ass. A person who lies as much as he does makes it hard for someone to trust anything they say. It ain't like I didn't already know the shit, but it fucked me up when it came directly from the horse's mouth. And in the middle of the baby section of Target at that!" Kota fumed.

"Jada ass ain't shit!" I joined in, getting slightly off task. I was supposed to be pissed at the fact that yet another one of my cousin's friends had fucked her over in a sense by fooling around with my brother when we made it clear that shit like that was unacceptable.

"I can't stand that bitch!" Mel concurred heatedly.

"I've been meaning to ask you what your beef was with her," Kota asked.

"First of all, I don't like how she did you, and before you open your mouth to speak on me fucking around with your brother, Breelyn, we were seeing each other for a long-ass time before I found out he was any kin to you all. There's a few other reasons as well, but I'll let Elijah talk to you about that."

"Ump," I smacked my teeth for the hell of it. I actually liked Mel a lot. I just disliked the fact that my cousin had friends who weren't always honest with her. She could front all she wanted. I knew that that shit with Jada and Montell hurt her deep, and when Kota B hurt, I hurt.

"Anyway, by the time I found out who his family was, I was already caught up," she sighed. "Ladies, this man was there for me when I was going through that whole ordeal with the school district. All the shaming and judgment in the media? He was my support in the background the entire time, and I will always love him for that. Who do you think broke that li'l nigga's legs after the truth came out?"

"Bitch, no!" Dakota exclaimed with an amused smile.

"Yes, bitch! All hoop dreams flushed down the drain just for lying on me." Mel nodded.

"That sounds like some shit his crazy ass would do." I couldn't help but laugh. My big bro went hard for those he cared about, so I had no doubt that he had love for Mel.

"I swear I was pissed when he did that because the boy was young and not thinking things through when he did the shit he did. Rah didn't give a damn though, and that was when I knew for sure that he loved me. He stayed trying to act like I was just something to do for the time being, but I knew better. Sneaking around was cool for a minute, but when you finally opened up to me about what went down with Jada trying Montell and her past dealings with Rah, I just didn't want to be added to the shady friend list, Dakota. I felt like shit for being yet another person to break your trust, so I kept quiet and broke it off. Plus, he wasn't trying to make us official so there was no need for me to come clean about it," she confessed.

"That's understandable," Kota chimed in while I nodded in agreement.

"I promise it was so hard keeping it from y'all, but my situation with Rah was toxic as hell for a long time. He did some shit to me that hurt me deep down in my soul, and y'all already know I'm not some punk bitch. Definitely not a chick who's going to sit back and let a man run all over me and treat me like anything less than what I feel I deserve. When I saw what he was about, I hit him where it hurt, his fucking ego. Kinda glad we kept shit between us under wraps because the three of us probably wouldn't have remained friends with y'all in the middle of such a volatile relationship. I guarantee both of you would have felt a way if you'd been privy to some of the things I did to get back at him when he toyed with my emotions. We're in a better place now, and we're done with the games. I'm just asking for a chance to show y'all that I'm different and that I really love him," she stated while looking to us for a response.

"Shit, it's cool with me. As long as you do right by him, we'll have no problems. I have love for you too, so I'll be telling his ass the same thing about you," Dakota said as she embraced Mel.

"And what about you, Greedy? You fucking with the kid or nah?" She grinned like a fool with her arms extended to me for a hug.

"I suppose so, but I'm gon' need you to chill with that Greedy shit. You don't know me like that," I stated with a straight face while they both looked at me like, "Really, bitch?"

"I'm kidding, damn! But for real, I understand why you didn't tell us, and I think you're a good look for my brother. Chile, if this were Jada out here pleading her case, I would have already mopped the floor with her ass. Besides, Elijah done already gave you a nickname, so you in the family. There's no turning back now," I joked as they both fell out laughing. "Fuck he get Judy from though?" I asked after our quick embrace.

"Girl, you better act like you know," Mel said before twirling around and pointing to that big-ass rump shaker she was toting around, making it clap a little for emphasis.

"That boy is a damn fool! Big Booty Judy!" Kota cackled loudly.

"He's so silly." I shook my head, finally catching on.

"Are y'all done or nah? Any way I could get my lady back now?" Elijah asked, peeking his big head out into the hall. Kota and I just flipped him off as Mel walked closer to him with a smile on her face that spoke of a woman truly in love. With his arms wrapped around her,

I watched as my brother placed soft kisses on her face and whispered God knows what in her ear. I had never in my life seen him look at anyone that way, and the love I saw there damn near melted my heart.

"What the fuck y'all got going on out here? Bring your fine self in here and dance with your man, Kota B," Giannis's ol' sucker-for-love ass said as he brushed past my brother to scoop up his baby mama. Hands clasped together and extended toward the ceiling, they stepped to the low sound of the song currently playing on the other side of the wall like they were some original Chicago steppers. They were too fucking cute, and I couldn't get enough of them. They kept up the groove until they disappeared behind the door. Elijah and Mel weren't too far behind them, rejoining the party inside.

Not quite ready to follow, I moved over to the window, and outside of it, I was met with the perfect view of my city from the twentieth floor. For a moment, I just chilled. It had been a while since I'd been alone with my own thoughts and been genuinely content with my life. Normally, I had to have someone around to keep me company or a man in my life to make me happy. Someone constantly telling me they loved me. I now loved my damn self, so everything else was extra. My heart wasn't 100 percent healed but I was on my way.

A lot had happened to me over the last year or so. I lost a love that I thought for a long time meant everything to me. Discovered a true love that I knew for a fact I didn't want to live without. I'd been hurt physically and was almost destroyed emotionally when I woke up from my coma to learn that my unborn child didn't survive the injuries I'd sustained from the accident. As bad as I wanted to give up and as low as I felt some days, I was glad that I didn't check out on this thing called life. At this moment in time, I was good.

I smiled because just as I was about to go inside to find my man, I felt him and the same symptoms as always. My heart rate went up by at least twenty beats per minute, and my palms became real clammy while the hairs on my arms and at the back of my neck stood at attention. Only DeMario Taylor could do that to me. He'd probably been there watching the entire time. I was always catching him being a creep, just staring at me with that same look in his eyes. With my back still to him, I spoke. "Babe, why do you do that?"

"I told you it's because I can't get enough of looking at you. Gotta make sure you're the real deal and not just a figment of my imagination," he whispered before pulling my back flush against his chest.

"Mmm," I moaned lowly as soon as that warm mouth and tongue of his grazed that spot on my neck that he'd become very familiar with.

"I know tonight's not the night because of your aunt and uncle's anniversary, but when do you want to share our good news with everyone?" he asked, making me smile harder, which I thought was damn near impossible.

"In due time, baby. Right now I just want to enjoy this time in our lives, just the two of us. That's cool with you?" I asked, turning in his arms to wrap mine around his neck.

"Whatever you want to do is fine with me, Breelyn." He pecked me a few times before continuing. "I was going to ask you how you were feeling, you know, make sure I'm doing what I need to do to keep you happy, but seeing that glow of yours return and that beautiful-ass smile on your face as I stood back watching, you answered my question. I know for a fact that you're good."

"I no longer have pain when I walk or difficulty breathing while performing the simplest tasks. My heart is healing from our loss, my family is straight, and I got my man. I'm better than good. I'm fucking great, DeMario." I cheesed hard as hell.

"And that's all that matters to me."

"I love you, babe."

"Not more than I love you, Breelyn Taylor," he told me before kissing me silly like only he could.

Rah

The party had died down some, and now a handful of us just sat around the main table, listening to my aunt and uncle share stories of their early years together, the good, bad, and ugly of marriage. From breakups to make-ups and being broke as hell sleeping on the floor of their one-bedroom apartment in the beginning. Incidents with shiesty friends as well as infidelity. They'd been through it all, which was probably why their bond was so strong.

"Kasey, baby, you remember this?" my Aunt Syl asked as "Saturday Love" by Alexander O'Neal and Cherrelle blasted through the speakers.

"OMG! I love this song. My parents played this song all the time when they were alive!" Mel said excitedly before she began singing along. Her losing her parents in an accident when she was only a teenager and me growing up without my mom was one of the things that bonded us over time. In my opinion it was harder for her because she was old enough to know what was going on when she lost her mom and dad, but when my mom passed, I was too small to understand what was happening. We met when we were broken and damaged, but since then we'd grown tremendously. That was my baby right there with her singing ass.

"Judy, sing that song for me one time. The one I like so much." I tapped Mel on her hip.

"I'm not about to sing in front of everyone, Elijah." She waved me off.

"You were just singing though," Greedy's smart-mouthed ass said.

"That's not the same thing, heffa." Mel shot the middle finger her way.

"Let me find out you be singing for this fool though." Dakota was too amused.

"Shut up, Kota," she mumbled before cutting her eyes my way.

Everyone was coming at her and it was my fault, but I couldn't help it. "Ay, if you don't want to sing it for me, sing it for my aunt and uncle. I mean, it is their anniversary," I said, putting her on the spot.

"You know you not shit for that!" She threw her head back in laughter as we all joined in.

"Come on, Mel, do it," Greedy encouraged her.

"Y'all leave this child alone," Aunt Syl said, trying to run interference for her.

"Sing it to me, Melanie," I said, looking deeply into her eyes. It felt like she was the only person in the room. The spotlight was on her, and I knew she didn't particularly like that, but I had to hear her sing that fucking song. She sang it to me in the shower years ago, and I believed that was probably the day I fell in love with her. I remember fucking her so good after that. I'd probably keep this to myself for life, but I sometimes played that on repeat when I was missing her. I snapped out of it when she placed her hands on both sides of my face and began to sing.

"Oh, give me just a minute, just a second, I gotta get it off my chest. Ain't no competition when you're in it. Let you know that you're the best."

My girl belted out the opening to Jazmine Sullivan's "Excuse Me" song like she was Jazmine herself. I knew she could sing. I knew this. I'd heard her sing plenty of times, and if you followed local Dallas music so had you, but she was killing the hell out of this song right now. She had me so caught up in the words and the sound of her voice that I didn't even notice I was gripping the shit out of her thigh. She removed my hand and sat her fine ass on my fucking lap, and I was wishing like hell that I hadn't put her on blast. She had flipped the script on me, and with all that ass of hers sitting on my dick, along with the soothing, soulful notes flowing from her mouth, a nigga was stuck. I was sure I was looking like a sucker to the fellas and maybe my family too, but I didn't give a damn.

"Make me wanna cook and clean, just to see you smiling at me. Baby, you don't even have to ask me. Don't care what the task be, if it makes you happy."

I almost laughed after that part because of how opposite of her this verse of the song really was. She was rebellious as hell and always fought against giving in to me, although most times she eventually did. And let's not even talk about that cooking part because her ass couldn't boil water. Even with all that, I was happy to be with her, flaws and all. She accepted mine, so I had no choice but to accept hers as well.

"Didn't I tell you they'd make the perfect couple, baby?" Auntie Syl nudged Uncle Kasey once Mel hit the last note.

"They a'ight. They ain't got shit on us though, love," my uncle joked as he pulled his wife to her feet. All the other couples followed suit except for Mel and me. My ass was stuck trying to give my dick some time to go down. "I'm just messing with you, nephew. And you, baby girl, have a beautiful voice," my uncle complimented my woman before turning his attention back to Auntie Syl.

"Thank you." Mel blushed, watching everyone make their way to the dance floor.

"I love you, Melanie Banks," I told her once we were alone.

"Elijah!" she gasped in surprise before covering her face with her hands. She even made a move to get off my lap, but I held her in place.

"Quit acting shy, girl, and tell me that you love me too," I teased, pulling her hands down.

"Boy, you know I love yo' ass," she laughed with tears clouding her eyes. I caught her off guard with my confession, but I had to let her know how I felt about her. Before she could say anything further, I grabbed her face to squeeze her cheeks hard as hell before shoving my tongue down her throat, causing her to moan desperately. Our relationship was just different. Passionate. Crazy. A little rough, like the way I was kissing her right now. Wasn't like Kota and G's or Greedy and Rio's. We did our own thing and loved one another in our own way. I just hoped she was willing to do this shit with me for the rest of our lives.

"Herb, I done told ya ass about getting drunk and acting a fool," Uncle Kasey's deep voice boomed, interrupting our lip lock. It hadn't even been five minutes since they had all walked away to go dance. I looked to the other side of the room to see my uncle standing a good three inches taller than his youngest brother as he reprimanded him.

"But, Kase, man, I ain't e'en did shit! How that flat-nosed bihh gon' tell me I can't have nun . . . nun else to drank?" he hiccupped and slurred in response.

I tapped Mel on the hip to get up when I saw Uncle Kasey back him into the wall as he continued trying to move around him so that he could go back to the bar for another drink.

"Nah, nigga, you done for tonight! Why the fuck would you pull some shit like this on tonight of all nights? I'm supposed to be celebrating with my wife, but I'm over here babysitting your grown ass. You need to get ya shit together, Kelvin!" Uncle Kasey called him by his government as he pointed a finger in his face. Uncle Herb couldn't do shit but drop his head in defeat.

"We got him, Unc. Go back over there with Auntie and let us worry about this. We'll get him home," I assured him.

"Where the fuck is Kenneth? Why do I always have to deal with this dumb nigga on my own?" My favorite uncle threw his arms in the air in frustration.

Speaking of Pops, he'd gone missing a little over thirty minutes ago. It was weird, because we'd been sitting at the table talking with him for most of the night. I leaned back to say something to Rio, and when I turned my head back around, his ass was gone. I hadn't seen him since. Looking around, I didn't spot him anywhere in the ballroom.

"Ay, Greedy, follow me to the front to get this nigga jacket. Mel ready to go anyway, so we gon' take Unc to the house with us and let him sleep this shit off. Aunt Janice will probably kill his ass if we take him home tonight," I said as she nodded knowingly. I didn't know why the hell my uncle even drank like that, because it wasn't shit for my auntie to jump on his ass or kick him out when he acted a fool like this. Even I was annoyed as I struggled to hold up his body.

"Where Auntie?" Greedy asked.

"Shit, she left a while ago. Guess she got tired of his ass talking shit and flirting with every female who walked by. Straight left his ass," Dakota answered as she and Giannis approached.

"You ain't never lied. I thought I was gon' have to fuck him up for rubbing on my lady's ass while they were dancing earlier. I ought to fuck you up too, Judy. Didn't even protest when his old ass was talking all nasty while he felt you up," I fussed as me and the fellas carried my drunk ass uncle toward the front.

"Shut the hell up, Elijah! I did check him! Plus it was obvious that he was drunk and probably won't remember any of this by morning," Mel replied, rolling her eyes.

"A drunk mouth speaks a sober mind, Mel. Nigga probably been fantasizing about touching that big, juicy booty of yours for years. Got a few of them drinks up in him and decided to shoot his shot," Dakota's instigating ass added, earning her an evil glare from me while prompting more laughter from the group.

"Y'all hear that shit?" asked an amused Giannis. We all quieted down once we made it to the desk and were met with a soft knocking sound and what sounded like moans.

"Hell, yeah! Somebody back there getting it in like a bihh," Rio offered childishly.

Whoever was supposed to be manning the desk was out of line right now if they were back there fucking while people waited in line for their coats. After ringing the bell twice and getting no response, my sister was like to hell with it and decided it was time to bust their asses out so that we could get up out of here.

"Breelyn, what are you doing?" Dakota asked when she noticed her moving behind the desk.

"Going to get our jackets so we can leave. I'm trying to get home to do the same shit this coat-checking nigga doing in this closet!" she said but kept moving as they laughed their asses off. Shit wasn't funny to me because I didn't want to hear shit about my sister fucking.

Leaving Uncle Herb with Rio and Giannis, I followed my sister so that I could get my shit as well. As I pushed through the coats, I heard voices that made me wish like hell that I'd stayed my ass up front and waited. I turned, and the sight before me caused my eyes to pop wide open and my feet to get stuck in place. I couldn't move, and I couldn't speak.

"Mmm, Ken, if we get caught, I'm never speaking to you ever again. Waitttt, oh, my Gawd, what are you doing to me?" she moaned loud as hell, making my skin crawl. Seeing him move in and out of her from the back snapped me out of the trance I was in, and I immediately squeezed my eyes closed, hoping to erase what I'd seen.

"I'm making your ass out a lie, woman. Talking about you'll never speak to me again. You know damn well this dick too good for you to play yourself like that," he grunted. The slapping of their skin together was almost enough to make me hurl.

"Elijah, why the hell you got your . . . Aww, hell nah, Pops!" Breelyn shouted as she came up behind me. "What the hell is wrong with this family tonight?" she groaned. Following her outburst, the rest of the crew made their way to the back as well.

"Dammit! Kenneth, I told your ass someone would come in, but you just couldn't wait!" Ms. Ivy swatted at him after quickly pulling her dress back down over her backside. My father's face was flushed red in embarrassment as he turned his back to stuff his shit back in his pants. I was way past mortified after seeing my father fucking. I mean, I knew he be out here doing his thing or whatever, but I just couldn't picture him or Ms. Ivy getting down like that. Especially together.

"Where the hell is Uncle Herb?" I asked, snatching my and my lady's jackets from the hanger and leaving my father and his fuck buddy there still fixing their clothes. Just minutes earlier I was whispering in my girl's ear all the freaky shit I wanted to do to her, but after seeing that, I was no longer in the mood. I just wanted to take my ass home and forget I ever saw what I saw.

"Oh, he lying down right now," Kota snickered as she shook her head at my pops.

"Glad they didn't use that bench, because we damn near broke that ho when we were in here earlier," Giannis said under his breath, but I heard him loud and clear.

"Ain't that it," Dakota laughed.

"Y'all some nasty mu'fuckas, mane."

It seemed that the people in my family were doing everything they could to raise my blood pressure tonight. What did they not understand about keeping me out of their sex lives? I didn't want to see or hear about the shit. Like, at all!

Just as I suspected, when I got up front, I found Uncle Herb laid out on the floor, looking a shitty mess. I left him there and slipped back in the ballroom to let my aunt and uncle know that I was going home. I found them still dancing in the middle of the room, in love and in their own world. They were relationship goals like a mutha.

I walked back out to find the fellas picking Uncle Herb up by his arms and legs and carrying him to the elevators. He'd probably have to stay with me or Uncle Kasey until Aunt Janice let him bring his disrespectful ass back home. That was their routine anytime he got out of line like he did tonight. I must say that this evening was full of surprises. My family was a mess, but they were mine and I was theirs. Call us crazy, ghetto, or whatever else you wanted to call us, but the love between us was way too real, and if you fucked with one of us, you'd better be ready to deal with all of us. Fuck what you heard!

Dakota

"Shit, Giannis," I hissed lowly as my honey strummed my swollen clit like he would the strings of a guitar.

Whatever song he was playing, my body was singing right along with him. Moments earlier he was positioned behind me, spooning my body, and the next thing I knew his hand was down the front of my boy shorts. Since we'd come in from the party, we'd been getting it in. It was like his ass never got tired, and despite how sore I was, my body still reacted to his touch and craved more of his loving. "I don't think I can go anymo . . . mmm," I croaked as I felt that all-familiar buildup brewing in my lower abdomen.

"Shut yo' ass up, girl. Ain't nobody trying to fuck you. You said that pussy was sore, so I was just being a good guy by rubbing out the soreness," he said seriously, causing a half smile to appear on my face at his silliness. "Besides, she saying something completely different from what's coming out of your mouth, Dakota Layne." When he bit down hard on my neck, that was all she wrote.

"Ughhh," I called out loudly as my body froze in antici-pation of what was to come.

"See what I mean?" he teased. "Talking about you can't go no more. You can go as long as I say. Ain't that right?"

The feel of his tongue in my ear pushed me over the edge. "Yesss," I cried out like the fool I was while my body shook out of control. I didn't know how the hell he did it, but my body seemed to be under his spell and would come apart on his command. I needed a break, but my traitorous yoni had thoughts of her own. We had shit to do though, and if we didn't get some rest tonight, the errands we needed to run tomorrow would be put off for yet another day.

"A'ight, I'ma let you rest, but I have a surprise for you," he whispered in my ear after allowing me time to come down from my sexual high.

"You know I live for a good surprise, so what you got for me, honey?" I turned to face him, attempting to mask

my excitement. I bit down on my lip when he brought his
fingers up to his mouth to lick my juices from them. He
was just nasty as hell for no damn reason, and I loved it.

"So, I know you were pretty pissed with me because
I didn't let you go to New York with Breelyn when she
went, and on top of that, we didn't get a chance to really
celebrate your birthday."

"Right."

"So I talked to Dr. Salaam again, and because she said it
was okay, I'm taking you on a li'l vacation."

"Really, honey!" I squealed. "Where are we going?" I'd
been itching to take a quick vacation before the baby
came. We had a long way to go, but Giannis had been
against any traveling up until now. I'd already talked to
the doctor, who said it was okay, but his ass wasn't trying
to hear it. I didn't talk to his ass for days after he flat-out
refused to let me accompany Breelyn to New York.

"That resort that you showed me a few weeks back in
Turks and Caic—" he started, but I was already straddling
his lap, bouncing up and down while planting kisses all
over his handsome face. "You gon' let me finish or not?"
he said with an accomplished smile gracing his face. I
loved that it made him happy just to make me happy.
How dope was that? To have someone in your life whose
sole purpose was to make you smile? It just didn't get any
better than that.

"Thank you so much for doing this for us, honey."

"Listen, Dakota, I know you think I'm crazy and that
I'm smothering you, but I can't help it. You and my baby
are the most important people in my life, so when I think
about the fact that I could have lost y'all had you been
in your car that day, it does something to my damn soul.
Hate to even think about the shit. I just want this pregnancy to be smooth and complication free for you. So
please forgive me for being too overprotective at times,"

he said before groaning in annoyance. "Come onnnn, man, don't start that shit," he said, placing his hands atop his head in frustration when he noticed I was crying, a waterfall of tears sliding down my fat-ass cheeks.

"I can't help it, Giannis. If I have to put up with your bossiness, then you need to learn to deal with my tears." I continued sniffling.

"You're right. I'm sorry, love. I'm just not used to your hard ass crying so much. I'll be glad when I get my OG back," he joked. "Fix ya face, baby girl," he said while wiping away my tears for me.

"Okay." I poked my lip out like a baby. "So who all going?" I asked as he threw his head back in laughter at my sudden mood improvement.

"Both of your cousins and their spouses, of course," he answered, causing me to squeal in delight. "I'll have another surprise for you beforehand, but you're not allowed to ask me about it until I tell you it's time for you to see it."

"Honeyyy, that's not fair," I sulked with my arms across my chest.

"Dakota." He called my name with a sharp glare.

"Fine. Thank you for whatever it is, Giannis."

I knew not to take that spoiled shit too far with this one. He'd give me anything in the world that I wanted, but acting out on my end was never tolerated. Who would have thought that I'd get off on a nigga having me in check like this? Pussy became soaked every time he came at me aggressively or put me in my place. Suddenly I was no longer tired, and the soreness I was experiencing earlier had somehow worked its way out. I was ready and he was willing, so we did our thing like only we could do it.

Chapter 20

It's Handled

The Crew

"Remember what I said, Breelyn. Once you press the red one, that's it," Rio reminded her as the crew entered the funeral home. Expecting her to be nervous, he called himself coaching her. Little did he know, it wasn't necessary. She was ready and had been since he'd told her the truth.

"I understand, DeMario," Breelyn responded as her heels clicked against the concrete floors of the long corridor they walked down.

Rio pulled back with his fist to his mouth as he watched the way her ass swayed from side to side in the high-waisted booty shorts she wore for the occasion. The bralette she wore told of the newfound confidence she'd acquired. Breelyn was no longer ashamed of her scars but was now proud of how strong she had to have been to survive what she had. The marks on her body told of her will to live and how far the Man Upstairs had brought her. Her whole vibe said she was ready to do work as she switched her fine ass through the building, her limp no longer noticeable. The women looked out of place, moving through the building that hadn't been in use for the last five years. Following a heavy rain the night before, water made that familiar drip-drop sound from the faulty roof. Water damage was evident from the stains along the walls and ceiling. You could smell the mold, and they probably should have been wearing masks the moment they entered the building. They didn't plan to be here very long, so hopefully it wouldn't affect them.

"Man, I can't wait to get my hands on this bitch," Dakota fumed as she moved in sync with Giannis, who was close by her side, wearing a menacing scowl that mirrored hers.

"Chill, babe. I already told ya ass if you get too worked up with my baby in there, I'm sending you to the fucking car to wait until this business is finished. Do we have an understanding, Dakota?" he reminded her.

"'Do we have an understanding, Dakota,'" she mumbled, making Breelyn and Rio snicker lowly.

"Now is not the time to play with me, li'l nigga. It took a lot for me to even let you come here tonight, but I wanted all of us to take care of this shit together once and for all," he said without turning to face her.

"Fine," she said lowly. His ass never let her have any fun. She planned to follow the rules because she refused to give his petty ass a reason to send her to the car for real.

"Nice of you mu'fuckas to finally join me," Rah sarcastically announced once they made it to the bottom of the stairs and into the open area.

Sitting atop an elevated steel table, he was surrounded by every type of torture tool known to man. Most of the shit had come from Rio's stash and was new to Rah and Giannis. Since they brought him here, they'd watched Rio inflict pain upon their victim. Some of the shit was hard for them to watch, but they knew as well as Rio did that his grimy ass deserved everything he was getting.

"Yo, bitch, shut yo' ass up!" he called over his shoulder at the whimpering female behind him. Her muffled cries for help did nothing to move the group of individuals now gathered in the room. Ol' boy had long ago stopped begging for his life. Rah had to check a couple of times to make sure he hadn't kicked the bucket. He was surprised that he was still hanging on with all the horrible shit Rio had done to him.

Without a word, Dakota walked over to the table where her cousin sat, eyeing the arsenal of weapons placed strategically on the table. Knives, guns, pliers, a blow torch, and so much more. She ran her fingers across a few of them, trying to decide which one she'd use to get the job done. She picked up the hot pink Smith & Wesson 9 mm, and she automatically knew that her man had put that there for her.

"Gracias, honey," she offered without looking his way as she moved the gun around to fully check it out. She was in love and already planning to retire her trusty .22 and put this one into rotation.

"*De nada, mi amor,*" Giannis spoke in perfect Spanish.

Dakota's mind traveled back to the conversation had only hours before as she and Breelyn sat in Giannis's office with him and Rio standing before them.

"So we're about to take y'all to see the first part of your birthday prese—" Giannis had started, but their cheering had interrupted his speech. "Chill with the bouncing in your seats, because this isn't at all what y'all think it is," he finished.

"What kind of gift is it if we can't get excited about it?" Dakota had wanted to know as she looked from her man to Breelyn, who had questions in her eyes as well. Here they were expecting this bomb-ass gift for birthdays that they hadn't gotten a chance to celebrate, and their men stood before them stone-faced and serious, acting as if they were about to deliver the worst news imaginable.

Leaning against the desk with his arms folded across his chest, DeMario spoke. "Breelyn, what would you say if I told you David was alive?"

Eyes bucked and heart pounding, she tried to gauge whether he was just fucking with her or being serious. Again her eyes went to Dakota, who had the same dumb-founded look on her face. "If you told me that David was alive, DeMario, the first thing I'd want to know is why you lied to me about taking care of him," Breelyn answered with an attitude.

"I never lied to you. All I said was that we found him and that he'd been taken care of, which he has been, but not in the way you think. And you never questioned me about it, so I left it alone."

"After all he's done and everything he's taken from me, why the fuck is he still breathing, DeMario?" Breelyn shot up from her seat to get in his face.

Her anger with him couldn't be masked at the moment. This man had been alive all this time, and the part that had her heated was the fact that Rio hadn't made good on the promise he'd made to always protect her. She wasn't feeling that at all. She thought about the possibility that he could have come back to finish the job he was unable to complete when he fucked with the brakes on Kota's car. She was lost as to why her man would put her and her cousin at risk that way.

"Because I wanted you to be able to take him out your-self. It wasn't shit for me to kill his ass, and I still will if you want me to. Just thought I'd give you the opportunity to handle that," he revealed as she softened her stance just a little. "The nigga was minutes away from death when we found him, and I've had him under twenty-four-hour watch as our street doc nursed him back to health only to start that slow torture process on his bitch ass." Rio gritted his teeth, anxious to get back to the spot to finish this shit. "Been fucking him up for a while now, but I want you to be the one to end it if that's what you want."

"Shittt, if she don't want to do it, I will," Dakota announced.

"Calm yo' ass down, OG Bobby Johnson. I got something for your li'l violent ass, too," Giannis joked.

"I knew you wouldn't leave me out, honey. So what'cha got for me?" Dakota batted those long-ass lashes of hers, causing Giannis to bite down on his lip as he became caught under her spell.

"See for yourself." He shook his head to snap out of it before grabbing the remote control and punching a series of buttons. The television mounted on the wall behind Giannis's desk came on, and a video time stamped the day before Breelyn's wreck began to play. "Rio and I were chopping it up the other night and it dawned on me that we'd forgotten to check the surveillance video from the house. With so much going on, it completely slipped my mind to take a look at it. Of course we already knew David's ho ass was behind the shit, but we were shocked as shit when we saw the bitch he had tagging along with him. I remember getting on your ass that morning because you didn't set the alarm like you told me you did before we went to bed." As Giannis spoke, the girls were anxious to find out who the hell he was talking about. What female did they have beef with who would want to hook up with David to do them harm?

"That funky bitch!" Dakota slammed a fist into her other palm once she made out the face of the female seen playing lookout while David messed around with her car in the garage. They had to be dumb as hell or smoking some good-ass dope thinking they would get away with the shit they were doing without getting caught. The camera Dakota installed herself after Montell started doing that weak shit wasn't well hidden and could be seen by anyone moving about the two-car garage. The sun hadn't even gone all the way down and her dumb ass was all out in the open, standing outside the side door, moving her head from side to side suspiciously while he did his thing.

"Don't worry, we caught up with her ass. Since they want to team up to break into shit and call themselves taking you out, they monkey asses gon' die together as a gotdamn team," Giannis added. They hadn't seen or heard from Jada's ass since everything had gone down, and with the way she had been trying to weasel her way back into their family and their lives, her disappearance was highly suspect.

"Her ass been missing in action for a minute. Word was that she moved back down to Birmingham with her people," Breelyn said.

"Yeah, but we caught up with her when she snuck back in town after spending some time down there with her son," replied Giannis.

"Her son?" Breelyn and Dakota answered at the exact same time. This was news to them. Jada had never mentioned or brought a kid around them, so they were so lost right now.

"Yes, and there's a whole lot more to that part of the story with her, but I'll let y'all get that information from Rah when we get to the spot."

"What the fuck can Rah tell us about her son, Giannis?" Dakota pressed.

"What I just say, ma? Talk to that nigga when we get there." he said, leaving it at that.

"And y'all just happened to run into her?" Breelyn questioned.

"Nah, the same bitch who told us where to find David dropped dime on Jada ass too," Rio responded.

"His baby mama?" Breelyn asked. She couldn't believe her ears when Rio told her months back that Shawna gave up David's location. She never thought she'd see the day when that girl was no longer down for David, but after the beating he gave her that resulted in her losing her baby girl, she was done with his ass. There wasn't that much love in the world as far as she was concerned, and for once Breelyn sympathized with her. She was a dumb ho when it came to David, but she'd finally put her and her son first, which was what she should have been doing from jump.

"Yep, straight ratted her ass out," Rio chuckled.

"Damn shame." Kota shook her head.

"So what's it going to be, Breelyn? I'm not trying to make you do some shit that you aren't comfortable with, because once you take a life, there's no way to give it back. It will change you, and I need to know if you're really ready for that. Just say the word and your man will handle it for you. You don't even have to set foot in the building if you don't want to," Rio said.

"No, DeMario, I want to do it myself. Therapy is helping me a lot, but I feel this is what I need so that I can fully move on."

"And you're sure about this?" he asked for clarification.

"I'm positive, baby." She smiled and kissed his lips.

"Well, let's roll. I'm ready to take care of this mess and go on my birthday vacation." Dakota had begun dancing around Breelyn playfully. Of course she'd joined in on the silliness as the men laughed.

Now in the warehouse, Kota was prepared to give Jada her issue. She was content with allowing Breelyn to get her revenge on David. He meant to hurt her but ended up fucking up Breelyn's entire world, so Dakota felt she deserved to be the one to end his life. It did her soul good knowing that his last vision before death would

be images of his beloved Breelyn standing before him
with the man she was sure to spend the rest of her life
with. After thinking things over, Dakota came to the
conclusion that David just wanted her to say he had her.
Seemed that the nigga had some type of sick fantasy
of being this pimp nigga with a harem of women at his
disposal, but he had them pegged wrong if he thought
they'd ever go for some shit like that.

"Damn, daddy, you messed him up pretty bad," Breelyn
observed as David's battered body was lowered from
some contraption that Rio's mental ass had paid to have
constructed some weeks back. With the control device in
hand, he stopped the chain right as David's feet were flat
on the four-foot box beneath him.

"Ahhh!" he immediately screamed out in agony.

Taking a closer look, Breelyn couldn't help cringing.
His ankles were terribly twisted and appeared to be broken, so being made to stand on them clearly brought him
a great deal of pain. She also wondered if he could see
her. His face was barely recognizable and his eyes were
swollen shut, so she wasn't sure. Head hung low with
blood dripping from one corner of his mouth, he was
mumbling something that no one could quite make out.

"Speak up, nigga!" Rio's mean ass ordered. "Don't
nobody understand all that damn mumbling."

"I'm surprised he can even talk with the way you yanked
all his damn teeth out yesterday with those pliers. I'm
glad we got over that shit we were on in the beginning. I
ain't trying to be on your bad side. Ol' psycho ass." Rah
shook his head at his homie. Had it been left up to him,
he would have hit David with a head shot followed by one
to the heart and been done with the shit, but Rio's extra
ass had to pull out all the stops while taking care of this
fool. He understood his rage, because the man had taken
his child away from him and hurt his woman. In Rio's
eyes, David had to suffer for that shit.

"K . . . kill me pleaseee," he begged in a voice that was barely audible.

"Oh, we definitely plan on doing that this time," Rio said in response to his desperate request. David had been brought to the brink of death several times and nursed back to health, but this time it was a done deal. There was no coming back after today.

Jada seemed to realize the predicament she was in, because she went from whimpering to a hysterical cry. She was realizing that the likelihood of her making it out of this building was slim to none. It was crazy how people who did so much dirt in their lives and worked overtime trying to bring others down became humble as fuck when it was time to answer for their deeds. If you were going to go around doing shiesty shit, own it and thug it out to the end. There was no use in crying when your past wrongs caught up with you.

"I'm definitely using this one on this ho," Dakota mumbled.

"Handle your business, baby." Giannis gassed his woman.

"Before I do that, is there something you need to tell us, Rah? This bitch supposedly has a child, and you're the only one who can give me answers about that? Fuck is that all about?"

"Umm, so yeah. I found out that this ho had a baby and—" he started but was interrupted.

"And what the fuck that got to do with you, Elijah?" Breelyn popped off. She was silently praying he wasn't about to tell them what she suspected since learning Jada had a son.

"It has everything to do with me, sis." He looked over at her sadly then gave Dakota that same look. It was clear he was hurting about something, so the girls decided to keep their over-the-top reactions to themselves for now. "I know what y'all are thinking, but I honestly haven't fucked on her raggedy pussy ass in years, so it ain't some shit that happened recently. I ran across her in the mall a while back and she had this kid with her. Li'l man looked to be about nine or ten years old, and it got me to thinking. The bitch was yelling at him and snatching him around just for asking her simple questions. She was acting like being around him was the last thing she wanted to be doing, so I just knew he wasn't hers, but I wanted to know who was dumb enough to trust her with their child. I followed them for the longest time before I got the courage to approach. As bad as I wanted to mind my business, I couldn't walk away for some reason, and I'm glad I didn't. When he turned around . . ." Rah shook his head and took a deep breath. "Just imagine coming face-to-face with a kid who looks exactly like you, who you never knew existed. I started to snap her fucking neck in the middle of the mall, and had she not had shorty with her, I would have done just that. From the moment we made eye contact, I felt a connection with him. I felt as if this was my son, but this simple bitch kept screaming he belonged to some other dude and how I needed to mind my business. I knew better though. We were fucking around, being reckless as hell back in the day, so it wasn't hard for me to put the pieces together. It was tough as fuck playing her close all these months, but I was scared her ass would run off before I got the truth about my son, so I did what I had to do. Had to damn near beat this ho up to get her to go do the DNA test, but we finally got it done and the results confirmed he's mine. Bitch ain't had him with her all his life. Had him living with her people out in Birmingham. Kinda shit is that?"

Rah chuckled heatedly, pissed that he'd been kept away from his seed. Jada wasn't about shit and he never had any real love for her, but he would never deny his child or want to be separated from him. He didn't understand her reason for keeping them apart, but all that had come to an end. She snuck back down South with the boy because her ass knew all along what the test would come back saying. Little did she know, Rah was waiting to snatch her up the moment she made it back to Dallas.

His next mission was to go pick up Kai. With the results in hand, he showed up to her family's place in Alabama, demanding his son be released to him. The nine he had pointed at her older sister, Jessica, ensured that he got what he came for. Since that time, Kai had been with him and seemed to be content with his new living arrangements. He was enjoying getting to know his father. He hated living in Birmingham with his aunt, but he hated being with Jada even more.

"So that's why Mel don't like her ass?" Kota asked, putting shit together in her head.

"Exactly. I told her about it as soon as I found out. Kai's at the house with her right now." He smiled, thinking about how cool his son and girlfriend had become since they'd been introduced to one another a few weeks back.

Breelyn and Dakota were both fuming at hearing that this girl had kept Rah's son away from him. You'd think with the money Rah had she'd be trying to hit him over the head with the amount of child support she requested or at the very least use the kid to earn her spot as Rah's woman. Lord knows she was crazy over him back in the day. And that's just the type of conniving person she was, so those things were expected, but not this. They'd never know why she did what she did, and at this point, it didn't really matter. This ho had to go, plain and simple. Dakota decided to ask Rah how he felt about it, but her mind was made up.

"Rah, I know this is your baby mama or whatever but—"

"Do yo' thang, baby cuz," Rah interrupted. "This ho don't want my son no way. He told me she stay putting her hands on him for no reason and telling him how she wishes he was never born. She's a waste of fucking space, so don't mind me. Handle your business, Kota B." He threw his hands in the air.

"Shit, that's all I needed to hear. So, Ms. Jada, as much as I want to untie you and whoop your ass, my man ain't having that, so I'm going to get straight to the point," she spoke to the bound woman who sat there trembling in fear.

There was no telling what she'd witnessed Rio doing to David since she'd been there, so her mind was probably racing with thoughts of what was to come. Fortunately for her, Dakota didn't plan to draw things out or make her suffer. Had she not been with child, things would have turned out very different, but Dakota's condition was Jada's saving grace at the moment.

"You wanted me dead, huh? Claiming you wanted to mend our friendship, but yo' ass was still plotting on me behind my back? I would ask you why, but I honestly don't give a fuck." She shrugged.

"Please!" Jada cried, knowing that her pleas were falling on deaf ears.

"Ain't no please, bihh," Dakota spat before unloading on her. Jada's body jerked in the seat as the bullets penetrated her tiny torso. With one final shot to the dome, Dakota was done and Jada transitioned to wherever evil people like her went when they died. Right as she placed her gun back down on the table, Giannis came and wrapped his arms around her waist from behind and kissed her neck while rubbing her small bump.

"A'ight, you've had your fun. Now let's go wait upstairs until it's done," G told her.

"Aww, honey, I don't get to watch the show?" she pouted, referring to what Breelyn was about to do to David.

"Nope. I believe Baby Williams has experienced enough action for the day. Rio got Breelyn, baby, so don't worry," G said as he pulled a reluctant Kota back toward the stairs after slapping hands with his boys.

Rah followed suit and got in line behind them to leave. As much as he wanted to be the one to get at David for what he'd done to his sister, he realized that was something that she and her man needed to do together. He would always be there for his sister and cousin, but it was high time that he relinquished his job as their protector and allow the men in their lives to take over. Shit, he had a son and his own woman to look after, and her hardheaded ass was enough trouble. With a body like the one she had, he planned to stay knocking niggas out anytime one of them stepped to her.

Back inside, Breelyn stood directly in front of David's damaged body as rage coursed through her veins. Of everything that he'd ever done, taking her child away from her had to be by far the worst. Every day she suffered because of it, and she was ready to let it go. She was just unsure if her being the one to take his life would make her feel any better. Before walking in here, she thought it would, but now she wasn't 100 percent positive that she could go through with it. She wasn't like Dakota. Sure she'd changed up a little and bossed up some, but she wasn't a killer. She couldn't even look at Jada as Dakota filled her body with those bullets. She was realizing that being sweet li'l Breelyn was okay with her, and her man liked that side of her more anyway.

"Daddy, I don't think I can go through with it." She shook her head, looking from David to her man, hoping he wouldn't be disappointed in her for backing out at the

last minute. Her tone was almost apologetic. All plans
she had to make her ex pay had suddenly flown out of the
window.

"I told you I got you, Breelyn. You ain't got to be
ashamed of what you're feeling. It ain't in you to take a
life, and I understand that. I actually prefer that. Means
I get to lay down any mu'fucka who tries to come for you.
That's what I'm here for, okay?" He smiled, pulling her
into him. He kissed her like they were alone and didn't
have one dead body in a chair and one on the brink of
expiring hanging before them. "You staying to watch, or
you want to step out with the others while I finish?" he
asked after releasing her.

"Oh, I'm staying. Just because I don't want to do it
doesn't mean I'm leaving. I gotta see for myself that he's
gone," she answered, moving toward the table.

"Nah, come here," he ordered, pulling her in front of
him.

With one hand around her waist he pressed the single
red button on the controller he held in the other, causing
the stand David's feet rested on to slowly descend into the
floor. Rio pushed that same button once more to pause it
for a moment to watch the man struggle to breathe as he
now stood on his tiptoes. It was then that Breelyn looked
up and noticed he had rope around his neck. The panic
in his eyes and choking sounds he made were things
Breelyn had never witnessed, but she couldn't turn away.

Before Rio could press the red button for the final time,
Breelyn reached up and hit it while smirking deviously
up at David as their eyes locked. The stand was now
completely gone from under him. Eyes bucked and red
as hell, he sweated profusely as the veins in his face and
neck bulged and pulsated. Hands tied behind his back,
blood now poured from his mouth. His body dangled and
writhed back and forth for a while before all movement

ceased. Now he kind of just swayed from side to side. Surprisingly, Breelyn kept her eyes on him the entire time, not wanting to miss a single second of his misery, pain, and death. For some reason she just couldn't pass up the opportunity to press that button, and she was glad that she hadn't.

"Thank you, baby," Breelyn turned in DeMario's arms and wrapped hers securely around his neck before kissing him so passionately that he dropped the remote from his hands.

"Damn," he said, shaking his head at her as she pulled away. "You know I'm tearing that ass up as soon as we touch down, right?" She nodded, wearing a sneaky smile. "G'on outside with Kota and have Rah and G come back. Let us get rid of this mess, and I'll be ready to go, a'ight?"

"Okay, but try to hurry, DeMario. This thong is a mess already. I might not be able to hold off until we get there," she purred into his ear, causing a groan to slip from his lips. Weird time and setting for her to be turned on, but that's the effect DeMario had on her.

"Quit fucking with my head, Bree." He smirked. Before he could grab her up like he planned, she quickly stepped back and began to walk away from him. Of course his eyes were glued to her rear end as it moved from side to side. There was always something about that mean-ass walk of hers. Shit was sexy as fuck to him, which was why he always walked behind her.

Once the guys joined him, they pushed the bodies into the oven one at a time, making sure that nothing but dust would be left of them. Rah purchasing this funeral home a few months back worked out perfectly for them because they were able to dispose of the bodies without having to move them from place to place. It was funny as hell seeing their homeboy go to school to be a funeral director, but niggas died every day, so he had the right idea. If he played it right, he could build a very successful business, and they were all proud of him. Now that this part was taken care of, they could move on and really begin to enjoy the good things happening in each of their lives.

"A'ight, fellas. Now that that's handled, it's time to put this bullshit behind us, hop on this flight, and enjoy some time in paradise with our women," Rio said, dapping them up.

"That's what the fuck I'm talking about," Giannis answered as they walked up the stairs to meet the girls.

"I'm glad we're finally moving on from this shit. Now it's time to chill," Rah said.

"Hell yeah! Rah got a kid who's damn near grown. G, my nigga, you got a baby on the way, and I'll be having tons of fun with Breelyn while trying to get on y'all level as we kick shit in Turks," Rio added, making Rah side-eye him. They knew that talking about sexing Rah's sister or cousin rubbed him the wrong way so they did that shit as often as they could.

"Y'all dummies swear that shit funny." Rah shook his head as they laughed. "I know y'all better bring y'all asses on before Kota and Greedy come in here and snap for making them wait too long." As much as the men swore they ran shit when it came to their women, everyone around them knew who really wore the pants in their relationships. That much was evident by how fast they made it up the stairs.

"Mane, what the hell you doing here, and where is my son?" Rah asked when they made it outside and he saw Mel posted up with the girls. She was looking like a fucking snack in the T-shirt dress she wore, which hugged her curves perfectly. He tried to mask his delight, but he was happy as hell to see her right now.

"He's already with your Dad and Ivy. Juaquin ended up canceling the show because the money wasn't right, and I hit your pops up as soon as I got word. You know they were too happy to get Kai," she answered while pushing herself off of his ride to come over to meet him halfway. "I didn't want to wait until tomorrow to see you," she replied, snaking her arms around his neck.

"I'm happy you're here, Judy," he said before kissing her lips softly.

The plan had been for her to fly out the day after tomorrow since she already had a commitment to sing background for one of her brother's groups. Rah prayed that the show would get canceled after she told him that there was a big possibility that could happen. Also, he was more than pleased that she'd taken it upon herself to make arrangements for his son and come here early to hop on the flight with the fam.

"A'ight, family, let's get this show on the road," Rio ordered.

Everyone happily followed his lead, making their way to their vehicles. They'd overcome many obstacles individually and collectively to get where they were, and now it was time to live, laugh, and love like there was no tomorrow. It was time to get back to life.

Epilogue

Sometime Down the Line

"Ha! Look at her chubby ass wobbling and shit," Dakota joked lowly while everyone stood out of the way, watching Breelyn walk from the restroom to her bed as she prepared to be moved to a different floor. They'd already packed up her belongings and the many gifts that had been dropped off by family and friends since she'd been there. After three whole days and two attempted labor trials to maybe speed things along, it was finally time.

"Kota, don't say that bullshit where my baby can hear you. Get ya wife, man," Rio directed Giannis. Breelyn had been self-conscious about her recent weight gain and he wasn't for anyone making her feel bad about it. Not even her bestie. After years of trying and let down after let down, the moment they'd been praying for was finally upon them.

Rio and Breelyn had recently celebrated three years of marriage. Their family was shocked to find out that the wedding they attended two years ago was actually the couple's one-year anniversary. Dakota was pissed when she found out and didn't speak to her for like a week after finding out. It wasn't really their plan to keep it from them for so long, but after about six months, they decided to wait to break the news the night everyone assumed was their first day as husband and wife. They had exchanged vows the

first time just days after they returned from New York following their fallout and reconciliation.

"Chill, Kota B." Giannis tried not to laugh.

"Man, fuck that. You know how long I've been waiting
to call that heffa chubby? I can't front though. My baby
boo still fine as hell. Big-ass belly and all," Kota added
with an approving nod.

"You ain't never lied." Rio smirked arrogantly, feeling
himself all of a sudden at Kota's observation. It was a
known fact that his wife was one of the finest women on
the planet. Breelyn Taylor couldn't be faded in his book.
Baby weight be damned. "Baby, can I get you anything?
Are you sure you're okay?" he asked Breelyn, who was
now laughing at a story being told by her nephew, Kai.

"DeMario, I promise you I'm fine," she assured him,
looking nothing like a woman who was now in active
labor. By now her husband was expecting her to be
cursing him out or crying out in excruciating pain, but
she was doing neither.

"Aww shit." DeMario shook his head while looking
down at his phone as he stood next to her bed as the staff
prepared to transfer her to the labor and delivery floor.

"What's going on, baby? Who is that?" Breelyn questioned.

"That fool Nyijah. He was asking if the baby was here
yet, and I told him no. Then his ass proceeds to inform
me that he would be in town tonight or some time tomorrow," he answered, still shaking his head.

"Okay, so what's the problem with that? I thought the
plan was for him to visit when I had the baby anyway,"
she pointed out. She didn't see what the big deal was.

"He said he's coming to stay for good. That's the problem," was her husband's reply.

To that news, the crew eyed one another in silence
knowing that all hell was going to break loose when

Nyijah came to live in Dallas permanently. For the past few years he and Val had lived separate lives, with her here in Dallas and him back in New York. She had some shit going on that no one had the courage to tell him just yet, but if he was moving here permanently, he'd find out soon enough.

The two weren't divorced yet but they definitely were no longer together. After another incident of "cheating" on Nyijah's part a few years back, Valencia decided that they no longer needed to be together. It was a long story, but since the breakup Nyijah had been trying his hardest to reconcile with his wife, but she wasn't having it. According to Valencia, it was a done deal. No one believed her because after all this time her ass still hadn't served him those papers.

"It's about to be some smoke in the Triple D." Giannis nodded his head knowingly. Over the last few years, the crew had become real cool with Rio's people during their frequent visits to Dallas. They'd also become privy to the extracurricular activities the couple participated in during their marriage. That was a whole other story for a whole other book though.

"Fuck yeah," Rah agreed.

"I'll have Dad and Dakota follow me this way and, family, you all can remain here until we get her settled in her room. Looks like we're finally going to meet baby Taylor tonight," the nurse announced excitedly once they made it downstairs.

Besides Val and Nyijah, another person not in attendance for the arrival of the newest member of the family was Breelyn and Rah's father Kenneth. A family emergency on his wife's side of the family was the cause of his absence. He had to be there to support Ivy as she mourned the loss of her nephew, who had recently been killed in a motorcycle accident, but he promised to fly back right after the service. It killed him to not be there for the birth of his second grandson, but Breelyn was very understanding and gave him her blessing to be there for his wife. She had a lot of love for Ms. Ivy, and she was glad that her father was finally happy.

The relationship between Kenneth and his children had changed drastically. He may not have been there for them when they needed him over the years, but he was going above and beyond to make up for lost time. He was a huge presence in their lives now. He was also the best Paw Paw on the planet to Kai, and he planned to be the same for DJ when he finally arrived.

"I can't believe this shit."

Dakota was in shock while studying the monitor an hour or so later. It clearly showed that Breelyn was having a very strong contraction, but her reaction to it was throwing everyone off. The mom-to-be simply closed her eyes, did some breathing exercises, and then resumed the card game she had going with Zyan. Her hair was still intact. Her face was still fresh and flawless with no signs of distress. It was the most astonishing thing. Kota was hating because childbirth for her was nothing like this. In her opinion, it was ten times worse than what Breelyn was experiencing at the moment. Her labor was so painful that she vowed to never have children again. Although she was thankful for her 3-year-old daughter Zyan, she had no desire to go through that a second time.

"Sis, you're taking this shit like a straight-up G," Rah commented while he stood by the window with his arms wrapped around Melanie's waist. They had been going strong since making things official. Rah was ecstatic that he chose love over fear and gave their relationship a try. He couldn't even front. These last few years had been the best years of his life. His son was growing up right before his eyes, and he was happy to be a part of that. As of yet, he and Mel didn't have more children, but neither was opposed to the idea of adding to their family. As far as Kai was concerned, Mel was his mother, and he never asked about what had happened to Jada. Rah had no idea what he would tell him if he did, but for now they didn't discuss it. Kai was happy, and as long as that was the case, Rah was cool. Making sure his son and Mel were straight was his priority these days.

"Y'all gon' quit underestimating my girl. I been saying this child is tough as nails. Unlike this child of mine. I thought I was going to have to hit her dramatic ass over the head with all the screaming and cutting up she was doing when she had my grandbaby," Syl recalled.

"Whatever, Ma. That shit hurt," Kota rationalized her behavior. She went so far as requesting the doctors perform a C-section on her after only three hours of labor. Giannis shut that shit down off the muscle. If his baby wasn't in any distress and it wasn't required, he didn't want her to go through any unnecessary surgeries.

"Ay, what was it that she kept screaming?" Rio chuckled.

"'This shit is so dumb. So fucking dumb!'" a few family members recalled in unison. Everyone fell out laughing, remembering how bad Kota clowned when she was in labor with Zyan. She just couldn't understand why having a child had to hurt so bad, and in her opinion it was just dumb. It was definitely something that they would reminisce and laugh about for years to come.

"That shit funny as hell," Chubb laughed. "Kota B swear she tough but be the first one in tears. Straight crybaby!"

"Ain't that it?" Breelyn chimed in, earning her the middle finger from her favorite cousin.

"Is that what y'all think?" Kota asked as if she were in shock. She looked to Giannis, who turned his face in the other direction, wanting no part of this conversation. His wife was a crybaby and he knew it. He just didn't want to be the one to tell her. "I hardly ever get emotional or cry. The only time was when I was pregnant with Zyan, but that was nothing but hormones."

"Baby girl, you know Daddy loves you, but I'm going to have to agree with Chase. You have always been a crybaby," he admitted as the family laughed and chimed in, each offering a memory of a time when she cried during her childhood.

"Oh, a'ight! I see how it is. And, Chubb, laugh now, cry later. You'll soon feel my pain, heffa," she retorted, shutting Chubb up immediately.

Surprising everyone, Chubb, who was the youngest of the cousins, recently confessed to getting pregnant after engaging in a one-night stand nearly three months ago. No one would admit it, but up until she spilled the beans, their entire family assumed that she wasn't attracted to the opposite sex. They weren't judgmental and wouldn't have cared if that were the case, but her tomboy ass threw them for a loop with that one. From what a few family members said, it was rumored that her baby daddy was connected and associated with some pretty important folk in Dallas. Thing was, no one had met him as of yet. All they knew was that his name was Big B. Rah was familiar with a dude by that name from when he was ripping and running the streets, but he was sure that this wasn't the cat his little cousin was pregnant by. He just wouldn't believe that his homie Marcus's right-hand man had hooked up with his baby cousin. His ass had a little sister who was just a few years younger than Chubb. There was no damn way. Again, that was a whole other story for a whole other book.

"Mrs. Taylor, are you ready to get this show on the road?" her nurse asked when she entered the room.

"Of course I am. I'm so ready to meet my baby boy," she answered excitedly while the family cheered. They were all exhausted after spending days at the hospital but still anxious to meet DJ. She was fully dilated, and now it was time to push. Everyone was escorted from the room except for Rio and Kota as they prepared to begin.

Later That Evening

"Giannis, I'm ready, baby." Dakota turned to him as she held her newborn baby cousin in her arms. Breelyn was finally getting some rest after days of being in the hospital. She handled the pain pretty well throughout labor, but the pushing at the end took a lot out of her. She was able to bond with her son for a while after he was born, and then she was out.

"You sure?" Giannis asked excitedly. Breelyn having DJ was making her rethink her stance, and she now felt she was ready. Plus, busybody Zyan needed a sibling to bug and boss around.

"I'm positive, honey. Hopefully we'll get a boy next time. DJ has to be the most laidback baby ever," she replied, snuggling him up close to her face.

He only cried when he first came out and the nurses were getting him all clean and ready, but since then he'd been quiet. Every now and then he'd open his eyes to look around at nothing in particular, and then he'd be right back asleep. The baby fever was all too real for Dakota right now. Even Mel and Rah had stars in their eyes when they held him. By next year there was sure to be a slew of babies born into the family.

"Man, guess who I just saw in the cafeteria when I was getting coffee?" Uncle Herb asked when he entered the room.

"Who?" Rio asked.

"That punk-ass nigga Montell," he answered, causing Dakota to roll her eyes and focus her attention back on the baby.

Word on the street was that he now had custody of his daughter, and his girlfriend, Erica, had recently had another baby for him. His other baby mama was locked up on child abuse and neglect charges, which was how he was able to gain primary custody. Dakota laughed hard as hell when she saw her mug shot on the news. It was messed up what she did to her daughter, and Dakota was glad she got her issue. She also meant what she said the last time she spoke with Montell and she was pleased that he had no problems following orders. They'd run into each other plenty of times since that last encounter, and he respectfully kept it moving and didn't speak to her at all. She was happy that things seemed to be going well for him and didn't wish any bad on him. She just didn't fuck with him.

The family hung around for a while before Rio asked to have some quiet time with his wife and son. Everyone was tired anyway, so they left with plans to return later the following day. As soon as the last person left, he got comfortable in bed with plans to join them for a much-needed nap. The movement in bed caused Breelyn's eyes to shoot open. She immediately smiled upon seeing his face then reached for the baby who had begun to whimper just a little.

"I love you, Breelyn. Thank you for giving me him. For giving me you. That may not make sense, and I don't even know what else to say right now, but I promise I've never been this happy or felt what I'm feeling at this moment. I owe that all to you," Rio told his wife as he witnessed his son latch on to her breast for a feeding.

"Babe, don't make me cry," she pouted. "It's me who should be thanking you though. For you. For him." She gazed lovingly at her son as he sucked away. "For showing me a love that I've never known or thought possible. Thank you, DeMario," she replied before placing a soft kiss on his lips.

Right when Rio was about to respond, his phone went off. Two seconds later Breelyn's cell vibrated on the bedside table. Picking both phones up, Rio unlocked his first. It was a message from Nyijah.

Nyijah: Be there in an hour or so. Caught an earlier flight out.

"Nyi is on his way," he yawned as he read the text she'd just received. Pinching the bridge of his nose, he held the phone up so that she could read the message.

Val: Hey, sis, I'm wrapping things up at Greedy's. After a quick shower I'll be on my way to see you and my baby.

Val: BTW, Von is coming with me, so please make sure your husband is on his best behavior.

"And the drama begins." Breelyn smirked.

"Indeed," her husband agreed.

The End

Thanks and Shout-outs

Heyyyy, good people! I just wanted to take a moment to thank you for reading and supporting my work. I'd like to apologize for the delay in getting this one out, but I really wanted to give you something I felt good about, and I hope you enjoyed it. Dakota and Breelyn's story is done, hunni. That's it! They got their happily ever after. Can't say they won't be mentioned in other books, but I'm just done telling their story. As you read, I brought one of the family members, Chase aka Chubb, to the forefront so that she could have some shine. Since she's family I'll give small peeks at what's going on with your favs. Did you all notice who Chubb's baby daddy is supposed to be though? Big B! Man, I'm going to have a blast writing about them because I'll get to give you updates on Marcus and Jakobi along with their significant others. I miss them so much! In addition to that, I can't wait to get feedback on what you all think of Valencia and Nyijah! I'm really excited to tell their story. All I'm going to say is that they have one crazy-ass relationship and end it there. Gotta save the drama for the book.

To the readers! You are the real MVPs! Without you I can't do what I do so thank you! Thanks to my hunni Michael for all the support and sacrifices you make to ensure I'm able to follow my dreams. My Mom for always holding me down! I luh you, baby! To The Squad . . . y'all already know! The support I receive from you ladies keeps me going. #SquadUp! Thanks to Blake, my publisher.

To my test readers (Kym, Nisha, Shunda & Ursula). Thank you! I appreciate you ladies keeping it real and honest with me. Genesis and Desiree! Thanks for listening to my crazy ideas, giving feedback, and the encouraging words. This industry gets crazy at times but I was super blessed to stumble upon some real ones. We have sooooo much work to do, ladies. In the words of Martin Lawrence . . . #WeAboutToBlowUp lmaooo

Big shout-out to my best friend Valerie and Baby Ayden! Thank you for allowing me to be a part of your childbirth experience. My girl was chill as hell at first (Breelyn) but when those strong contractions started coming back-to-back she turned into Dakota lmaooo! This shit is so damn dumb! I love you, baby, and I'll never forget that.

To stay up to date on upcoming projects, snippets, visuals, cover reveals, and so much more, subscribe to my mailing list and follow me on all my social media platforms.

Website:
www.authorshantae.com

Facebook:
https://www.facebook.com/shantae.montgomeryknox

Twitter:
https://twitter.com/OneDimpleTae

Instagram:
https://www.instagram.com/onedimpletae/

Snapchat:
Author Tae`   **31901064898093**

Periscope:
@TaeKnox